HER
LAST
WHISPER

BOOKS BY JENNIFER CHASE

Little Girls Sleeping

JENNIFER CHASE

HER LAST WHISPER

bookouture

Published by Bookouture in 2019

An imprint of Storyfire Ltd.
Carmelite House
50 Victoria Embankment
London EC4Y 0DZ

www.bookouture.com

ISBN: 978-1-78681-832-4
eBook ISBN: 978-1-78681-831-7

For the hardworking and diligent cold-case detectives
that refuse to let cases remain unsolved.

PROLOGUE

A heavy evening mist clung to the windshield of the police car, obscuring the view of the forgotten neighborhood. In the few occupied houses curtains were drawn tightly leaving only thin cracks of light seeping around the edges. Some homes even had bars across the windows. This small rural community had been ignored by the rest of the lively, growing town around it for too long. It was in desperate need of attention and restoration.

Deputy Stan Miller flipped on the wipers to clear his view, only to smear streaks of dirt across the windshield. He let out an annoyed sigh and turned the wipers to a higher speed—making it worse—and then off again.

"Now you've done it," said Deputy Karl Windham beside him, and Miller laughed in spite of himself after a long and uneventful night shift.

"You're going to criticize *me*?" Miller joked. "Me? The guy who has your back?" He sat up straighter, sucking in his waist and adjusting his seatbelt; it was no use pretending he hadn't put on a few extra pounds recently.

"It's the kiss of death out here tonight," complained Windham watching out the side window as the mist turned to light rain.

"I bet it was Sheriff Scott's idea to double us up, with all those recent ambushes on cops around the state."

"It probably has something to do with the mayor's office. Who knows? You know how they don't tell us anything, even though we're the ones putting our asses on the line every shift." Still gazing out of the window, he watched a dark figure dart around a garbage can and disappear into the darkness, then he turned his attention to a skinny cat scurrying along the sidewalk, nose close to the ground tracking something.

The rain got heavier as they drove deeper into the Basin Woods Development. There were no other vehicles on the road. No lights in the distance. Only darkness.

"You hungry?" asked Miller.

"I wouldn't turn down a cup of coffee," replied Windham.

"Me neither."

Deputy Miller took his eyes off the road for a moment to check the time and looked back just in time to see a slender woman stagger into the road ahead of them. She stopped still in the headlights. Her long hair, wet from the rain, was plastered against her head and around her face. She wore only a pair of panties and a tattered tank top. She looked terrified, dark eyes pleading in the glare of the lights, her mouth forming words they could not hear.

"Hey!" yelled Windham to his partner. "Stop!"

Miller jammed on the brakes, making the patrol car bounce to a stop inches before hitting the young woman. Weak and unbalanced, she fell to her knees. In the glare of the headlights, both men could clearly see the dirt embedded on her face and neck, the blood seeping from wounds on her hands, elbows, legs, and feet.

Deputy Miller turned to his partner with wide eyes. "What the…?" Jamming the vehicle into park he picked up the radio. "Dispatch, this is 3741, we have a possible 10-16 at Lincoln and Travis. Will keep you updated. Copy."

"Copy that," replied Dispatch.

He nodded to Windham who swung open the car door and ran to kneel beside the woman. "Miss…" he spoke gently. "Are you alright?"

She shook uncontrollably. Her head and shoulders drooped while her mouth tried to form around a word.

"Can you tell us what happened?" Windham said.

He gently touched her shoulder and she flinched away from him. "It's okay. You're okay now," he reassured.

"Truth... truth... the *truth*... you don't understand... otherwise..." she finally managed between gasps for breath. "I told the truth..." she muttered.

"What truth?" asked Deputy Miller who had retrieved a blanket from the trunk and now stood a few feet away.

She stopped speaking and slowly looked up at the deputy, her eyes filled with fear. Then she whispered, "I told the truth... I told the truth... told... *the truth.*"

Both deputies carefully helped the woman up and gently wrapped the blanket around her.

"What's your name?" asked Windham.

"A... Aman... Amanda," she said slowly.

"Okay, Amanda. We want to help you. Can you tell us what happened?"

"I tried..." she whispered. "It was..." Her voice trailed off.

Deputy Miller opened the back door to the patrol car as his partner gently guided her to sit down in the backseat. Miller handed her a small bottle of water and, after a few moments, her eyes focused on the officers and her breath began to steady.

Deputy Windham kneeled down to her eye level and asked, "Amanda, can you tell us what happened to you? Do you *remember* what happened? Anything?"

She shook her head as more tears welled up in her eyes.

"It's okay."

"A blue door with white trim," she said quietly. "A big box..."

"What else, Amanda? Can you remember anything else?"

"There was a fantasy tree..."

Confused by the description, the deputy tried to make sense of it, pushing gently to pry out any more details from her. "Can you tell us what happened?"

Taking a couple of deep breaths, she finally spoke: "I was k-kidnapped."

CHAPTER 1

Six months and three days later...

Monday 0705 hours

Detective Katie Scott drove her Jeep into the Pine Valley Sheriff's Department parking lot and turned off the engine. She sat for a moment gathering her thoughts as she stared through the windshield at the rusty chain-link fence in front of her. She took several long, deep breaths to steady her anxiety. Today was her first day in her new job and her nerves were jangling.

Am I good enough to head the cold-case unit?

Katie had always wanted to be a police officer and ultimately a detective. This was her chance to prove, not only to herself but to anyone that doubted, that she could.

Can I mentally handle the caseload?

Katie had been through tough times, losing her parents, losing friends on the battlefield, but she never backed away from a challenge even when she knew it would leave a scar. She would do everything possible to find the culprits responsible for their crimes. Two years as a patrol officer and nearly four years as an Army K9 handler had brought her to this moment, to this job. Today was finally the day when she would lead the cold-case unit.

Angst tingled through her body, calling distant memories of the battlefield; images filtered into her brain, her senses heightened, the faint smell of expelled gunfire filled the air. Though she had a better handle on it now, her PTSD was a burden she would most likely carry with her forever. She'd purposely never been officially diagnosed with post-traumatic stress disorder, afraid of the burden and stigma that came with it. For now, she pushed those images from her mind.

After the missing person's case she'd been involved with barely six months ago, Sheriff Wayne Scott had ordered her to take some personal leave before beginning her new position. She didn't want to admit it, but the rest had done her some good. Though her now elevated pulse told her otherwise, she was refreshed, rested, and ready to take on any assignment, no matter how big or small.

Glancing down at the passenger seat, she smiled at the sight of her new leather briefcase, coffee thermos filled with extra-strong java, and her freshly pressed suit jacket. She wanted to take a moment before everything changed.

Her cell phone buzzed with the arrival of a text from the sheriff:

Go to forensics first.

Sink or swim… she thought to herself as she grabbed her things, making sure her holstered gun and detective badge were secured properly at her waist. Exiting her car, she hurriedly slipped on her jacket. She might not feel like a detective yet, but at least she was going to look like one.

Quickly walking through the main entrance, she waved to the receptionist and crossed a large open area to the farthest corner where there was an unmarked door guarded by a small video lens, now directed at her from above. She pressed a button and waited for the door to unlock.

Hearing the click, she pushed through the door and made her way down the narrow wooden staircase leading to the main room in the forensic division. Katie figured that the sheriff must already have a case for her and wanted her down here to see some of the physical evidence first. She had spent some time in forensics working the missing girl case, so the area was familiar to her.

"Hello?" she called out as she hit the last step.

Silence.

"Hello?" she said again. "John?" She addressed the forensic supervisor. "Sheriff Scott?"

Again, no answer.

Katie let out a breath and looked around, her enthusiasm fading. "Anyone around? Hello?"

Walking down the long hallway with closed office doors lining both sides, she looked back and forth, calling out again. She was just about to turn around when a yellow sticky note on a door caught her attention.

DETECTIVE SCOTT ==>>>

Katie smiled. "Okay, what's going on?" She knew something was up. She didn't immediately recognize the handwriting, but thought that it most likely belonged to John.

There were two doors at the end of the hallway, opposite one another. She had never been to that part of the forensic lab before and assumed it was more offices or storage areas. When the department had originally built the forensic unit, it was slated for a larger staff than it had currently.

"Okay, no one better jump out at me," she said, grabbing the handle of the door on the left and pushing it wide. The room was empty except for the custom built-ins at the farthest side of the work area and a sink.

Disappointment and confusion flooded through her. She had imagined her first day would start with combing through old and new files, matching evidence, and reading through folders filled with detective reports. This was definitely not how it was supposed to go—a cryptic scavenger hunt.

Glancing at her watch, she was now officially twenty minutes late for the first day on the job. Putting down her briefcase, she reached for the other door and opened it.

"Surprise!" yelled the group huddled in front of her.

Katie stood in complete shock staring at all the friendly faces including the sheriff, Deputy McGaven, Denise from records, John from forensics, and a couple of other deputies.

"Look, she's speechless!" laughed Deputy McGaven who had worked with her during the previous missing girl cases.

"Now that's a first," replied Sheriff Scott.

"What is all this?" she asked gaining her composure. "I don't understand." She gaped at the dusty old office, which had two large work desks and two chairs, several tall filing cabinets, a bookcase, and a few storage areas. A large freestanding ink board stood in the corner. She took in the desktop computer, laptop, and miscellaneous office supplies beside two extra-tall stacks of boxes, which she assumed were filled with unsolved case files. The room must have been a storage area before the furniture and boxes were moved into it.

Sheriff Scott came forward and announced, "This is your new office, *Detective* Scott."

"Here?" she said.

"Over the past two months, there has been some rearranging of the detective division, including a new person joining the staff," the sheriff explained.

"But I thought—" she began.

He continued, "So we thought working in the forensic area would be perfect for you. You would have all the cold-case files and evidence closer to you, and it's a *much* bigger office, so we could add another person if needed. But that would be a little further down the road."

"I really don't know what to say," Katie said. "This is… this is absolutely amazing. Thank you."

Everyone expressed their congratulations and began to file out of the room one at a time.

Denise gave Katie a hug and said, "Congratulations. You deserve this. Now remember, I'm just up there if you need any searches done that you don't have time for." She laughed and pointed upward to the administrative level.

"Hey, great office," stated McGaven and gave her a high-five slap.

John approached her and smiled. "Well, I guess I'll be seeing you a lot more around here. Congratulations." He left.

Katie was left alone with the sheriff. She took a quick look around to make sure everyone had gone before she said, "Uncle Wayne, this is amazing. I can't believe I get to work here."

"Well, by my calculations you will probably be out a lot following leads."

"You're probably right," she said.

"At least this way you don't have to turn your spare room at home into a crime scene office anymore."

Katie looked around again, now seeing a vase of spring flowers sitting on one of the shelves with some cards lying next to it. "What case do you want me to work first?"

"Detective, that's entirely up to you. The top boxes are the ones that I've pulled out for first consideration, but after that I'll just let you follow your nose. Keep me up to date. I would like an official report on my desk at the end of every week, unless there's something that I need to know about immediately. If you're going anywhere out of town or rural, please let me know so we can keep track of you."

"You got it."

"I have several meetings to get to. And I don't have to remind you how much your parents would have been so proud of everything you've accomplished," he said. "I still feel like they're here in spirit." He paused for a moment, and then he was gone.

She retrieved her briefcase from the hall, shed her suit jacket, and stood alone in the middle of the large musty office. It was time to get to work bringing closure and justice to as many victims' families as possible.

CHAPTER 2

He traveled through the crowd with confidence, causing people to make way for him as he walked. It always gave him a thrill; the brush of a shoulder, the light graze of a fingertip, the distinct odors that proved everyone was truly unique.

Sweet perfume.

Day-old Scotch.

Fresh laundry.

Sweat.

All were part of the fantasy he held close; his personal collection of what made each individual who they were. Their truth. He felt the tension of the lunchtime crowd—hunger; desire; loneliness; hatred; longing; wanting—and craved the unadulterated reality they hid from everyone else. Their most personal secret.

He smiled at a pair of women as they casually passed by him. One smiled back and the other, more interesting to him, looked away. Curiosity burned inside. *What was she hiding? What did she dislike about him so much? What did she dislike about herself?* The questions piled up, but he knew how to keep his insatiable curiosity in check.

Standing in line for a coffee, he noticed ahead of him a brunette with honey-colored highlights clipped into place with an elegant gold barrette. He watched her lips, doused with a carnation pink lipstick, move gently as she ordered her drink. Leaning closer, he took in her dark gray suit and pale pink blouse, unbuttoned to give a little hint of what was underneath. He inhaled. Lilac. Clean oatmeal soap.

He heard the coffee kiosk employee call her Tess.

Tess, beautiful Tess. I wonder what deep dark secrets would come tumbling out of you at the right time?

He shadowed her as she walked away, careful not to draw attention to himself. Following. Learning. Finally on the hunt again...

Tess...

CHAPTER 3

Monday 1300 hours

Looking around at her new office space, it dawned on Katie that with no windows, there was no sound or natural light. The room was in desperate need of something living—perhaps a couple of plants would help. She wondered if the forensic division—John and his two technicians—minded her taking up space in their area at the police department. It was somewhat unorthodox, but she felt that it was going to work out well for her. She was a bit of a loner, so the quiet suited her just fine. In fact, she felt rather at home.

Sitting at her desk, perching on the edge of her too-big leather chair, Katie felt she needed to do something physical to calm the flurries in her stomach and slightly shaky hands. She rolled her chair back and swiveled toward the two towering stacks of boxes. A mismatch of sizes and styles, the boxes looked ready to fall at any moment. Splitting them into four smaller stacks, she noticed that a couple of the boxes had the distinct musty smell of old paper. It saddened her that these were some of the oldest cold cases, those that had little hope of ever being solved.

The quietness of the basement wrapped itself around her. No voices. No whoosh of air conditioning above her head. No sound of cars rattling outside. The only noise she could hear was her own breath as she adjusted the furniture in the room to better suit her needs.

She turned the two five-foot desks to face one another—that way she could use the extra space when she opened evidence boxes. She pushed the ink board over to the other corner where it would be easy for her to begin making her notes and wouldn't take up any more precious space than necessary.

Along the back wall were long Formica counters and a sink. Originally designed for a forensic technician, they were now cluttered with yet more cold-case boxes. She opened the cupboard beneath the sink and found some paper towels to wipe away the heavy dust around the room. The old cupboards had a sharp sour smell as if they hadn't been opened in a decade.

When everything was set up, Katie decided to start by getting all her new employment paperwork out of the way so she could get to work on the case files without interruption. She quickly initialed each page to indicate that she understood the regulations of her duty as a police detective. It included the insurance coverage, back pay, vacation time, overtime, and union information. She recorded her previous work experience as a patrol officer at Sacramento Police Department as well as her time in the military. Most sheriff departments required a minimum of four years' law enforcement experience to apply for a detective position, but her previous experience, college degree, and military time were more than sufficient. It also helped that the department had received glowing letters from her previous supervisor at Sacramento PD, her co-workers, and even the mayor for her dedication and hard work on the missing girl case.

Just as Katie's vision was beginning to blur from tedious box checking, there was a knock at her door.

Chad Ferguson appeared in the doorway and walked directly into Katie's office. His infectious smile, light sandy hair, and his immediate warmth made him the center of attention in any room.

"Hey there," said Katie as she rose from her chair to greet him. She had known Chad since they were eight years old and he was her closest childhood friend. There were very few childhood memories that he wasn't in. They had dated in high school, but then life had taken them in different directions. Both had left Pine Valley for a while and had returned recently at around the same time. She wasn't exactly sure how to define their relationship now.

"I wanted to see you," he said.

"I'm glad you did." She couldn't keep his constant gaze. Since seeing him again, after the last terrifying outcome with a serial killer, she still felt a surge of attraction.

"Interesting office…" He gazed around.

Katie laughed. "It's different. I was just trying to rearrange it so that it didn't feel like I was in someone's basement."

"Well, I won't keep you from your work." He glanced at the well-worn boxes. "I wanted to say congratulations in person and invite you out to dinner tonight."

Katie leaned against her desk, taken aback. She had wanted to keep things between them unromantic until she'd settled in to her new job and civilian life a bit more. And even then, she wasn't so sure if she should jump into a serious relationship.

"I can see you're hesitating. Maybe we can go out to dinner another time?"

"No, no. Dinner sounds nice," she countered, trying not to let her voice rise another octave.

"Well, actually…"

Katie knew that look, had seen it many times when they were growing up; his blue eyes twinkled irresistibly and signaled that he had something really important to share. "Spit it out," she said. "C'mon, how long have I known you? You have something important on your mind."

"I thought we could celebrate *both* of our new jobs."

"What? You finally were hired full time?"

"Yep, you are looking at an official full-time firefighter for Sequoia County. No more picking up short gigs here and there," he said with some relief to his voice.

"That's great. I'm so happy for you." She gave him a quick hug.

"So that means we both have something to celebrate," he said.

"Absolutely."

"Pick you up around 7.30 p.m.?"

"Uh," she hesitated. "Sure. See you then."

He walked slowly to the door, barely turned the corner, and then leaned back into the room and said, "Detective Scott, I think this job agrees with you. I wouldn't have left here with anything except a yes for dinner."

CHAPTER 4

Monday 1745 hours

Katie had lost track of time as she piled her large work desk with thick file organizers and corresponding banker's boxes, sorting everything by urgency and solvability. She not only wanted to read through the top cases pulled personally by the sheriff, but also familiarize herself with the kinds of cases that generally went cold. It wasn't only homicides; there were sexual assaults, burglaries, missing persons, and one arson case that took place when she was a teenager.

As she scanned the case overview notes, she realized that there were some significant problems and stumbling blocks with almost every case. It made them extremely difficult, especially some of the older ones, which had missing evidence and insufficient detective notes, and where many of the prime suspects and witnesses were deceased or missing.

She turned on her desktop computer and waited for it to warm up, instantly recognizing the database that she had spent time updating when she had returned home from the military and her uncle, the sheriff, had suggested she fill in at the records division until she figured out what she wanted to do. She had been assigned to enter all types of police data from investigation files, patrol reports, crime reports, warrants, and various traffic citations, so she was one step ahead when it came to learning the ropes.

After careful consideration, Katie decided that she would create a streamlined spreadsheet for the overview of cases, and it would make it easier for her to write weekly updates for the sheriff. She quickly created a system using her own version of abbreviations, solvability rates and key case information and got to work.

In the first box she opened, the ones suggested by the sheriff, there were several files she skimmed through. The first case involved a missing person from ten years previous: Sam Stiles, thirty-four years old, who worked at Palmer's Auto Repair, left work early feeling unwell one day and was never seen again. The sheriff had made a notation that Stiles was known for fighting in bars, usually over card or pool games. There were a few leads from friends, co-workers, and patrons at the bar he frequented regularly, but all leads petered out and then the case eventually went cold. No forensics. No eye witnesses. Sam Stiles never resurfaced; the family still checked with the sheriff's department every year on Sam's birthday to find out if there were any new leads.

Katie sat back in her chair and mulled over the facts of the case. Ten years was a long time, but perhaps a fresh look would pull up something now the dust had well and truly settled. Or, perhaps not. She put the folder aside for now and opened another file for a kidnapping and assault case from only six months ago.

Six months and a cold case already?

Katie read the brief overview of the case to make sure that it hadn't been misfiled. There was a note inside that read: *undetermined—victim uncooperative—cold case*. Not something that she had ever seen before.

Her interest piqued, she began to read the account carefully. The original report was typed, double spaced, and sorted neatly into sections of a special file folder. It had been written by Deputy Karl Windham, one of the two officers who had discovered the victim that night. Katie didn't know the officer personally, but was impressed by how thoroughly the report was written and the detailed recording of events. There were even some initial photos.

The victim was Amanda Payton, a thirty-one-year-old nurse working for First Memorial Hospital, who had run out into the road in the middle of the night, scarcely clothed and was almost hit by a patrol car. The two officers, Deputy Windham and his partner Deputy Miller, were the ones who had first contact with Amanda. She'd been disoriented, covered in dirt and blood, and had difficulty conversing with the officers. She kept repeating the phrase, "*I told the truth.*"

Reading through the rest of the report, Amanda claimed she had been kidnapped from her car at a grocery store, held for over a week by a man whom she never saw, then escaped that rainy night and was luckily picked up by the police. After taking Amanda back to the station to warm up and make a full report, the deputies went back and thoroughly searched the area she had cryptically described, but they never found anything to corroborate her claim of kidnapping and being held against her will. The deputies looked at houses with blue doors and white trim, near large tree landmarks, for evidence of the bedroom, of restraints, or anything to indicate someone had been imprisoned. There was nothing; none of her remaining clothes, blood, or paraphernalia of the perpetrator was found. The deputies had taken extra efforts to search for anything that indicated any type of criminal activity and anything confirming Amanda's story, but their attempt came back negative.

Amanda was later admitted to the South Street Psychiatric Hospital for a seventy-two-hour hold, which was routine observation for any victim who had shown severe anxiety, unable to sufficiently explain what had happened, and unable to assist in the investigation surrounding their circumstances. Deputy Windham had made the call to take Amanda to be checked out.

Reading on, Katie saw that there was little investigation into her kidnapping claims due to the lack of evidence corroborating her story except for her injuries. It made Amanda's case almost impossible.

There were some follow-up phone calls to Amanda's place of work, to her supervisor Dr. Jamison, and to Amanda personally after she had been released from the psychological evaluation—but she wouldn't cooperate further with police because they were asking so many questions and she sensed they didn't believe her. She claimed that she just wanted to put the horrible incident behind her. The investigation was left at a standstill and was ultimately shuffled into the backlog—then into the cold cases when no more leads materialized. Katie looked up from the file, trying to take it all in.

She thumbed through the photographs that the hospital and deputies had taken of Amanda. The lighting was poor, but it was clear there were dark bruise marks around her wrists and ankles consistent with restraints over a period of time. Her neck was scratched in a way that could possibly have been caused by some type of restraint. The toxicology report was clean—no drugs: prescription or otherwise.

After the photos, there was a notation that the rape kit had not been used to test Amanda for signs of sexual assault. Katie shuffled back through the original report from Deputy Windham where Amanda had specifically told the officers that she *wasn't* raped. Flipping back to the forensic evidence reports, it had been reported that the hospital had taken her remaining clothing, bra and panties, and packaged them to be transported to the forensic division at the sheriff's office. The report didn't have test results or proof that the clothing ever arrived.

Were they misplaced? Backlogged?

Katie looked at the photos again and studied the injuries and wondered if they could have been self-inflicted. But the more she stared, the more she was convinced by the angles and depth that someone else had perpetrated those injuries. It was possible that the injuries were sustained in another way—even consensual. But if Amanda didn't want to further cooperate, there was nothing the police could do to move forward.

Katie wanted to talk with Amanda to hear what happened in her own words, to see for herself if she was telling the truth. The last thing she wanted was a case like this to fall through the cracks, leaving a violent perpetrator on the loose. She knew firsthand that women were often reluctant to report attacks and sexual assaults. She had seen cases when she was a patrol officer; and in the army, she had heard about women raped and assaulted with little investigation. There was no way she would let that happen with Amanda Payton's case. She would make some enquiries and if it proved that there was more to Amanda's story, she would keep digging.

Looking at the personal information that the deputies had gathered from Amanda at the time, Katie called the phone number listed. The call immediately went to a recording announcing that it was no longer a working number. She called it again to make sure, but with the same result. Out of service.

Katie wrote down Amanda's last known address: 1127 Brickyard Street, apartment #14. It was almost 6 p.m. and the block was on her way home. Grabbing her briefcase and the office keys, she left.

CHAPTER 5

Monday 1815 hours

Katie drove her assigned police vehicle to the downtown area and looked for Brickyard Street going northeast. Traffic was heavy, but as she drove steadily through the inching sets of cars, weaving in and out of the lanes occasionally, she realized that it felt a bit peculiar and somewhat freeing to be moving through her first investigation on the first day. She felt a little rush of independence break through her nerves.

It had been only six months since the suspected kidnapping and it was likely that Amanda still lived at the same residence. Katie composed some questions in her head, running them through as she drove. She needed to be compassionate about her approach; kidnapping or not, it was obvious from the photographs that Amanda had been through some type of trauma. If what she told Deputy Windham was true, the case needed a much closer investigation and Katie wanted all the facts before deciding one way or another.

She slowed the sedan and made a right turn from Main Street onto Brickyard Street where many remodeled old and quite large residences had been turned into apartment complexes. Pine Valley had been growing significantly over the past ten years and always pushed to accommodate more people. Mature trees dotted the sidewalks giving shade to the flowers blooming from low-lying bushes.

She drove another block until she found number 1127: a two-story development painted dark brown with white trim. She searched for a parking spot on the street, driving around the block twice until she found one. Most of the cars parked along the street and in designated parking spaces were small compacts to mid-size SUVs. It was clear that the neighborhood was made up of the average working force mixed with young families.

Getting out of the car, Katie watched as cars sped down adjacent streets, racing to get home. Several teenagers rode down the sidewalk on their bicycles talking and laughing with one another. She kept walking until she stood at the gate entrance to Amanda Payton's apartment. Quickly surveying the area, she noticed the bushes and flowering vines had been trimmed recently but the stepping stones were cracked and some were missing. Someone had left a roasting pan filled with water as a makeshift birdbath.

The gate hinges screeched as Katie pushed it open and walked through. Amanda's residence was located on the first floor around the other side of the building, so she continued along the path, her heart sinking as she approached apartment number 14 and saw there was a "for rent" sign taped to the front door. Peering inside the small side window revealed a living room and galley kitchen, with what must be the bedroom and bathroom behind one of the two closed doors. It was completely empty and she could smell a hint of some type of cleaning solution.

Damn.

Pulling out her cell, Katie called the property management telephone number listed on the door notice. It immediately went to voicemail which rattled off many of the available rental units. Hesitating a moment, she ended the call without leaving a message. She was about to leave when a voice above her said, "Are you looking for Amanda?"

Looking up, Katie saw a young man in his late teens, with dark brown hair, leaning over the second-story railing staring at her. He rested his skateboard against the iron barrier, a playful, curious look on his face.

"Hi," Katie said, tilting her head back to see the young man more clearly. "Do you know her?"

"Yep."

"You live here?"

"Yep."

"When did she move?"

"About three weeks ago." He leaned farther over the railing to get a better look at her.

"You wouldn't happen to know where she went?" Katie asked.

"Nope."

"If you had to guess," Katie prodded.

"You a cop?"

"I'm a detective."

"What do you want with Amanda?"

"Just wanted to talk with her," she said. "She's not in any trouble."

"No?" he said.

"No, not at all. I thought she might be able to help me with a case I'm working on." Katie sensed that he knew more than he let on, and that he might be toying with her.

"What kind of case?" he persisted.

"I'm not allowed to discuss it."

"Did Amanda do something?"

"Not at all," Katie countered quickly and confidently.

"Oh."

"Are you sure that you don't know where she moved? It would really help me out."

"Um, maybe with her friend Emily that she works with."

"You have a last name?"

"I think Day. She has blonde hair and used to come here a lot." Katie felt her cell phone vibrate in her hand.

"What's your name?" she asked.

"Simon."

"I'm Detective Katie Scott from the sheriff's department—nice to meet you. Thank you, Simon, for your help."

Katie turned to leave.

"Detective Scott?" he called after her.

Looking up again, Katie said, "Yes?"

"I hope you find who hurt Amanda and put them in jail."

Katie hesitated and wasn't completely sure how to respond. She nodded. "I'm going to do my best."

After Katie returned to her vehicle, she made some brief notes. It wasn't a complete dead end; she could enquire about Emily at the hospital.

Her phone buzzed again; she answered it.

"Hey, I'm at your house. Are you going to be late?" said Chad.

Katie had forgotten about her dinner date.

"Uh…" she whispered.

"You forgot, didn't you?" he teased, not sounding surprised or upset.

"I'm so sorry."

"No problem."

"You want to reschedule?" she said.

"No. I'll wait. Besides, I can play with Cisco while you get ready."

"Okay. I'll be there in about fifteen minutes."

"Is that with or without sirens?" he said.

"Always with."

"I'll just chill. Bye," he said playfully.

Katie ended the call and let out a sigh. She should have rescheduled the dinner, but it was too late now.

As she drove to her house, Katie's mind began to churn through ideas about what did or didn't happen to Amanda Payton.

CHAPTER 6

Monday 1920 hours

As she drove up her driveway, Katie saw Chad's large black Jeep parked outside with the driver's door open, his long legs hanging out. He was clearly taking a nap.

"That is so Chad," Katie quietly said to herself and smiled as she cut the engine and got out of the car.

Chad's smiling face appeared as he sat up at the sound of her door shutting. He had changed into a nice pair of khakis and shirt. "Hey, how's the town's newest detective?" he asked.

"How do I even answer that?"

"Any way you like."

"It's exciting… terrifying… all rolled into one."

"That's a good answer," he said as he followed her to the front door. "It's truthful and insightful."

A loud, rapid barking greeted them.

"Take it easy, Cisco," said Katie as she inserted her key, turned it, then rushed inside to enter the four-digit alarm code while a jet-black German shepherd ran circles around her, whining in delight.

"Every time I see Cisco, I almost forget how handsome he is," stated Chad as he shut the door behind him, nearly knocking over some photos. "And a war hero too," he added as the dog obediently followed Katie into the kitchen.

"I'm sorry, Chad. I have to feed Cisco, let him out for a bit, and then I'll quickly change. You sure you don't want to do this another time?"

"No worries. I can still entertain myself. I don't have to be at work for another twenty-four hours. No, make that twenty-three hours," he said, browsing a bookshelf that ran along one of the walls outside the kitchen. The books were arranged chronologically and meticulously organized by size. Mostly various novels of mystery and adventure, but there were historical, dog training, and photography books as well.

"Hmmmm, let's see," he said as he ran his fingers along the books' spines.

The living room consisted of a comfortable oversized couch with a neatly folded blanket on the back, flanked by two leather upholstered chairs with matching embroidered floral pillows, perfectly placed in opposite corners. The hardwood floor was covered by a large multicolored rug and two pieces of artwork filled the walls. One was a landscape painting and the other was a vintage oversized photograph of Pine Valley taken from an elevated location.

There was a small narrow table decorated with several photographs; one of Katie aged five with her parents, one of her graduating from the police academy, and a group photo of her and Cisco with her army company taken at a military base.

Katie prepared the dog's dinner and then hurried to her bedroom, partially stripping off her dark pant suit as she moved down the hallway and disappeared into her bedroom. She could hear Chad reading the synopsis of a mystery novel out loud to Cisco and making funny voices for each character. "I'll let Cisco out," he called from the living room.

Chad had hardly changed from the kid she had met so many years ago in elementary school; light-hearted, fearless, and always charismatic. They'd been inseparable then—fishing, building forts, hiking—but now they had found their way back to each other. She wondered if they could ever be the same—together? They weren't kids anymore. So much had happened in their lives. Was it just a comfortable place to be because of their shared pasts?

Katie washed her face, reluctantly and inexpertly applied makeup, and unpinned her dark hair from her practical work hairstyle. She removed a few dresses from the closet, stared at them and then put them back. Finally she decided on a pretty sleeveless blouse, dark pants, and low heels that wouldn't hurt her feet. She quickly changed.

She stood in front of the full-length mirror and stared at her reflection; she didn't feel comfortable dressing up. The truth was she felt more relaxed in jeans and a T-shirt doing training combat maneuvers with Cisco.

Was that who she really was? All she was? A soldier?

Was that the person that Chad really wanted to be in a relationship with?

There it was.

Again.

When Katie asked herself tough questions, or when she stepped out of her immediate comfort zone, a creeping anxious feeling took a hold of her. A tingling in her extremities, quickening of breath and strange dizziness caught her by surprise. No matter how many times it happened, it always filled her with dread. The fear of the unknown. Her legs weakened, pushing her to pace about the bedroom trying to outrun the feeling.

The room closed in around her. She knew that it was her imagination, but she instinctively readied herself for a fight-or-flight scenario.

No… You're not welcome here.

These feelings made her want to run—anywhere. No destination in mind, just leave and keep going. She thought that she was mostly over these episodes, but faced with undue stress, they often came charging back.

Feeling her cheeks flush, she hurried into the bathroom to splash cold water on her face. As she blotted herself dry, she stared at her reflection, freshly applied mascara pooling under her eyes.

What am I doing?

I can lead an army patrol, but not get ready for a date?

Katie touched-up her makeup and waited a few more minutes until her complexion had returned to a more normal color. Just as she was leaving her bedroom, she grabbed her favorite gold bracelet, the one with several garnet stones, to put on for luck. She stared at her wrist, suddenly reminded of the photos of Amanda Payton—her bruised wrists and ankles. Were those restraint marks consistent with being held against her will? Or self-inflicted wounds to gain attention?

It was too soon to tell.

Cisco's cold nose touched her hand and shocked Katie back into the moment, realizing that Chad had gone quiet and must be waiting for her in the next room. Pushing work from her mind, she grabbed a small purse with her essentials and a lightweight jacket. Cisco's amber wolf eyes looked up at her as if to say, "you're going out without me again," but Katie reassured him with an affectionate scratch behind the ears before she left the bedroom.

"Hey," Chad said as he stood at the end of the hall. "I thought I was going to have to call my buddies to do a welfare check." He smiled broadly. "But I can see it was totally worth the wait."

"Thank you."

Looking at his watch, "We'll just about make the reservation."

"Reservation?"

"Yes, that is what one does when one wants to celebrate at the best Italian restaurant in town and score a great table that's not next to the restroom."

"Celebrate?" she asked.

"We've both recently been employed in jobs that might get us killed…"

"That's a good line to begin a toast."

"We're living the dream…"

Since it was early in the week, Little Gino's was only half filled with patrons. The intimate tables were covered with crisp white linens and decorated with swan-shaped napkins and little candles. Italian art adorned the walls, with an entire mural of a quaint Italian village along one side.

Katie suddenly recalled that she had been to this particular restaurant before, what felt like a lifetime ago before she did her tour in the army.

"What are you thinking?" asked Chad, his head cocked, eyes looking deep into hers when she looked up. Katie laughed and blushed. "Whatever it was—it must've been a doozy," he added.

"I was just thinking about how long we've known each other."

"And?"

"Well, don't you think it's interesting how much we both loved Pine Valley as kids, then suddenly we couldn't wait to leave. And now, somehow we are both back…" she mused.

"Well, I don't know. Things change. Priorities change."

Katie ran her hand over the red cloth napkin. "Things happen for a reason."

"I agree. But I don't think of it as a *coincidence*."

"Talking about coincidence," said Sheriff Scott as he approached the table with an attractive woman on his arm.

"Uncle Wayne and Aunt Claire," said Katie. "It's nice to see you." She was relieved that the conversation was momentarily sidetracked.

"Why don't you join us?" asked Chad.

"Oh, no we wouldn't want to crash your party. Besides, we came here for a nice quiet dinner," the sheriff said.

"They look so cute together," said Claire. "Let's go get our usual table and let them have some privacy."

"Of course."

"But Katie, honey, I still want to have a girl's lunch soon," her aunt said.

"I would love that."

"Nice to see you both," said the sheriff as he steered his wife away from the table.

Katie smiled, watching them walk away.

"Now, they're the cutest couple in town," stated Chad. He turned his attention back to Katie. "How did they meet?"

"I'm not sure and I don't know a lot about her background. After my Aunt Elizabeth divorced him, he was so sad until he met Claire. His entire life turned around and here they are almost eight years later."

The waiter came to their table with two glasses filled with red wine.

"Thank you," said Katie. Taking a sip, the wonderful flavor of the Californian wine melted into her taste buds. "Wow, this is delicious."

"I'm glad you like it." He leaned forward and lowered his voice. "I confess, Detective, I asked one of my buds back at the firehouse what would be a good bottle of wine."

"Are you trying to impress me with honesty?"

"Are you profiling me?" he said lightheartedly.

"It's a bad habit."

"Well," he began and leaned back in his chair. "I figured a great dinner and good wine would lessen the blow of getting dumped."

"Dumped?"

"Yeah, I figured you're just waiting for the right moment."

"Chad, how long have we known each other?" she asked.

"Twenty-something years."

Katie stressed, "I would never string you along, but…" She glanced across the restaurant and saw her aunt and uncle holding hands across the table, both completely engaged in the other. She wanted to have a relationship, strong and secure, but she had to get some things straight in her life first. "I… just don't know where things land right now."

He leaned forward and touched her right hand. "Remember when we were about twelve and my mom was diagnosed with cancer?"

"Yes, of course." She remembered that time well. It was the only time she had ever seen Chad cry.

"It turned out okay and she beat it, but at the time my world came crashing down around me. I still remember that day like it was yesterday. You were my best friend and I knew from the moment I poured out my heart to you that you were someone I could always count on." He watched her carefully as he spoke.

Katie closed her eyes for a moment. There had been so much drama and so many difficult times, but they had managed to get through it. "I know… you were my strength when my parents died. So much heartache…" she began, not wanting to remember.

"I know you've been pulling away."

"After what happened during that missing person's case, and after what happened in the army… I just… don't know… if…"

Chad leaned forward and gently squeezed her hand. "It's okay. I don't ever want you to feel uncomfortable or pressured. I just want to spend time with you. I know there are things that you haven't shared with anyone, but you know I'm here for you—always. We've always been there for one another and nothing is going to stop that now—no matter what."

Katie didn't know exactly what to say. She felt like she was walking a tightrope that could break at any moment. There were unresolved things that she needed to talk about but she didn't know if she could do it. Deep down, she knew that her heart belonged to Chad, it always had, but her handle on her fear would dictate how the relationship would ultimately end up.

"I just want to be here with you." He squeezed her hand. "After all, it's a celebration." He raised his wine and tapped Katie's glass to lighten the mood. "Here's to the new jobs, and new adventures."

Katie reciprocated. "Cheers." She smiled as she felt the relaxing effects of the wine after a long day melt her anxiety away.

Here's to new adventures…

CHAPTER 7

Tuesday 1015 hours

The next day, after contacting Deputy Windham and setting up a time to meet with him before his patrol shift, Katie decided to keep digging through Amanda Payton's file—her work, friends, and family. She keyed in some search parameters for Emily Day and patiently waited for the information to filter through. It looked like she still worked at the First Memorial Hospital where she met Amanda and had a clean record apart from having been arrested for assault and trespassing two years ago. The judge gave her leniency with time served and six-month probation.

It struck Katie that there weren't any similar reports or background records run for Amanda in her file. Perhaps they were lost or misfiled, or maybe the original detective didn't think it was important to run them. Clearing the search boxes, Katie ran a fresh criminal record check for Amanda. And what came back surprised her.

Amanda had been involved in several altercations of battery, one resulting in her obtaining a restraining order against a Raymond Alvarez five years ago. She'd called the police on three occasions claiming that he had beaten her up—later she retracted her statement and said it was all a misunderstanding and she was mad. The other two incidents were similar situations where she later retracted her statement. Katie sat back and allowed the new information to simmer—it didn't make her look that reliable.

A soft knock on her door interrupted her thoughts.

"Come in," she said.

A stocky deputy with close-cropped sandy hair dressed in uniform entered. "Detective Scott?" he addressed.

Katie stood and said, "Yes, please come in." Extending her hand, she continued, "Nice to meet you, Deputy Windham."

He shook Katie's hand and took a seat across from her.

"I appreciate you taking the time to talk with me."

"No problem, anything I can do to help."

Katie shut several file folders and pulled the one for Amanda Payton, leaving it front and center on the desk. "I came across this kidnapping case for Amanda Payton from six months ago."

The deputy nodded. "I'm glad you're looking into it," he said.

"Why do you say that?" she asked.

"Something didn't sit right with me."

Katie opened the deputy's incident report. "I read your report several times and you were very thorough. I really appreciate the photos you and your partner took of Ms. Payton and the scene at the time."

He leaned forward. "You have to understand. That entire incident was difficult to forget. I've never had an experience like that with a victim."

Katie realized that her patrol experience of a little over two years paled to what the deputy must have witnessed in his decade of service.

"Why don't you tell me what happened in your own words as you remember it?" she said.

He sighed and appeared uncomfortable. Pausing a moment to get his thoughts together, he began, "My partner and I, Deputy Miller, were patrolling the Basin Woods area on third watch. It was raining on and off. There was no activity, no calls for service, and we were thinking about getting some coffee. What seemed like out of nowhere this young woman stumbled into the street barely dressed and we almost hit her. We stopped to help her and got her into the patrol car and asked her repeatedly what happened. We saw her injuries on her wrists and ankles. She was absolutely terrified and wouldn't talk to us at first, but she finally told us her name, some landmarks where she had been held, and that she had been kidnapped."

"Why was this case dropped so quickly? She claimed to have been kidnapped."

He sighed. "Detective Petersen, the detective who caught the case, felt that there was nothing more to it without corroborating evidence and Ms. Payton had since been uncooperative. Basically there was nothing more we could do. Since he didn't want to close the case, he downgraded it to a cold case to keep it open in case new evidence became available."

Katie frowned. "I haven't spoken to Detective Petersen yet, but it's obvious that's the next step."

"He's…" the deputy stopped talking.

"He's what?"

"Detective Petersen has been here a long time and he's a good cop. He doesn't take well to people questioning his work, shall we say. I'm just giving you a heads-up."

"Noted. Thank you." Katie had never been intimidated yet by a senior police officer, and she wasn't going to start any time soon.

Deputy Windham readjusted his weight in the chair, obviously uncomfortable with having spoken ill of one of his fellow police officers.

"I made a few calls. Amanda has quit her job and moved," she said.

"That could mean she made everything up and doesn't want to be found, or it could mean that she's scared to death that her kidnapper will come back." He looked away as if thinking about why she moved so abruptly.

"Since Detective Petersen downgraded it to a cold case… Maybe her story was created for you to believe her or at least sympathize with her. The house where she was held, you couldn't find anything fitting her description?" Katie asked.

"There are certain things you learn on the street. After ten years on the job, I have a good sense of when people are lying and when they are telling the truth," he said shifting in the chair. "It's the things they say, don't say, mannerisms, and slight gestures. I've seen it all."

"So do you think she was lying?" Katie watched the deputy. He had a way about him that was compassionate and calm. It was difficult not to like him immediately.

"Quite the opposite. I think she was absolutely telling the truth."

"Why?"

"She told us details—landmarks and specific details about the house—all without hesitation. My partner and I searched the streets for houses with blue doors with white trim. We found several, but found no evidence to suggest someone had been held there or had recently escaped. I knew there had to be something we were missing—anything to corroborate her story. But nothing surfaced. We tried, but the only outcome was understandably her frustration with us and then she stopped cooperating altogether," he said.

Katie nodded in sympathy. "I see you noted that when you first had contact with her, she kept saying the word 'truth.' What do you think that means?"

"I honestly don't know. She kept repeating it, claiming over and over again that she's telling the truth."

"You truly believe that she was coherent and wasn't giving you something she had dredged up in a fantasy? Although her toxicology was clean—no drugs—prescription or otherwise."

"She didn't appear to be under the influence."

"Maybe something went wrong with her date or with someone she's known for a while? A sex game that got out of hand?" Katie pushed.

"I don't think so. Something really spooked her—she was afraid and was still reeling from her experience when we found her."

"I'm just trying to see both sides of the story. I'm going to pursue this case. It comes down to whether or not she made everything up and is lying to us, or if she wants this terrible experience behind her."

"I see where you're going with this, but that was what, six months ago, and I still feel the same way right now as I did that night. She was telling the truth," he stated again.

Katie nodded. "I think there's something more here too. I'm going to find her and talk with her and see if she can tell me anything new, or if she sticks to her story. If you think of something that I should look into, please don't hesitate to let me know."

"I will." Deputy Windham stood up, making his uniform belt squeak from the numerous items he had attached, including his holstered gun. "Detective, there's one thing I do know for sure."

"What's that?"

"Amanda Payton was scared to death of something, someone, and she might run because of it."

After Deputy Windham left, Katie picked up the phone and pressed the double-digit number for the detective division. The phone rang once before someone answered, "Detective Division."

"Hi, Alana," said Katie.

"Hey, Detective Scott. How are you?"

"Can't complain. I was wondering if Detective Petersen is in?"

"He sure is. You want me to transfer you?"

"No, I think I'll come up for a visit."

"Great."

"See you in a little bit," said Katie and she hung up.

Outside the door to the detective division, Katie clutched the Amanda Payton file to her chest feeling conspicuous and somewhat of an outsider even though she was an investigator just like them. She'd received quite a lot of heat from a fellow detective when she'd originally been called in to help with the missing girl's case. Thankfully, he was no longer working for the sheriff's department, but she knew there were still others who resented her because her uncle was the sheriff.

Before she could knock, there was a buzz and the door unlocked. Stepping inside, the floor was a buzz of activity with several detectives talking animatedly about the latest bust, and Alana talking alone with a uniformed deputy.

"Oh, Detective Scott," she said as she caught Katie's attention. "Go on down to the second door on the right." She gestured and then resumed her conversation.

In front of a closed door decorated with a cheaply made name plate—Detective Sergeant David Petersen—she took a deep breath and knocked.

"Come in," stated a deep voice within.

Inside, she found a thin man with dark hair sparsely covering the top of his head hunched over a pile of paperwork. His tie and jacket were draped over the only other chair in the office.

"Detective Petersen?" said Katie.

"Yes," he said never looking up. "What can I do for you?"

She hesitantly closed the door, leaving a couple of inches cracked open. Taking another step closer to the desk she said, "I'm Detective Katie Scott. It's nice to meet you."

Still the detective didn't look up.

"I wanted to ask you a couple of questions about one of your cases—which is now a cold case."

"Shoot," he said.

"Well," she began, contemplating how to balance her need for answers with a level of polite respect.

Detective Petersen finally looked up and stared at Katie. "What's on your mind, Ms. Scott?"

Katie noted that he didn't address her as detective and decided to dive straight in.

"Do you remember a case from six months back involving a woman named Amanda Payton?"

"Payton," he echoed, searching his memory. "Oh, of course, the woman that reported that she had been kidnapped and held against her will; then she managed to escape."

"Yes," she said.

"What do you want to know? The reports are self-explanatory."

"Well, for starters, I noticed there weren't any background checks run on Ms. Payton, and I wanted to know why."

"Didn't need it. We looked into her claim, which was unfounded, and then she retracted her statement. End of case."

"Yes, but the evidence…"

"I know you've got the glamorous job combing through our old cold cases, but you're going to have to realize that some cases don't warrant further investigation. There are more cases, current cases with real evidence, that need our attention."

"Why is this a cold case, and not a closed one?"

"No cooperation from the victim. We can't investigate unless we can talk to the victim. It's cold in the hope that maybe one day she'll change her mind."

Katie chose her words carefully as she changed tack. "Detective, what was your impression of her condition? Did you not feel the bruising on her wrists and ankles added significant weight to her story?"

He let out a loud sigh. "Look, if someone—a victim or not—doesn't want to work with the police there's nothing more that can be done—unless they change their mind or if solid evidence comes to light. We did our due diligence. If your look through the case finds otherwise, then so be it."

"Due diligence? That's interesting. I thought we were here to help people and keep them safe? Did you ever think that maybe she's terrified that the person who abducted her is going to return?

Capture her again, or worse, kill her this time? Did you ever think that she's devastated that no one believes her?"

He looked up at her with disdain. "Was there anything else you wanted to know about the case, Ms. Scott? Otherwise I'd like to get back to solving *real* crimes with *reliable* witnesses."

"No, I have everything I need. Thank you, Detective, for your *precious* time."

CHAPTER 8

Wednesday 0715 hours

The next morning, Katie walked out to the police training area and met with a tall, dark-haired, older man, Sergeant Blake Hardy, who was in charge of the five police K9 units for the sheriff's department. The large six-acre cyclone-fenced training area was located just two blocks east of the sheriff's department. It consisted of routine drill items for climbing, scaling, tunneling, and various other obstacles for agility and endurance. There were two different sized sheds on opposite ends of the training area and it was surrounded by trees, giving this barren space a little of the Pine Valley charm. The cool morning was refreshing and helped to ignite Katie's spirit of beginning a new day.

Hardy turned to see Katie approaching and smiled. "Hello, Detective Scott."

"Sergeant," she nodded. "Thank you for letting me and Cisco crash your training this morning."

"No problem. It's nice to have a war veteran here to show the rest of these mutts how it's done."

"Cisco has been so bored since we came back, this is exactly what he needs."

"You're up next after Deputy Ryder."

"Great," she said, turning to watch the action.

Dressed in dark gray SWAT pants, dark T-shirt, and sporting a leg-holstered sidearm, Deputy Ryder held the collar of a dark sable German shepherd named Nitro. The dog barked loud, high-pitched and in rapid succession, the unmistakable call of the working police dog, and bounced up and down on his front paws. Thirty feet away was the decoy, a dog trainer dressed in an oversized protective bite suit, who was moving in the opposite direction away from the K9 team. The fifty-pound-plus suit impeded the trainer somewhat, causing him to waddle as he moved.

"Sheriff's Department! Stop or I'll send the dog!" the officer yelled and then repeated the warning. When the man in the suit didn't stop, he let go of the dog's collar, hissing, "*Fass*," meaning *attack* in German.

Nitro took off at a full pelt, leaped up, and bit down on the decoy's shoulder, dragging him down to the ground with all of his propelled weight.

Deputy Ryder jogged up to his partner and yelled for Nitro to let go: "*Aus!*"

Immediately the dog let go and trotted back to the officer to sit at attention.

"Good boy, Nitro," said the deputy, tossing the dog his favorite ball.

"Great work!" yelled Sergeant Hardy.

Katie clapped and said, "Nice job."

Deputy Ryder jogged up with Nitro heeling at his side.

"You've been working with him. He comes off the bite well," complimented the sergeant.

"It's all about the ball," the deputy said. "It's so much better than the burlap training stick."

"Glad to hear it," the sergeant replied. "Deputy Ryder, this is Detective Katie Scott."

"I've heard about you." He smiled. "It's nice to meet you." He shook her hand.

"Same here," Katie said.

"Okay, Scott, you're up with Cisco."

"Great." She walked back to her Jeep and took Cisco out on the leash. Putting his favorite toy in her back pocket, she walked out to the working field.

"Do a stop and frisk," suggested the sergeant.

Katie knew the drill well. She waited for the decoy to come in close and commanded Cisco to lie down: "*Platz.*"

Cisco pressed his body to the ground as Katie approached the decoy and started to pat him down, pretending to search for something. As she worked her way around his body, the decoy grabbed her suddenly and they struggled. Cisco was by her side in an instant, grabbing the decoy's sleeve between his teeth and dragging him down hard to the ground.

"Stop moving!" yelled Katie to the decoy. Then to Cisco, "*Hier.*"

Cisco immediately let go and padded over to Katie, finishing off with a neat heel sit.

Katie turned away from the decoy as Cisco held close next to her left thigh. Suddenly, out of nowhere the decoy grabbed Katie by the shoulders and spun her around. They began to struggle again, mimicking a surprise attack to simulate what could easily happen to a police officer out on patrol. Cisco didn't miss a beat, jumping up to assist Katie and dragging the decoy back down to the ground.

"Cisco, *aus,*" Katie ordered. "*Hier.*"

Cisco ran to Katie's side and waited patiently for his reward—the ball.

"Good boy, Cisco. Atta boy," she said, giving him a quick pat on the side.

"Awesome bite," said the decoy trainer.

"He's a great dog, Scott. His speed and agility are impressive for an older dog," stated the sergeant.

"He has always been fast and he's not showing signs of slowing down. Thank you for allowing us to train today. I can tell he's happy to be back doing some work, even though it's just training." Katie looked over at Cisco, panting with his favorite yellow ball in his mouth, and smiled.

CHAPTER 9

Wednesday 0915 hours

Tess Regan wanted to go home. She wanted more than anything to quit and never see her co-workers, her job, or her boss ever again, but it had been the only job she could get after she was let go from her previous company, and she desperately needed the money. It was mind-numbing work, processing medical insurance claims day in, day out, but insurance was a necessary evil; loathed by those who paid in but never claimed, and those that claimed and never got near enough to cover whatever they had insured. At least, that was what Tess thought as she stared around her small cubicle, her narrow desk not wide enough to balance all her claim folders, searching for an excuse to leave her desk. Retrieving office supplies, using the restroom, or stepping out for a coffee, anything to catch a break from her gloomy existence.

Tess wanted more—to be special. She was going to be thirty-four in two months and she felt that her life had hardly begun. She was drowning in debt and her boyfriend of more than three years had decided that morning that he wanted to move on in his life. In other words, move on from her. She had no savings, no relationship, and had been estranged from her parents and brother for more than five years. Even her best friend from college had been slowly distancing herself. Tess had never felt so alone.

She got up from her desk, sidestepping the pile of spreadsheets on the floor that she needed to process before the end of the day;

the sadness she carried felt like deadweights dragging at her feet. She felt empty. She wanted out.

Walking through the office, Tess glanced around but no one looked up, no one noticed as she slipped like a ghost down the long hallway and pushed open the communal restroom door. Once inside, she locked the door and stood motionless for a moment gazing at the image staring back at her in the mirror.

Who was this girl?

She studied the contours and shape of her face; eyes set neatly apart, nose not too big or too small. Absently, she rubbed her lips together, watching the lipstick slowly fade. She wondered if her hair was too light, too brown, and should be worn loose around her shoulders instead of twisted up, pinned with her favorite sparkly barrette.

Did it really matter?

There was nothing left.

Tess slipped a retractable razor blade from her pant pocket— staring at it, contemplating what she wanted to do with it. How would it feel against her skin? Her neck? Would it hurt? How long would she stay conscious if she cut too deep? She pushed her thumb against the blade, moving it in the light to cast shapes on the bathroom wall and wondering whether or not to take her own life.

CHAPTER 10

Wednesday 1325 hours

Even though she hadn't spoken to Amanda yet, Katie was slowly beginning to create a preliminary profile of the perpetrator in her case. If this person who had taken Amanda against her will really existed then the kidnapper was someone who had a heightened sense of predatory behavior.

In the file, Windham had written out Amanda's account of what had happened the night she was taken. She left the grocery store and was sure that no one was around or had followed her. It was late, just before closing, and the parking lot was mostly deserted. She unlocked her car and just as she was about to get inside someone grabbed her from behind, overpowering her and taping her mouth and eyes before dragging her to another vehicle. She believed that she was put inside a trunk and driven to the location that she had escaped from. Her car was later towed and impounded. According to the paperwork, she had paid the fee to retrieve her car seven days after the initial report was filed.

Katie started to list out a rough idea of the abductor's profile. Nothing was set in stone, but it helped her to see the behavior evidence and pertinent questions more clearly—allowing for updates and changes when necessary.

Predatory Behavior versus Opportunistic Behavior (most likely PB). Male. Age? 30-45?

Previous? Unknown at this time. Not enough information. (NEI)
Educated? Not necessarily. (NEI)
Clever. Devious.
Organized. Prepared. Quick/Efficient. Practiced?
Planned? Had tools/tape, car, and abandoned location.
Fantasy oriented? From childhood? Adolescence? From own
received mental/physical abuse?

Skimming through the report again, Katie read that Deputy Windham stated Amanda claimed she was tied to a bed, and that the man had taken the tape from her mouth but not from her eyes and repeatedly whispered into her ear phrases like, "you want to tell me the truth" and "tell me your secrets" and "the truth." After the man left, she claimed she yelled for hours to no avail, but she could hear faint sounds of traffic in the distance.

Katie added to the list:

Signature—Bondage. Taped victim's eyes. Women in distress—at
his mercy.
Whispers to victim—to hide identity? Or, part of his fantasy?
Truth? Meaning? Perpetrator's fantasy? Wanting confessions?
Taken somewhere remote—no one heard her screams. No
indication of soundproofing: traffic sounds.
She was found near Basin Woods Development—abandoned
housing area slated for tear down and rebuild—county in
stalemate over budget. (Further Research)
Kept her eyes covered—Abductor didn't want his identity known
and/perhaps didn't want to look in her eyes.
Traffic/cars? Rural enough where no one heard screams, but traffic
could be heard? (Need Research)

Katie stood with her hands on her hips reading the list. She tilted her head to one side and wondered if it was a crime of opportunity—whether Amanda was selected or just was in the wrong place at the wrong time. Was it someone she knew? Or someone she came into contact with regularly at work, home or in her spare time? As a nurse she'd spend the majority of time at the hospital working shifts, but that hardly narrowed the field with constantly changing employees, patients, and contractors.

Pulling out a county map, Katie estimated that is was approximately five miles from Amanda's apartment to the hospital. She drew a five-mile radius around the hospital and apartment and studied what was included within; mostly residential areas, shopping malls, and several office buildings. She let out a sigh.

Logging off her computer, she grabbed her jacket and briefcase and headed towards the exit. She peeked into one of the examination rooms as she passed, seeing John deeply immersed, staring into the eyepiece of a microscope, his body completely still. She was going to say goodbye, but decided not to interrupt him.

Out of the building and into her car, she reminded herself of the last known address for Emily Day from her arrest record, which was located at 543 Forest Avenue, apartment #10.

After winding her way through Pine Valley for almost fifteen minutes, she finally took a left turn onto Forest Avenue and found the apartment building at 543. It was pretty with carefully tended shrubs and intricate black wrought-iron fencing. The full bloom of a bright pink bougainvillea climbing up the side of the building was quite spectacular, reminding Katie of an English country garden she had once seen in a magazine. It was beautiful and extremely inviting to anyone who happened to visit.

Katie found a parking space on the street and quickly made her way to the apartment building, the aroma of fresh flowers like a sweet and citrus cup of herbal tea. From what Katie could ascertain, there were eight small apartments on the ground floor and four larger apartments on the second level. The #10 apartment was located upstairs, so Katie took the metal staircase on the side of the building and rehearsed a few things in her mind that she would ask Emily—and Amanda, if indeed she was staying with her friend.

Katie pressed the doorbell. At first, she didn't think there was anyone home until she heard footsteps slowly approaching. The door opened a few inches and an attractive woman with dark hair peered through the crack. With relief, Katie immediately recognized Amanda Payton from the photograph in her file.

"Yes?" she said quietly as her eyes darted around and then rested on Katie.

"Amanda Payton?" Katie said gently.

The woman's eyes grew bigger at the sound of her name; it was clear that she had been crying from the smudge of makeup beneath them.

"Ms. Payton, I'm Detective Katie Scott from the sheriff's office. May I have a moment to speak with you?"

"What about?" she said, though her tone indicated that she already knew.

Katie glanced around. "I think it would be best if we spoke inside. May I come in?"

Amanda stared at her for a few tense moments as if contemplating what to do. Tears welled up in her eyes. "No. I won't be called a liar again." She slammed the door shut and locked it.

Katie blinked at the door. It was clear that Amanda was still quite distraught and scared, and that she knew that the sheriff's department wasn't exactly on her side. But Katie wasn't going to walk away. There was something to Amanda's story, and she was going to try to get to the bottom of it. Taking a breath, she knocked on the door again.

No answer.

She knocked again, harder this time.

"Please, Amanda. I'd really like to speak with you. We can figure this whole thing out—together."

There was some movement inside, but the door remained shut.

Katie hung her head and tried to think how she would feel if something that terrible had happened to her and the police let her down. "Amanda, you don't have to talk to me. I won't force you," she said. "But I want to help you. And I *do* believe you."

Nothing.

Katie glanced around, leaned in closer and lowered her voice, sensing that Amanda was just on the other side, still listening. "I know what it's like to be scared. I went through a lot in the military and I've only just been able to start working again. It's scary. I keep fighting with myself—internally—about whether or not I'm going to be able to handle it all. But here I am."

She waited.

"Amanda, at least let me try to help you."

Katie was just about to turn and leave when she heard the rattle of locks and then the door opened a few inches.

"I suppose you're not going to take no for an answer," Amanda said.

"Please, I only have a few questions," Katie replied.

Amanda gestured for Katie to come inside, where she could hear someone humming above the sound of a hairdryer.

"Is Emily here?"

"She's about to leave."

Katie perched on a straight-backed chair in the living room, leaning slightly forward and keeping her focus on Amanda. It was obvious that the woman was nervous as she fidgeted about the room before settling down on the couch next to a wooden end table. On it was a vintage lamp, a small beaded purse, a box of Kleenex, a small water glass, and two prescription bottles.

The living room was small and led into an open kitchen. The furniture, two chairs and a couch, were all different in material and print, which gave an eclectic vibe. There was a neatly folded quilt and pillow on one end of the couch, which was obviously where Amanda slept.

Katie began, "Ms. Payton, I'm here about your case and I wanted to ask some follow-up questions. If you're up to it?" She knew that she had to move forward slowly to allow Amanda to open up in her own time.

"Okay."

"I read the deputy and detective's reports but I wanted to ask you a couple of questions of my own, especially now that some time has passed."

"I... I... can still hear his voice in my head. It's always there," Amanda interrupted.

"Did he seem to know you?"

"What do you mean?"

Katie treaded lightly and said, "Well, like did he know about things in your life, where you worked, the things you liked, or where you hung out?" She waited patiently.

"Well... I'm not sure..." Her face turned pale as if she had never thought about that before.

"Please, just take your time and think about it."

Amanda sat quietly, not really focusing on anything around the apartment as her gaze wandered. "Maybe he did mention something about my job."

"Like?"

"Like, it didn't pay enough. Nursing wasn't a good fit for someone like me. He kept telling me to tell him the truth, as if everything I said to him was a lie." Her voice wavered.

Katie took her small field notebook from her jacket pocket. "Did he remind you of anyone you worked with at the hospital?"

"I don't think so."

"Are you still employed there?"

"No. I quit a while ago. I didn't feel safe. I started feeling like he might be watching me."

"What do you mean?" Katie asked.

"I felt someone was following me, watching as I came and went. I couldn't take it anymore."

"Did you ever see anyone suspicious?"

"I don't know. It might just be me, but I feel like he's around every corner... I can't live like this..."

"What about your apartment? Maybe someone you've seen coming and going from there?"

"No. I... I don't think so..."

"Is there anyone who might want to hurt you? Or anyone that has ever threatened you before or since then?" Katie pushed. "I'm sorry, but I have to ask these questions. Maybe you might remember someone, an incident, something that didn't seem important at the time, but maybe now might."

Amanda sighed and said, "No. I've wracked my brain but I can't think who would *do* something like that?" she said, almost on the verge of crying.

"The report said that you were tied up for about a week. Five or six days? Is that correct?"

"Yes. I... I think it was five, maybe six days. I'm not exactly sure. It was hard to know the amount of days—when it was day or night. It seemed like a lifetime." She hesitated, taking a deep breath. "I really don't know why you're here asking all these questions. I've answered these already. Do you have any suspects?" she countered.

"No, but I'm looking into your case," Katie said. "During the entire time you were held, you never once saw his face? Not even a glimpse?"

She shook her head and shuddered at the very thought of him. "No."

Katie made a couple of notes about Amanda's answers and her obvious still terrified demeanor.

"Why are you dragging all this back up again? Do you at least have any new leads?" Amanda sat back in fear. "Did another woman come forward? Or worse…"

"I need to gather all the information that I can get from every possible source," Katie said gently, trying to keep her voice calm and to maintain Amanda's focus. "Amanda, I'm on your side. I want to find the person that did this."

"You didn't answer me. Did another woman come forward?" she asked directly.

"No," Katie replied. "But I'm going to be looking into other cases for any similarities to your case, so that's why I need to know every little thing that you can remember. Anything that will help me."

"D-did he kill someone?" Her body trembled as she ignored Katie's answer.

"There haven't been any homicides that would indicate a link. You or any other woman should never be afraid because of what he did—and I'm going to do everything I can to catch him for you."

Amanda's eyes filled with tears as she nodded, appearing to understand what Katie was telling her.

"Is there *anything* you can remember that's not in your report— no matter how small it might seem to you." Katie reverted back to her field training and how important it was to use all the senses. "Smells? Something you might've touched? Any little sound? Anything at all?"

"I don't know—I told the deputy everything," she said. "But… maybe there was this smell, like spring, or something."

"What do you mean?" Katie asked.

"Flowers. Honeysuckle or lilac, something like that. Wait, no, it was jasmine. I'm sure of it."

"Was there a window open? It was still summer. Or was it only when the man was there, like he was wearing cologne or used a particular soap?"

Amanda's mood suddenly changed, shaken by Katie's probing questions, at being forced to take herself back to that moment. "I can't talk to you—I can't keep going back to that time. There's nothing more I can tell you that I haven't already told the police. Please… please just go."

Katie rose from the chair. "Amanda, I assure you that I'm going to do everything I can to catch this man."

"So how many police officers are working my case? Huh?" She paused, waiting for the hint of a response from Katie. "It's just you, isn't it?" Tears welled up in her eyes again.

"For now, I'm working your case, but I can assure you that I have more detectives at my disposal." Katie knew that she was stretching the truth a bit, but she needed to gain Amanda's confidence. She was doing everything she could, and would continue to do so.

"Detective Scott, is it? Please leave." Her voice was now stern.

Katie wanted to reassure her in every way possible, but she was just as concerned as Amanda was about this man still roaming for potential victims. She reached into her pocket and retrieved a business card. "My personal cell is on the back. If you think of anything or just need someone to talk to, please don't hesitate to call me." She put the card on the small end table next to the prescription bottles. She couldn't see the name of the type of medication.

Amanda fought back tears with her arms crossed in front of her, hugging herself for dear life.

Katie was going to say something more, but realized that there was nothing left to say. She had done everything she could—at least for now.

When Katie reached the front door, Amanda's quiet voice stopped her before she turned the knob.

"He said that I would *never* be without him. That he would come for me. And I know that he will eventually kill me. I'm getting everything together to leave California and move to Idaho, where I have a cousin that has agreed to help me, and take me in until I get back on my feet. I'm changing my name."

"I know there's no reason for you to believe me, but I will catch him. So for now, please stay around people like your friend Emily here. Don't go out at night. Don't go anywhere alone. I will contact the patrol sergeant who oversees this area and ask him to have officers drive by here on a regular basis." She paused. "Take care of yourself. I'll be in touch."

CHAPTER 11

Wednesday 1830 hours

Katie hurried to the entrance of the 1893 Gideon Historic Building. The three-story brick building had been an old hotel and boarding house in the late 1800s and through the 1920s and contrasted with the rest of the downtown block of modern offices. She stepped up on to the creaky porch and entered the main area, admiring the ornate staircase in the center, and taking in the original light sconces and crown molding as she walked across the antique hardwood floors.

Although it was difficult to completely shut out her Amanda Payton investigation, she wanted to enjoy a couple of hours with her uncle. It had been their tradition for many years—as long as she could remember—to spend one afternoon every month roaming around various art exhibitions. They'd been lucky to get tickets for this special black-and-white photography exhibit sponsored by several top film and local entertainment companies.

As her eyes adjusted to the low lighting in the gallery, the soothing classical music playing in the background made Katie relax for the first time in days. She didn't immediately search for her uncle, but rather, allowed herself to become captivated by the outdoor scenes depicted in the photos. The series was titled *Stepping Outside* and showed many landscapes, buildings, random people, and close-ups of various objects found outside. Her instant favorite was an image of an old porch, which was slightly skewed giving it an otherworldly view. The building had been halfway restored and you could see the old and new; the dilapidated wood and peeling paint in stark contrast to the new boards with shiny nails.

Katie stepped back a little and studied the photograph from afar.

"Fascinating, isn't it?" said her uncle as he gave her a quick kiss on the cheek.

"It really is, depending on which way you look at it."

"I've read an article about a couple of these photographers and how they get their inspiration. It's a great exhibit. Unfortunately, they're only here for a couple of days."

"I'm glad we didn't miss it."

"You okay?" he asked.

"You know the rules. No shoptalk until I've seen everything and have a hamburger and chocolate shake in front of me."

"Of course," said the sheriff. "C'mon, let's start over here." He guided Katie to the far end and they began to work their way around the gallery.

"Okay, spill," said the sheriff sitting across from his niece at their favorite diner.

"That didn't take you very long," said Katie chuckling.

"How was your first week?"

"You read my report, didn't you?"

"Of course, but I'm asking you."

"You know, Uncle Wayne, there's a thin line between asking and interrogating," she said lightheartedly as the server dropped off a chocolate shake for her and a root beer float for her uncle. She savored the ice-cold drink for a moment before she began, waving a spoonful of whipped cream around to punctuate her point. "I'm beginning to see why no one wants to investigate cold cases."

"What makes you say that?" he asked.

"There's many directions you can go. The big question is where exactly to start."

"Now you see why they are *cold* cases."

"This case bothers me though."

"Which one?" he asked.

"Amanda Payton's abduction. There's something unusual about it," she said trying to overcome her ice cream headache.

"Do you think she's telling the truth or trying to cover something up?" The sheriff watched her closely, only taking his eyes off her to quickly glance around the room to make sure no one was listening.

Katie leaned back, taking a break from her ice cream. She was amazed that her uncle was so on top of these old cases. "I'm in agreement with Deputy Windham. I think she's absolutely telling the truth."

"I saw your formal request with the watch commander to have patrol drive by her residence on a regular basis. Good work. I agree with your decision."

She leaned forward and lowered her voice slightly. "I went to see her. She's petrified he's coming back for her. You can see it in her eyes and in her body language. It's truly disturbing."

"Is there any possibility that she might be suffering from some sort of cognitive disturbance or illness? Schizophrenia?"

The server with long dark hair braided down almost the full length of her back dropped off two large burgers and a giant basket of French fries. "Anything else?" she asked.

"No, we're good. Thank you," said Katie.

"Thank you," her uncle said as the waitress left.

Taking a big bite, Katie wrestled with her food before she answered her uncle. "No," she said, wiping her mouth. "I believe that she experienced something terrible and her story is credible, but..."

Finishing her sentence, he said, "But finding corroborating evidence is the problem."

Katie nodded. "I'm inching closer though." She took another bite. "Are these burgers getting better, or what?"

Swiping a French fry through a mound of catsup, he said, "It seems like it. I only eat here when I'm with you." He smiled. "Maybe it's the company?"

"Uncle Wayne, are you buttering me up so I'll tell you all my cold-case secrets?" She laughed.

"I know how driven you can be. This placement is a little different than the other detective positions. You're allowed some leeway and to oversee your own schedule."

"And?"

"I don't say this lightly. Please be mindful—and careful. Understand?"

"Of course."

"I mean it." He stared directly at her, eye to eye, to emphasize his concern.

Katie softened. "I understand. There's always going to be some risk, but I'm making the right choices. Thinking before I leap."

"That's what I'm talking about. You are so single-minded about solving these cases," he said.

"Isn't that the point?" She ran her finger up the side of the cold glass. "You promoted me to this position for a reason—I'm not like other detectives."

"Don't force me to make it a temporary position." He suppressed a little laugh.

"You would do that?" she said surprised.

"All I'm saying is be a little bit more conservative and don't jump in headfirst with everything."

"I know you're right. There's just a lot to digest right now and the suspect pool is too general and too large—which is frustrating."

"I did some checking to make sure that there wasn't some rule against it."

"Against what?" she asked. Her curiosity piqued as she swallowed another bite.

"I know that some of your field investigations can take you to places alone—sometimes after hours—and I think that it might be a good idea to bring Cisco with you during those times."

"Is it okay to bring him to my office?" Katie was intrigued by the idea, and she knew full well that Cisco would love being with her instead of at home alone.

"No, but you can house him at the department's kennel when you're working, and then take him when you head out somewhere."

"I know Cisco would love being there, like he has a job again—even if it was just a kennel."

"He's a great dog and I know you've been taking him to some of the K9 training."

"Yes, actually Sergeant Hardy asked me to join in whenever I like."

"Good. But I still need for you to include in your weekly reports the days that Cisco is with you and in what capacity. Understood?"

"Got it," she said. "Don't worry, I promise I will be careful out there."

CHAPTER 12

Thursday 0845 hours

Katie stood in her office staring at her whiteboard. It helped her to recap all the information she had first thing in the morning, to walk around her office and take it all in; not something she'd be free to do upstairs in the detective division.

She sighed, realizing how lucky she was to have such free rein working cold cases; but she was also frustrated at herself for not producing results fast enough. She knew that there would be the occasional stumbling blocks, and leads that would go nowhere, but this case was extra-complicated because she was dealing with the incident in the past *and* the ongoing threat in the present. She needed to come up with a strategy that would keep everything on track.

As she thought about all her options, the phone on her desk rang, startling her. Tentatively she picked up the receiver and held it to her ear. "Detective Scott."

"There's been a homicide. I need you out there," stated her uncle.

"Me?" Katie was momentarily confused why she was being informed.

"It's Amanda Payton. Someone found her body early this morning."

Katie's heart pounded against her ribcage. "Where?" she said, trying to sound calm and professional.

"A young couple out running this morning found her body at a vacant lot near Whispering Pines," he said.

"There's been an ID already?"

"Her purse was found nearby with her driver's license and her identification from the First Memorial Hospital."

"I see," said Katie, her mind whirring. "Who's running the case?" she asked.

"Detective Bryan Hamilton."

"I don't know him," she said, trying to put a face with the name.

"He's new to the department, a transplant from Stockton PD."

"I guess my cold case just got hot," she said.

"That's why I need you."

"I can get all the information that I've been accumulating on Hamilton's desk before he makes it back to the station."

"No, you do not understand, Katie. I need *you* to go to the crime scene and work the area with Detective Hamilton. I've already spoken to him and he's waiting for you."

"Oh."

"Did you hear what I said? He's waiting for you right now." Her uncle's voice was commanding.

"I'm on my way," she said, already halfway out the door.

CHAPTER 13

Thursday 0945 hours

Katie drove as fast as she could to the empty site near Whispering Pines that was destined to be the town's new shopping mall. It was a pristine area that really represented the beauty of Pine Valley, with trails that bypassed around the vicinity and accommodated a large section of California pine trees. It wasn't really called Whispering Pines. That was what most people called it because of the sound that the trees made when the wind blew—the sound of someone whispering.

Katie tried to focus as she readied herself for what she had to do next. It pained her so much that Amanda's fears had been realized, that she couldn't help her, but for now she had to think only of the task in hand.

Slowing her vehicle as she neared the area, Katie could see the first responders and crime scene unit were already there, which made parking tight. She had no choice but to park farther away and then walk, which gave her a little time to try and compose herself before working her first official homicide crime scene with a detective she had never met before.

Standing with the driver's door open, she clutched the side of the car to steady herself as the breeze chased up the dust from the larger vehicles ahead of her, dredging up a long-buried memory.

The heavy dust mixed with scorching heat was something that was always difficult to deal with, but you had to forge ahead no matter what. It was forever in your eyes, mouth, and lungs. All of us were exhausted—even Cisco seemed tired as he kept the grueling pace towards a small village that had been known to be on our side. We passed a little girl and her mother preparing food in a big metal pot outside their house. It smelt delicious and I smiled as the little girl pointed at Cisco as we passed.

My eyes locked with the mother and I felt her gratitude spur me on. But something made me look back before we turned the corner. Then came the explosion. In an instant, mother and daughter were gone…

Katie blinked in shock, gulping back the memory she had packed away so neatly in her past. Her boots felt like they were filled with lead, but she forced herself to reach for her small field notebook and a pair of latex-free gloves; she had a job to do.

Weaving around several vehicles, she finally reached the small number of deputies that had assisted in securing the scene, and now were busy keeping bystanders away from the area. Katie recognized Deputy Windham among them, and when their eyes met, he made his way over to her.

"Detective," he said with a serious expression.

"Is it really her?" she asked, though she already knew the answer. He looked somber. "I'm afraid so."

"I'm here to assist Detective Hamilton."

"Oh course, he's over there." The deputy pointed in the direction past the morgue van.

"Thank you," she answered in a voice calmer than she felt.

As Katie neared the crime scene, she was shocked to see that the body was still in its original position. She had expected it to be already loaded into the van. She swallowed hard, knowing she would have to see Amanda Payton's body up close. The reality of the situation knotted her gut as she remembered reassuring Amanda that she would have patrol drive by her home to keep her safe.

Katie focused on the tall man with dark wavy receding hair talking to one of the deputies. He was in his mid-forties, she guessed, and was dressed better than most of the detectives. He looked in her direction. His expression was somber as he watched her approach.

"Detective Katie Scott?"

"Yes. Detective Hamilton?" she replied.

"Bryan."

"Nice to meet you." She shook his hand. It was firm, the strong handshake of someone trying to assert their claim.

"I know all about you," he said, clearly not amused that he had to wait for a rookie detective to arrive to support *his* crime scene.

"And what's that?" Katie countered, wanting to get everything out in the open so that they could get on with the investigation.

"You found those missing girls single-handedly. At least, that's what the sheriff said," he taunted.

"Nice of you to say, but I certainly wasn't alone."

"That's not the way I heard it," he mumbled.

Katie changed the subject. "I hope that I'm not overstepping. I was told that I'd be assisting you on this case." She tried to be diplomatic and keep her voice even.

"The sheriff explained the situation," he said and walked back to the body. "You knew her?"

"I met with her just yesterday to talk about her kidnapping case and to see if I could get more information." She tried to keep her voice steady as she followed him over to the edge of the scene and allowed herself to glance quickly at the body for the first time. Amanda was naked, her beautiful, lithe body facedown in the grass. Katie didn't flinch, aware that everyone around was watching her closely.

"She was definitely afraid that this… might happen," Katie managed as the image of the smiling mother and child in Afghanistan flashed through her mind. She looked away from the crime scene and was relieved to see John on his knees organizing evidence containers, waiting for the go-ahead to begin processing the scene—waiting on her to do her job.

"Well, let's get started. I assume you've done this before?" Bryan asked.

"What's your procedure? I can tell you what I see and then we switch positions," she said.

"Be my guest." He pulled a small wire-bound notebook from his inside jacket pocket to jot down notes. "After you…"

"Okay," she said, looking back down at the body, seeing it properly for the first time. There was no avoiding what she had to do next. Silence fell. No one spoke. Even the police radios had been turned down.

Amanda's head was turned to the right, exposing several rows of reddened marks across her pallid neck. Her dark hair partially obscured her face, arms bent close to her torso with palms down, pressing against the earth, and her legs straight close together. She looked more like a mannequin than the woman she had spoken with barely twenty-four hours ago.

Katie pulled on her gloves, hoping that no one noticed her trembling hands. She needed to focus on the small details, the same way she had done in the army when she searched specific areas for tripwires and bomb devices. Keeping her focus narrowed and thorough would help her manage the full horror of the situation unfolding in front of her.

Katie knelt close to Amanda and carefully pulled her wet hair away from her neck and face to reveal more of the marks on her throat. "It appears to be strangulation with these ligature marks on her neck—someone strangled her from behind. Whatever was used is consistent with the restraint marks you can see on her wrists and ankles. Rope or twine." She gently picked up Amanda's arm and studied the marks on her wrists, which were faint but distinct.

Katie moved around the body, working in a clockwise rotation.

She scrutinized Amanda's entire body and couldn't see any other wounds, only the pooling of blood at the bottom of her torso and the back of her legs as livor mortis set in and the slight stiffening of her arms and body indicating the early stages of rigor mortis. "Judging by the lividity, she was killed somewhere else and dumped here afterwards—this is the secondary crime scene. But what I'm not sure…" She looked at a strange mark on the side of the woman's back, near her waistline; a long imprint with two lines going vertical.

"What is that?" asked the other detective.

"Not sure, but it could be something that she was forced up against when she was restrained. Like some type of furniture, outdoor railing, or maybe a car?"

"Forensics will get photos," he said.

"I'm not one hundred percent sure, but it appears that these restraint marks were post mortem. The medical examiner will be able to tell," she said.

"Why would he restrain her if she was already dead?" He took a couple of notes. "Why?"

Katie studied the marks on the body and then noticed an almost imperceptible thread wedged under her middle fingernail. She turned and said to John, "We need to bag her hands before she gets put on the gurney. I can see some foreign fibers under her nails."

John nodded as he continued to wait until she was done with her initial scene examination.

"Good eye, Detective," said Hamilton, but his voice still wasn't friendly.

"Wait… there's something else," she said, taking her pen and cautiously prizing up Amanda's pinky and ring finger to reveal a crumpled piece of paper curled into her fist.

"What is that?" the detective asked.

"I think it is…" she hesitated. "It looks like a business card."

"Whose?"

Katie flattened the card and was taken aback. "Mine. I gave her my business card when I spoke with her."

"Why would the killer do that?"

"I'm speculating, but whoever did this must know I was looking into her case. Maybe they want to send a warning?" Katie swallowed hard. Seeing her name clutched in Amanda's lifeless hand sent chills down her spine. As if on cue, a gust of wind blew through the area causing the pines trees to sway and whisper around her.

"How would they know that you would be working this homicide?" he asked.

"I just spoke with her only yesterday and gave her my card. Maybe she kept it on her? It's like he's telling us he's the one in control, that this was the way it *should* have been," she said.

"What do you mean?"

"Well, Amanda escaped from him once, so maybe he set this all up to re-enact what should have happened if she *hadn't*."

"Posing? A recreation?"

"Something like that. It's like he's letting us know that he corrected a mistake, one he won't let happen again. Interesting."

Detective Hamilton turned his gaze to the body and seemed to be lost in thought—could he not see what she saw?

"What was the weather like early this morning? Was there any heavy mist or rain?" she asked.

"I don't think so, it was like it is now. Overcast and cool."

"So why is her hair so wet?" She leaned forward and smelled Amanda's hair. It had a strange chemical smell, almost like rotten eggs. Like the smell that they use for propane so that you can detect gas leaks. "Her hair smells like sulfur."

Katie stood up and began to survey the area. The body was far away from anywhere where a car could easily park without being seen. Looking around her and following the most probable path, she jogged up a small hill where a car would have been able to park and dump a body early in the morning.

"What's up?" Hamilton shouted up to her.

"Why aren't there any drag marks leading to the body? The grass is flattened where someone walked, but no identifying shoe or tire marks." She slowly walked back toward the body studying the ground. "I think the killer must have carried her to this spot. I think the location is strategic for him. I don't know why—yet. But with the extra weight, why no footprints? Unless they wore something to cover their shoes."

"Like crime scene or hospital booties?"

"Yeah. Our killer is cautious and mindful of what he's doing. Everything is so neat. It's calculated, know what I mean?" she said.

"Very impressive analysis for a rookie detective. No offense."

Katie laughed; it helped to relieve some of her tension. "None taken, Detective. We need to cover the body in case this wind kicks up any harder so that we won't lose any potential evidence. I would also increase the search area by fifty percent."

Detective Hamilton made a couple more notes and snapped his notebook shut. Katie took one last look at Amanda, glad that her eyes were closed, and not staring at her as if to say, "why didn't you help me?"

CHAPTER 14

Thursday 1415 hours

"Hi," said Katie to the sheriff's assistant. "He wanted to see me."

She replied with a smile, "Go right in, they're waiting for you."

Katie continued toward the partially closed office door where she heard several men's voices. She opened the door and saw her uncle, Detective Hamilton, and Deputy McGaven standing together. They turned at the interruption.

"Hi, everyone," she managed.

"Please come in and close the door," the sheriff said. "Take a seat."

Everyone followed suit and sat down. No one spoke, waiting for the sheriff to make his point.

"Okay, we're all busy so I promise this will be short and sweet," he said with a crisp authority to his voice. "I've given this a lot of thought and I think this is the best and most efficient way to proceed."

Katie felt reassured that both Hamilton and McGaven appeared to be just as much in the dark as she was about the meeting.

"Amanda Payton was originally a kidnapping cold-case being investigated by Detective Scott," the sheriff began.

Hamilton and Katie nodded in agreement.

"So what I would like to do is to have Katie take lead on her homicide." He paused. "And I would like for Hamilton to take over lead on the serial burglary and assault cases that are pending."

Everyone remained quiet—each digesting what the sheriff had just told them.

Detective Hamilton shifted his weight in his seat, but he remained silent.

"But I have no problem with—" Katie started to say.

"I know you don't want to step on anyone's toes," the sheriff quickly countered. "I really want Detective Hamilton to oversee these other cases, and the Payton homicide needs someone's full attention. It's no secret that we've lost a lead detective recently due to misconduct during the missing girls' case, and the budget isn't getting any closer to allowing for me to hire or promote the two additional detectives we so desperately need."

Katie sat quietly; she wasn't sure if she agreed with her uncle's decision.

"So why am I here?" asked McGaven, cutting the tension in the room.

The sheriff laughed. "I haven't forgotten you, McGaven. I would like for you to partner with Detective Scott on this case. There's plenty of work for the both of you and you seem to work well together. I've spoken to both your patrol sergeant and the watch commander, so they can make the appropriate scheduling modifications in your temporary absence. You'll need to complete the special assignment you had been working on first, but that shouldn't take more than a day or so."

Katie smiled. She knew that he would be the best partner for her and was glad that her uncle had appointed him to her case. McGaven had been assigned to work with her in her first case for Pine Valley PD. It had been a rocky start, but they both managed to work things out.

McGaven looked shocked, then a slight smile broke out on his face.

"Unless of course you want to remain on patrol," said the sheriff, now also smiling.

"I would love the opportunity to work this case. Thank you for thinking of me, sir."

"Okay, we're all in agreement here?" the sheriff said. "No problems?"

"Do we even have a choice?" said Hamilton. It was clear he was annoyed by a rookie detective taking over a homicide, but there was little Katie could do about it.

"Good. Let's not waste any more time," the sheriff said. "You're all dismissed."

Katie was heading for the door, her mind rolling, when Hamilton stopped her. "I suppose you'll want all of the information I have forwarded to your office downstairs," he said with sarcasm in his voice.

"Thank you," she said, pretending not to have noticed his tone. He was going to need a little time to cool off, she understood that.

McGaven jogged up beside her and it was easy to see that he was eager to get started. "So," he said. "I get to work down in the depths of the forensic basement?"

"How many detectives get to do that?" she asked.

"It's kind of like law enforcement's version of the bat cave."

"C'mon, Robin, we've got a lot of work to do. So hurry up and finish your current assignment," Katie reminded him.

"Hey, wouldn't it make more sense if you were Robin and I was…"

"Don't press your luck."

CHAPTER 15
Thursday 1530 hours

As promised, everything in the Amanda Payton homicide file was delivered to Katie by one of the administrative assistants. Obviously, Detective Hamilton wasn't in the mood to offer any personal insight about the case. She couldn't blame him for feeling put out.

Katie opened the brown folder and scanned everything collected in the few hours since leaving the crime scene. Hamilton had already begun to run a background on Amanda and he'd compiled a list of people he wanted to interview. There was also a printed copy of Amanda's original police report regarding her kidnapping. It was clear to Katie that the detective knew how to run a homicide investigation and he was quick to get started, knowing that the first three days were the most important. After that, physical evidence becomes non-existent and people's memories become fuzzy, or they just don't want to cooperate with police.

Taking out her notebook, Katie jotted down the people to talk to along with their contact information: Emily Day (Amanda's best friend/co-worker), Dr. Jamison (boss at First Memorial Hospital), Marco Ellis (ex-boyfriend), Dr. Smith (psychiatric hospital), Abigail Sorenson and Lisa Lambert (friends/co-workers). There was no mention of immediate family; no parents, no siblings, no next of kin that the detective was going to contact. But a hastily scribbled name, Bradley Olson, was added in as a cousin out of state in Connecticut, and Melissa Roe, another cousin in Idaho, who Katie remembered Amanda mentioning that she was going to be staying with; an aunt was contacted but she was traveling abroad and was unavailable. Otherwise, Amanda didn't have any other immediate family.

Katie finished reading the file and found sticky notes indicating that they were still waiting on forensic results and the autopsy report. One particular note piqued her interest, an evidence number: PAY321. There was no further explanation and she didn't want to call Detective Hamilton for help just yet. She leaned back in her chair realizing that she needed to combine all the information she had gathered from the cold case with the homicide file to make sure that she didn't miss anything. Nothing was going to fall through the cracks on this case—not on her watch.

Katie tapped her pen against the side of her jaw; she stood up and added a few notes to her profile of the perpetrator on the board:

TRUTH? What does this mean to the perp? Why did Amanda repeat this?
Other definitions of TRUTH: fact, certainty, honesty, loyalty, devotion. Opposite: dishonesty lies, deception.

Katie contemplated the entire list. She wanted to have a confident direction before McGaven joined her, then she would divide the duties between them to cover more ground.

First, she needed to check out the evidence locker. She slipped the sticky note with the identifying number into her pocket.

Katie left the forensic section and hurried down the long dim hallway leading into the property and evidence unit. It was an area that she hadn't had a chance to visit yet.

She reached the door to a caged office with two desks and a wall full of filing cabinets leading into a large storage area. It looked more like a bunker than an office or storage facility. There was no one there.

"Hello?" she called out.

Silence.

She tried the door and was surprised to find it unlocked. Walking inside, she stood at the entrance and said again, "Hello? It's Detective Scott."

Looking around, she saw two neat piles of reports along with a thick clipboard filled with identifying numbers. Everything appeared neat and organized, which was a good sign. Even the trash can had been recently emptied.

Katie pulled the small piece of paper out of her pocket— PAY321—and decided to search for it herself. The clipboard had similar identifying numbers, each with three letters followed by three to four numbers.

She wasn't sure of the protocol, but didn't think that pulling an evidence container would cause any problem, so she entered the storage room: a huge area with specially made shelving units that went up two stories. Boxes and large plastic containers with lids sat on the shelves.

Katie wandered down two rows until she figured out which section matched the number she was looking for. Moving a ladder attached to the ceiling, she climbed up to the fourth shelf and found a box identifying as PAY321. She hauled it down and took it to a narrow metal table at the end of the row.

Flipping over the lid, Katie peered inside. There were two plastic evidence bags, each with a garment of clothing inside and an evidence receipt taped on top detailing the chain of custody. They were Amanda's tank top and panties, which had been sent from the South Street Psychiatric Hospital where she had been taken after the night of her alleged escape. She rummaged through the rest of the box finding several forms signed by Detective Petersen who had checked the box stating, "not to process." He had claimed that the victim retracted her original complaint. There was a note indicating if more evidence came to light, including witnesses, then the items would be processed.

Katie let out a breath, put the clothes back inside the box and closed the lid. The first thing she needed to do was get the garments tested and to visit the South Street Psychiatric Hospital.

Katie left a note on the desk for the evidence and property manager identifying herself and stating that she had taken the box to her office to have forensics test the evidence.

"Hi," said a stocky man in his thirties. "What can I do for you?"

"Hi," she said. "I'm Detective Scott and I was just leaving you a detailed note."

He looked at the box and eyed the identifying number.

"I'm sorry if I've broken protocol. I'm working cold cases and I got caught up in some new evidence that needs to be tested right away."

The property manager stared at her for a moment. She thought he might take the box from her. Instead, he smiled. "Don't worry about it. It's totally understandable. But, please don't make it a habit. I'm responsible for all the evidence."

"Of course. What's your name?"

"Bob."

"Nice to meet you," she said, heading out the door.

He nodded as he took a seat at his desk, carefully writing down the information on the clipboard.

CHAPTER 16

Thursday 1550 hours

He reveled in crowds, taking in each individual identity—everyone had a story to tell, a truth they were hiding in the way they dressed, a secret look, even a particular smell. Most people paid little or no attention to him. He had always been overlooked. That worked well in his favor and let him go about his work in peace.

He opened the lower cupboard in his small bathroom and pulled out every type of cleaning solution he could find—from hand soap to heavy-duty disinfectants. Each smell brought back vivid memories that he didn't want to forget. At last he found what he was looking for: a jasmine pump soap. It had always been his favorite scent, reminding him of a much different time in his life.

Turning on the hot tap in the sink, he waited until steam rose and the temperature was as hot as it could go before putting his hands under the water.

Scalding.

Red hot.

Burning his already-weathered hands, he marveled at how red his fingers became. Almost unbearable, but that was the way he liked it. He wanted to wipe away everything.

He pressed the hand soap dispenser three times for a generous lather. Washing his hands for nearly a minute, he slowly rinsed them under the hot water.

Taking a paper towel, he dabbed his skin dry, wanting to keep the integrity of the scent alive.

He smelled his palms, taking in a deep breath and savoring the scent.

He put the soap away, lingering a bit, before he turned off the light and left the room.

CHAPTER 17

Friday 0930 hours

The South Street Psychiatric Hospital resembled more of a jail than a medical facility for the mentally ill. The large building with two separate wings was painted an odd beige color that made it look like something half finished with only a primer coating.

After parking, Katie adjusted her badge and the gun hidden underneath her suit jacket to look as composed and experienced as possible. She didn't have a purse, so she put her small field notebook in her pocket along with a pen. Locking the vehicle, she headed towards the bleak main entrance; everything was monochrome, even the dry, pale grass blended in with the lack of color from the building.

Katie pushed through one of the glass doors and found herself in front of a reception booth manned by a young woman with a stern face. There was a small glass area with a round hole in the middle to communicate through.

"Hi, can I help you?" she asked without a smile.

"Hi, I'm Detective Katie Scott from the sheriff's department. I spoke with you on the phone earlier. I wanted to talk to the person who admits all patients brought in by the police for seventy-two-hour psychiatric watch."

The receptionist didn't even look up as she slipped a visitor badge and one sheet of paper through a space at the bottom of the window. "Please put your name, badge number and department here, and date and sign the release form here."

Katie quickly scribbled her consent to relieve the hospital from any liability if she got hurt, maimed, or killed during her visit.

"Please check any firearms and personal items, cell phone, keys, *any* personal items in there." She gestured to a small room with several lockers.

"Thank you," said Katie as she clipped her visitor badge to her jacket. "What's the name of the person I'm meeting?"

"Dr. Trent Smith, he's the supervising physician on duty." The woman turned away and began sorting through paperwork.

"Thank you," Katie said and moved to the special room where she relinquished her gun, keys, notepad, pen, and cell phone. Making sure the metal box was locked, she retrieved the key, depositing it into her pant pocket.

It suddenly struck Katie that she was entering into a dangerous, unknown place. She pushed the thought away from her mind as she waited for the heavy security door to unlock. A small camera lens was above her head and she knew someone monitored her carefully, no doubt, at that exact moment.

Katie watched as a heavy-set security guard opened a series of doors for her. "Please wait," he said as he re-locked the door behind her, making it clear she couldn't escape without assistance. Taking the lead, he turned to her. "Dr. Smith's office is this way."

Katie didn't know what disturbed her more: some of the patients wandering around in a type of fugue state, or the unpleasant odor of full bedpans. There was a faint hint of some type of air freshener, but its potency was no match for the stagnant space.

Katie kept her focus straight ahead as she followed the orderly into another area with minimum security, which housed the administrative and doctor's offices.

The burly man stopped at the door and said, "Here's Dr. Smith's office." Without a smile or another word, he left Katie at the closed door with cheap lettering displaying "Dr. T. Smith."

Looking up and down the deserted hallway, Katie then knocked on the door and heard a male voice call "Come in," from the other side. She turned the knob, unexpectedly cold in the stuffy heat of the hospital.

The office space wasn't what Katie had expected at all. In her mind, she thought it would be similar to the police department with neutral government-funded desks and chairs. But Dr. Smith's office was nicely decorated and quite tasteful with a dark mahogany desk and matching credenza and bookshelf. There were several potted plants and two pleasant seascape paintings that hung on the walls. Katie noticed that the two painting were originals, vaguely familiar, with the artist's signatures. The doctor obviously came from money. It was curious to her why he was at a mental health facility and not a cushy private practice.

"Detective Scott?" said the man behind the desk. He also wasn't what Katie had expected, dressed in dark jeans and a polo shirt. His dark features and light blue eyes—which made him appear to be looking through you, not at you—left Katie somewhat unnerved.

"Dr. Smith?" she said.

"So… tell me, what can I do for you?" He leaned forward on his desk with his arms crossed leaning on his elbows.

"I've been recently assigned to a homicide case at the sheriff's office. A woman who claimed to have been kidnapped and held against her will—then she escaped. Now she is dead."

"I see," he said without a trace of recognition. "And where do I fit in here?" He squinted as he scrutinized Katie more closely.

"I know all about doctor–patient confidentiality, but…"

"But what, Detective?"

Katie took a deep breath and felt defeat creeping into her investigation. "Look, I want to be honest with you."

"Please do."

"The person I wanted to discuss with you is Amanda Payton. Her kidnapping was a cold case, but now it's… it's a murder investigation."

"Okay," he deadpanned. He leaned back in his big leather office chair. "I get the impression that there's more to you than just police work—maybe you've been in the military?"

"Good guess." She disliked being scrutinized like this, especially by a therapist.

"No, not a guess," he corrected. "An educated deduction."

"I see." Katie managed a pleasant smile. "I can always go to a judge, but I don't think it's necessary."

"No, I don't think that will be necessary."

Katie remained silent.

"There's really not much to tell—I reacquainted myself with her file after you contacted the hospital ahead of your visit. And I assume that you already know most of it."

"I'd like to hear from you," she said. "I'm sure there are things I'm missing." She wanted to appeal to his expertise, pretend to be his subordinate.

"Well, she was brought in by two of your police deputies claiming she had been kidnapped and held against her will—but as luck was on her side she managed to escape." He picked up a gold pen with his right hand and rubbed his thumb along the side of it, clearly an old habit. "Let's see, she was highly agitated, coherent, fatigued. She was mildly dehydrated and needed a complete meal and fluids, but otherwise her physical health was satisfactory. We tended to her minor cuts and abrasions, but nothing needed stitches."

"And her mind?"

"Well, as you can imagine, she was unstable because she had been through a trauma. She kept repeating the same word over and over…"

"Truth," Katie said calmly.

"Yes! That was it. Ms. Payton whispered that word—*truth*."

"What did you do?"

"Well, what we always do. I gave her a sedative and she eventually went to sleep. The next morning she had more cognitive ability and I didn't think that she needed any further medication besides a mild sedative to take home. No use complicating things any more than they need be. I suggested that if she needed someone to talk to, she should come in for outpatient therapy." He had a half-smile on his face as he watched Katie.

"I see. Was there anything unusual or something that alerted your attention?"

"I'm not sure what you mean—alerted my attention?" He toyed with her.

"Meaning… something she did or said that seemed out of the ordinary—under the circumstances, of course," Katie said evenly.

He took a moment to think about it but Katie thought he was pausing for dramatic effect. "Nothing that needed to be notated."

It was Katie's turn to pause, but she thought about how it related to the perpetrator and not to Amanda. "One last thing."

"Shoot," he said.

"Has anyone else who has been admitted in the last six months claimed the same story as Amanda Payton, of being kidnapped and held against their will?" It was a spur of the moment question that popped into Katie's head.

"None that I can recollect… wait, except…"

"Except?" Katie perked up.

"A woman that was brought in about two months ago shared a similar-ish story, but I don't think she can help you much."

"Why not?" Katie asked.

"She doesn't know her own name and we still haven't been able to identify who she is."

CHAPTER 18

Katie followed Dr. Smith down several hallways—each time he unlocked doors and then re-locked them behind him. She counted five in total, which made her edgy, feeling as though the walls were closing in around her. They passed several uniformed doctors and nurses who all seemed to avoid contact, not showing any curiosity about Katie's presence. The farther they moved into the hospital the more patients Katie noticed; some watching television, while others worked at small tables with puzzles or games.

After making a quick left, Dr. Smith stopped at a door with a small viewing window, checked the clipboard on the wall and signed his initials.

"Well, here we are," he said.

"Thank you." Katie tried to force a relaxed smile.

"Of course, Detective, anything I can do."

"What do you call her?" she asked.

"Jane, as in Jane Doe, until we find out her name."

"Dr. Smith, where was Jane found and what was the approximate date?" she asked.

"It's my recollection that she was found near South Lincoln. I don't know the name of the street. And as for the date, it was about two and half months ago."

"She was found near the Basin Woods Development?"

"I believe that's correct. I'll have to check my notes to make sure. I can email you some information. Would that be sufficient?" he said.

"Yes, please, that would be helpful."

"Whatever you need, Detective."

Katie thought that was a strange response, but smiled politely and hoped that he meant what he had said.

He called to an orderly. "When Detective Scott is finished, please escort her back to the main entrance."

He nodded and took up position next to Jane's door to wait.

"If you have any further questions, please don't hesitate to call me directly," the doctor said, not waiting for Katie's reply before turning on his heel and heading back down the corridor.

Katie gave an apologetic smile to the orderly before giving the door a polite tap and twisting the handle.

The room wasn't as dreary as Katie had imagined. A large window with protective wire allowed for natural light to spill in even though it was overcast outside. A small writing desk and chair was in one corner, and a two-shelf bookcase sat across from it. There was a side table with a paperback with the cover torn off, a paper cup filled with water and a straw, as well as a torn pill packet.

The woman sat on a twin bed, feet on the ground, motionless, her head hanging forward. She wore light gray sweatpants and a white long-sleeved T-shirt that appeared to be two sizes too big on her slight frame. Her dark wavy hair was pulled back in a loose ponytail. Her posture and downturned expression made her seem much older than she was—but she wasn't really any older than thirty or thirty-five.

"Hello?" said Katie.

The woman remained still, dark-ringed eyes fixed on the floor, clearly heavily sedated.

"Jane, are you up for a visit?" Leaving the door slightly ajar, Katie looked around at the bookshelves and noticed that there were books about cats, gardening, and cooking; old and extremely worn, they were most likely donated. "I'm Detective Katie Scott from the sheriff's department. I wanted to chat with you for a bit. Is that okay?"

No response.

"I'm working on a case that you might be able to help me with," she continued.

Jane kept her head down and eyes averted.

Katie tried to think on her feet. "Do you like to garden? I wish I had more time to work in my garden," she said. "I'm surprised everything hasn't died, but I love my roses. My mom always loved roses. That's probably where I get my love of them." She sat gently next to her on the bed. "Jane, do you like roses?"

At last, just as she was thinking about leaving, Katie heard the woman speak.

"What color are they?" she quietly said.

"What?" Katie turned in surprise.

The dark-haired woman raised her head, staring directly at Katie, and asked again, "What color are your roses?"

Katie smiled and said, "Yellow."

"Like Texas?"

"You mean the yellow rose of Texas?"

She nodded.

"Are you from Texas?"

She didn't acknowledge one way or another and it was difficult to read her body language.

Katie tried a different approach. "Have you got roses in your garden?"

"Yes," she said softly.

"Do you remember where that is?"

She shook her head, but Katie had a distinct feeling that she wasn't being truthful. There was a spark of something in her eyes.

"What other flowers do you like?" said Katie.

She paused a moment, appearing to be thinking, and said, "Irises and peonies."

"Yes, I agree. They are so beautiful and come in so many different colors," said Katie. She casually walked to the window. "It's nice your room has a big window. Nice lighting. Indoor plants would do well."

Jane nodded and now watched Katie with tired, cautious eyes.

Katie glanced to the door to make sure the orderly was out of earshot and decided to change the direction of her questions. She said, "Do you know why I'm here? I'm working on a case of a woman who had been kidnapped and held against her will. Amazingly, she escaped."

Jane's hands began to fidget on her lap, averting her eyes so that Katie couldn't see her expression.

"My case only has a few unsubstantiated clues, but the victim is extremely scared that her attacker might come back—in fact—she believes one hundred percent that he *will* come back."

Jane remained quiet.

"I don't want anyone to feel that way. Do you?"

Jane glanced at Katie, just for a moment, but long enough for Katie to see the truth in there—the fear.

"If you're scared, we can protect you," she whispered so that the orderly couldn't hear her. "*I* can protect you."

But Jane only sank further back into herself. Her eyes fixed firmly back on the ground, her hands now still and lifeless.

It was no use; maybe Jane wasn't the link she needed, wasn't a victim of a kidnapping like Amanda's. Katie stood up to leave, but to her surprise, Jane grabbed hold of her wrist, hard, for a moment, and looked her directly in the eye in a way that could only mean *please help me*.

Katie didn't react, fearful of losing the moment and bringing unwanted attention from the orderly. Very carefully, suddenly aware that there might be cameras in the room, she said, "I would like to come back for a visit. Would you like that?"

Jane nodded and said, "Yes, that would be nice."

"Well, I'll come back in a couple of days."

The orderly poked his head into the room and said, "Detective, you ready yet?"

"Just a moment. It was nice meeting you, Jane. I wish I knew your real name." Katie turned her back to the door and mouthed the words *I will help you* to Jane.

Katie left the room, Jane's pleading eyes burning through her mind. She knew that there was more to her story, but there was nothing that she could do without a name and without a concrete link to Amanda's death.

Weaving her way back through the layers of doors and indistinct corridors, Katie finally entered the administration area and retrieved her firearm. She looked at the time and only then realized that Jane Doe had pressed her thumb hard into its face, leaving a fingerprint behind.

Clever.

Reaching into her jacket pocket, she pulled out a small folded bag, slipped off her watch and deposited it inside for safekeeping until she got back to the forensic office.

Katie hurried out to the parking lot, her mind whirring over what she'd just encountered, and almost didn't see the folded paper neatly tucked between the weather stripping of the driver's window. She cautiously pulled out the message, instinctively only holding it by its edges. The note was written with a blue ballpoint pen with heavier blotting on some of the words in slanted cursive writing:

You're on the right track.

CHAPTER 19

Friday 1300 hours

Katie returned to the office with more questions than answers. Pulling up a chair in front of her computer, she rebooted it to search for anything related to Jane Doe. Even with no ID, there had to be a police report. She quickly keyed in the search parameters from two months ago for a person who had been picked up and transported to the psychiatric hospital.

Her first computer search was unsuccessful.

Damn…

Katie tried again and this time used "Jane Doe" as part of the search parameters and opening out the date bracket. There was a hit. A Deputy Curtis had picked up a woman near South Lincoln and Second Street at 0200 hours a little over two months ago.

That was on the southern edge of the Basin Woods Development, which was the same approximate area where Amanda had been found. There wasn't much written in the report, so she would have to speak with the deputy. It was unclear from the report if fingerprints had been taken at that time. And if they were, the results were not in the file.

Katie printed out the report, firing off an email to arrange at least a phone meeting with Deputy Curtis as soon as it was convenient.

She stood up and walked to the counter, where she laid out her watch and the anonymous letter from her car next to the box of Amanda's clothes. She quickly filled out a chain of custody report and made sure that the new evidence was bagged properly. Everything was to be done by the book and she wanted to deliver these items to John in the forensics lab in person.

Katie watched intently as John's steady hands first removed the watch and laid it on an exam table, careful not to touch the band. He then opened a small round container with dark fingerprint dusting powder and swirled his circular brush into the mixture before dusting the watch all over.

"Is that a full print?" she asked, amazed by John's expert handling.

"It's a good clear image, but it's about sixty percent of the entire print of what looks like the left index finger." He prepared the sticky tape to transfer the print to an index card.

Katie was a bit disappointed. "Oh," was all she could say.

"Not to worry, Detective. There's more than enough to search the databases. Have patience." He smiled.

"That's great." She glanced at her copy of the short report filed for Jane Doe to make sure she hadn't missed anything.

"It may take a while. And there's no guarantee we'll find a hit if she hasn't been arrested or fingerprinted before." He finished the transfer and admired the print like a piece of art.

"I'll take anything I can get," said Katie, meaning it.

"This was no accident. Your Jane Doe knew what she was doing. It's not the natural angle of a finger when grabbing someone's wrist," he said. "You see, it would be like this if it was a normal grab." He took Katie's wrist and demonstrated, then turned his grip, pressing his index finger on the top of her wrist where her watch face would be. "And not like this." It showed Katie that Jane did indeed understand that she was leaving a print, just as she had suspected.

"That helps a lot—thank you."

"The result time will vary. It could be a few hours or days, and in some instances weeks."

"Would you know why her prints weren't originally processed?"

John went to his computer. "When was she picked up?"

"A little over two months ago."

"Jane Doe was the victim's name on record?"

"Yes."

John clicked through several layers of software until he found what he was looking for. "Oh, I see what happened."

Katie waited for his explanation.

"We unfortunately have a backlog for fingerprints. I'm embarrassed to say that they are a couple of months behind. It's the hazards of having a small forensic department with two employees—not enough hours in the day."

"That's only two months. She was picked up more than two months ago."

"Well, we didn't print her; the South Street Psychiatric Hospital did and they sent them to us. Since there wasn't a rush on the prints, they took their time. It looks like we received them six weeks ago." He kept reading. "And, it looks like there were also two garments sent for processing, a bra and panties."

"It wasn't stated in the report."

"No, the hospital should have sent them to us. I'll make a call and see what the holdup was."

"Oh, okay. Whatever it takes. That brings me to another issue." She gestured to the evidence box. "I'd like these two pieces of Amanda Payton's clothing examined, along with the garments from Jane Doe when you get them. I think there's a link between them."

"Done. I'll make sure it's done myself."

"And the letter?"

"That's a bit trickier. I will be spraying a solution called ninhydrin which will react to the amino acids in the fingertips into a purple-like color. It can take a while for any prints to appear, and there's always the chance the sender wore gloves."

"Thank you, John. I really appreciate you making time for this with everything else."

"No problem. You can quit thanking me." He looked up at her and smiled a little too long.

Katie felt herself begin to flush, so she turned to leave. "If you get a match, you know where to find me." She quickly left the lab.

CHAPTER 20

Friday 1545 hours

After calls to both of Amanda's cousins—Bradley Olson, and Melissa Roe—which didn't result in any new leads as neither of them had seen her for a year, Katie tried calling Amanda's supervisor, Dr. Kenneth Jamison. The phone rang and rang but no one picked up. She tried the hospital's front desk and was able to obtain his work schedule; twelve-hour shifts for the next three days. Looking at the clock, Katie estimated she had time for a quick trip to the First Memorial Hospital while she waited for forensics and the autopsy report on Amanda Payton to come back. McGaven would soon be joining her to help do some of the legwork and divvy up the duties, but for now she wanted to amass as much information as possible.

The traffic was extra heavy as people hurried to leave work early to get home and start the weekend. As Katie inched her way downtown past office buildings, restaurants, and shopping malls to where the hospital was located, she realized that she hadn't spent much time enjoying the area since she had been home from the army. Downtown gave a contrast to the more rural areas around the outskirts of the county, but it was pleasing to live somewhere with the balance of both. Pine Valley was also taking great strides to revamp, remodel, and redesign the older and rundown areas. There was a large park meandering around the downtown area, called Adirondack Plaza, where you could walk, jog, cycle, or just sit on one of the many benches and enjoy the scenery. Trees, blooming flowers and two large fountains were the main points of interest. As Katie drove past the western area of the park, she saw a group of joggers dressed in brightly colored running gear and a large group of children playing on one of the playgrounds.

Finally the traffic lessened and she was able to pass through three traffic lights, making her way toward the hospital. The low evening sun reflected off the buildings and windows making them sparkle. Ten minutes farther and she could see the huge hospital.

After parking, Katie stepped through the large automatic doors and quickly scanned the reception for signs directing her to the intensive care unit where Amanda had worked as a nurse for the past six years. She caught the elevator to the third floor and made a beeline to the main desk area where there were two nurses on duty.

"I'm Detective Katie Scott from the sheriff's office here to see Dr. Jamison. Would he be available?" She didn't think she needed to flash her police badge at this point.

The bored-looking nurse with the name tag identifying her as Ruth, RN, didn't look up from her paperwork. "He's here. Not sure where at the moment. Do you want me to page him?"

"That would be great. Thank you."

Katie moved to an area out of the way and waited. She could have taken a seat, but she wanted to assess the place and watch the employees go about their work. It was busy for a Friday afternoon and the stifling air made Katie feel uncomfortable, reminding her of the psychiatric ward she'd been in just that morning.

Over the intercom she heard, *"Dr. Jamison, please come to the front nurses' station 10-43."* Then again, *"Dr. Jamison, please come to the front nurses' station 10-43."*

After fifteen minutes, it appeared Dr. Jamison was too busy in the chaos all around her to answer her call. She knew that a 10-43 was a request for information and not a medical emergency. So she walked back to the nurse station and asked, "I don't want to take up your time, but did you know someone who worked here—Amanda Payton?"

For the first time, Ruth looked up from her work and stared Katie in the eye. "Of course. What do you want to know? I heard she was killed—such awful, awful news," she said, suddenly warm.

"Yes. She quit. Do you know anything about that?" Katie asked.

"Well, I wasn't surprised."

"What do you mean?"

"Look," she said, "I didn't have anything against her, but she was one of those types that always had some kind of catastrophe in her personal life. She quit without any notice and we were already shorthanded here." The nurse took a deep breath. "If you want to know more about her, try Marco Ellis, he's an intern downstairs."

"Thank you, I appreciate that," said Katie, recognizing the name from Hamilton's list of contacts.

"All the way to the basement," the nurse called after her as she made her way to the elevator.

Katie rode down in the crowded elevator listening to two young nurses complaining about their patients. No one paid any attention to her and it struck Katie how many people could enter and exit the hospital on a daily basis. In a place like this it would be easy for someone to blend in without anyone ever noticing.

The elevator arrived on the ground floor and the two nurses quickly exited, leaving her alone to ride the rest of the way down, where the doors opened into a deserted hallway. Stepping out, Katie realized suddenly that "basement" meant the morgue and a familiar feeling trickled up through her arms causing her breath to catch. She fought the urge to get back in the lift and head back to the living. This was a place she didn't want to be. But she needed to be.

The light illuminating the hallway dimmed as Katie's focus narrowed. Her mouth went dry. Tongue sticky. Gums parched.

The familiar slow attack of the anxiety that surfaced every time she was in an unknown area with no quick escape. She licked her lips.

Thirst overwhelmed her. Back at the army headquarters, her uniform weighing down on her like she carried an extra hundred pounds of dust and grief, all she could think about was water. Cisco pressed close to her left thigh. Eyes bright, ears perked, alert and strong. No matter how difficult or dangerous the situation, he was always there for her. He perfectly read her mood and her fears, and, most importantly, he always knew where the bad people were.

She passed a few members of her team in a daze and continued down a long hallway, her feet dragging with exhaustion, not really realizing she had taken a wrong turn until, looking to her right, she saw stretchers with sheets covering them, bright crimson blooms seeping through. Her knees buckled beneath her...

Katie blinked away the memory and tried to focus on the job in hand. Where would she find Marco Ellis? Was he a doctor intern, or a student intern?

"Excuse me," came a voice from behind her. "Are you looking for someone?"

Katie turned and saw a handsome young man wearing a blood-spattered lab coat. Her blood went cold at the sight and she blinked again. "Yes, please, I'm looking for Marco Ellis."

"That's me," he said, eyeing her badge. "What can I do for you?"

"I'm Detective Katie Scott with the sheriff's department."

"Okay?" Clearly, he was suspicious of her but remained polite.

"I'd like to ask you a few questions about Amanda Payton?"

"Yes, I know Amanda. Is she okay?"

"Is there a place we can talk privately?"

"Please, follow me," he said and opened one of the closed doors.

Katie followed Marco into a large room where two bodies lay on gurneys. One was an old man, maybe in his eighties, with excessively wrinkled skin, and the other was a middle-aged woman. Both bodies were in the middle of autopsies with their torso area split wide open, a technician carefully weighing the internal organs and recording results.

Marco walked along another hallway passing supply rooms and other exam areas. He stopped at another door that led into an office. He waited for Katie to enter before he closed the door behind them. The office was small and littered with folders and paperwork on a good-sized desk. He took a seat in the leather chair. There was an audio recorder set up to make easy recordings of the cases for an administrative assistant to transcribe.

"Please have a seat, Detective Scott," he said.

Katie sat down in a molded plastic chair, sorting her thoughts for the questions she wanted to ask, being careful not to give away any private information.

"I'm sorry to inform you, but Amanda Payton was found dead yesterday morning," she began.

"What?" He was barely able to respond. "How? Where?"

"Yesterday her body was found—and the investigation is currently under way. I'm sorry, but I'm not authorized to talk about details."

"Oh… no, Amanda…"

"How well did you know her?"

He moved slightly in his chair before he answered. "I met her a couple of years ago."

"And how close were you?"

"We went out a few times and spent time together here at lunch and during breaks."

"Did you want more—a more serious relationship?" she said.

He hesitated and answered carefully. "I thought so, but it became clear that we weren't compatible for the long haul."

"When was the last time you saw her?" Katie watched his mannerisms and listened carefully as he answered.

"It was a couple of months ago, a few weeks after she quit. She was really upset and came down here to tell me that something really bad happened to her—some type of attack."

"Did she give you any details?"

"No, she just said she thought someone was trying to find her."

Katie paused a moment, observing Marco and deciding that he was likely telling the truth. His eye contact was a bit inconsistent and she couldn't tell if he was deceiving her or not. "Did she say why or who?" She watched his hands, which he kept wringing, rubbing his thumbs against the sides of his index fingers, unable to keep them still.

He shook his head. "I tried to get her to tell me, but I wasn't sure if she knew. But I can tell you that she was scared—really terrified."

"Was she dating anyone?"

"I don't think so."

"What makes you say that?" Katie asked.

"It's what she said, how she was hiding and scared to go out, especially at night."

"What do you think?"

"About?"

"You've known Amanda for a while. Did this behavior seem normal, or out of character?"

"See, that's just it. The way she had been acting, even before her attack, didn't seem like her. I don't know what to tell you, Detective. I think she was very afraid of someone."

"Do you know her friend, Emily Day?" Katie asked.

"Don't know her personally, I'm sorry. Amanda mentioned her a few times."

"Is there anything that you would like for me to know?"

"I can't think of anything," he said and leaned back, clearly upset.

Katie stood to leave. "Thank you, Mr. Ellis, I appreciate your time. Here's my card if you think of anything that might help us; please call me anytime." She handed him a business card.

"I hope you find him," he said as Katie left.

Katie rushed back to the elevator, pressing the button frantically as she waited for it to return.

When the doors finally opened, she rode the elevator up and exited out into the bustling ground floor hallway. She rushed to finally step outside and took a few deep breaths—still seeing the bodies on the gurneys and smelling death.

CHAPTER 21

Early Saturday morning

Katie had a difficult time trying to sleep, tossing and turning, worrying about what to do next in Amanda's homicide investigation. Every time she closed her eyes and tried to rest, she could see Amanda's body at the crime scene. Facedown. Naked. Katie's name on a business card clutched in her hand.

Why Whispering Pines?
Why strip the body?
Why restrain her after she died?

Katie finally relented and threw her covers back, letting the cool air from the room float over her body. Cisco grumbled from his chair in the corner of the bedroom but didn't want to rise just yet. Katie sat up, swung her feet to the floor and headed to the shower to try to clear her head, but all she ended up doing was reworking the case from the beginning, the very beginning; the moment Amanda stepped in front of the patrol car. Katie's mind jostled between that night and Amanda's final resting spot at Whispering Pines, searching for a link. But only one thing became clear: she needed to visit where it had all had been set in motion.

Katie drove slowly through the abandoned neighborhood, formerly known as the Basin Woods Development, on the south end of town. It had been a thorn in the side of Sequoia County for several years now, the total opposite of everything Pine Valley resembled. Even in the daytime the houses appeared more like props on a film set than what was once a thriving residential area. It was unclear to her why they never invested in improving it, except that the land was probably more valuable than the cheaply built houses that sat on it. That was typical for California property.

Still rolling slowly, Katie saw there were subdivisions with chain-link fencing cordoning them off, but much of the neighborhood was old and falling down, decorated with rusting "no trespassing" signs. The copy of Deputy Windham's police report lay on the passenger's seat beside her, the addresses of the local houses they had searched highlighted, and also land parcel identifications from the county. Katie had also printed out an assessor's map showing the addresses with an overview satellite map and had studied them carefully before heading into the derelict neighborhood.

Cisco popped his head up between the two front seats, ears alert and eyes clocking anything that didn't appear normal down both sides of the street. His anxious panting made it clear that he wanted to get to work.

"Okay, big guy, this is just a fact-finding expedition. That's all. No running into houses to get the bad guys or searching for tripwires or bombs." She laughed as she spoke to Cisco like she would a human partner.

Cisco let out a disappointed grumble followed by a high-pitch whine.

"Yeah, I know. It can't be fun *all* the time."

Katie noted that according to Amanda's statement she had referred to landmarks of a *big box* and a *fantasy tree*. She also described the house with a *blue door* and *white trim*.

Slowing her unmarked patrol vehicle, she saw what appeared to be a big box housing telephone lines for the area. The two doors hung ajar with wiring spilling out of it.

Katie continued, surveying the houses along the way. There wasn't as much graffiti as she'd expected, and most windows hadn't been broken out. A couple of the houses actually looked like someone could still live there, if it weren't for the red notices from the county, warning of the abandoned and condemned houses, attached to all the front doors.

Old trees lined some of the streets and one street in particular had three large trees straight down the middle of the road—the trunks were massive, almost the girth of a car and she had to maneuver her vehicle around them.

Katie stopped the car.

The tree at the end was a type of oak that was twisted and gnarled in such a way it looked like elves might've inhabited the inside of it. The fantasy tree?

"Okay, Amanda. I see your landmarks, but what I don't understand…" Katie mumbled to herself as she thought about how Amanda could have seen these things on a dark, rainy night and in the frenzied state she was in.

Had she been there before?

Katie saw the blue door and white trim house Amanda had described, and the deputies had discovered and searched. A quick look at the map confirmed it with the police report.

She pulled to the side of the road, parking where her vehicle would be visible and give her clear access to leave. Cisco whined as he moved back and forth in the backseat, preparing himself for a drill.

"You're going to have to sit this one out," she said and got out of the car.

Katie stood still.

The first thing that struck her as strange about the area was that there were no sounds. She strained to hear traffic from a nearby freeway several miles away, but the silence was deafening.

Katie ran her hand over her gun handle, which was in its usual position on her hip, and adjusted a small remote device on her belt that K9 officers used to open the back door to their police cars to release their four-legged partners if an emergency were to arise. Sergeant Hardy had arranged for Katie to use the unmarked police K9 vehicle with the lever release whenever she had Cisco with her.

She took a couple of steps and stopped. Just like she would do when moving into enemy territories in Afghanistan, she slowly turned three hundred sixty degrees, surveying her position, looking and listening for anything that seemed out of place or unusual. Satisfied, she proceeded to the small house.

Pushing the front door open to let some light in, she crushed an old Styrofoam cup to form a makeshift door stop, jamming it under the open door to hold it in place. An overwhelming smell hit her senses hard, making her cover her nose and mouth. The odor of musty, disintegrating garbage and urine made her stomach flip.

Why hadn't Amanda mentioned the bad smell? Why did she smell jasmine? It had been six months since the attack, but it was clear that it had been a lot longer than that since the house smelt like "spring," as Amanda had described it.

She walked to the only front window that had vertical bars loose enough for someone to squeeze through.

But why not escape out the front door?

Katie focused her attention on the front door where there were geometric holes that had once housed two extra locks that were now missing. It was difficult to ascertain if the locks were part of the dilapidating house or if someone had removed them recently.

Taking a couple of deep breaths from the clean outdoor air, Katie then turned and headed deeper inside the house to search the bedrooms. The once low-grade carpet was now torn and curled from the baseboards causing it to buckle and fold beneath her feet in several areas.

The living room was empty except for some old trash that had been there for months and a couple of spray-painted initials from local gangs muddying the walls.

There were no pieces of furniture or anything that indicated anyone had been living there during the past six months or longer. A small bathroom missing the toilet and sink separated the two small bedrooms. As with the rest of the house, the rooms were empty and there was no indication that there had been furniture or anyone living there within the last year or more. The thicker old carpet didn't show any signs of a bed, table, or chairs having left indentations.

The rooms felt smaller than she thought they would be—even without furnishings. Disappointed, Katie walked through the rest of the house and into the kitchen. There was nothing to indicate anything criminal happened in the house or that anyone had been residing there—or held against their will. If there had been, the abductor cleared everything after Amanda had escaped.

No blood.

No remnants from the abductor's restraints or tools.

No bed.

Would it be worthwhile to have John dust for prints? She didn't think so: it had been too long. Fingerprints were the most fragile piece of forensic evidence and it was highly likely that if there had been any, they would have been contaminated from time, the weather, and any squatters.

Katie walked around the kitchen near the pantry area and her eye caught something on the floor. She bent down and picked up three small white adhesive pieces, each about an inch long. Rubbing them against her thumb and forefinger, they felt springy and elastic, most likely the remains of a waterproof sealant. It was possible that the type of caulking might have been transferred from someone's shoes or fallen away from something removed, but it was relatively new.

Cisco's distinct deep bark interrupted her thoughts.

She looked up just as the front door slammed shut with such a force she heard the remains of broken windows rattle and portions drop to the ground. On a still day like this, it couldn't have been a gust of wind. Someone must have slammed it.

Cisco's rapid bark echoed throughout the empty neighborhood.

She raced out of the kitchen through the living room to face the closed front door. Her imagination spiraling. She grabbed the handle, expecting to find it locked, leaving her trapped inside, but surprisingly, it turned easily in her hand.

Pulling her weapon, she flung open the door to—nothing. There was no one waiting or running down the street. She ran to the road and scanned every direction—looking for anything to indicate someone had been there.

Nothing moved.

No one was around.

She looked at Cisco breathing heavy at the slightly opened window—he began barking again. Katie knew he had seen who had slammed the front door and he had smelled their scent as they ran by.

Without hesitating any longer, Katie opened the back door and Cisco leaped out. She grabbed the long twelve-foot lead from inside the car and quickly snapped it onto him.

"*Suk*," she said—the command meaning trail. Knowing that there wasn't much time, they took off with Cisco in the lead; his nose pressed against the ground as he gained momentum. Katie trailed behind him holding the leash and eyeing the houses, side alleys, and anywhere someone might be hiding.

Cisco slowed down after an intense ten minutes of darting this way and that. They were back at the main road again and the trail had gone cold. Katie looked around and saw no sign of a car or anyone running. She never heard the sound of a car speed away, or even a motorcycle. If the person was on foot then they would have seen them. The only thing she could think of was the person must've ridden away on a bike. What other explanation could it have been?

Walking slowly back to the car still catching her breath, Katie found a folded piece of paper lying on the ground next to her driver's door. She carefully picked it up and unfolded it. Written with the same cursive writing in blue ink as the other note, it read:

You're closer, red hot now.

CHAPTER 22

Monday 1045 hours

Tess was late for work. Really late. She'd overslept. After calling in and giving an excuse that she had to make an emergency visit to the dentist and wouldn't be in until after lunch, all she could think about was going back to bed once more. Her brain was foggy and felt like she was in an endless loop of despair with no way to get out. She sat down on her couch with her head in her hands, trying desperately to forget that morning barely three months ago where it all began.

She had been getting ready for work when the phone rang. It was a police sergeant calling from the hospital. Tess's sister, Laurie, had been found unresponsive in her apartment after a neighbor couldn't get an answer at the door. They'd found Laurie in the bathtub, unconscious, having cut her own wrists.

Tess had rushed to the hospital, but it was too late. Her little sister had been successful in taking her own life. She remembered standing in the emergency area where Laurie's body still lay on the gurney—lifeless, frail and so alone. The hospital staff, seemingly uncaring, left Tess to run around trying to get answers herself until a janitor came in to begin cleaning up after the doctors failed to revive her. Blood was spattered everywhere and a hot rage welled up inside her—she wanted someone to pay for what had happened to her sister, so she lunged at the unsuspecting cleaner, beating on him and knocking him down. It took at least a minute or more before a couple of people arrived to pull her away.

Tess was still grieving, but someone had to be blamed for what had happened to her beautiful younger sister. Tears streamed down her face at the memory, but after a few deep breaths she managed to stop and pull herself together a little. She took a moment to stare at a photograph on her coffee table, of her and her sister on holiday two years ago, before going to the kitchen.

Tess rinsed her coffee cup and placed it in the sink. She realized that she didn't want to end up like her sister—she wanted to try to make her life work and have a chance to be happy. She had up and down days, but soon they would get better. Her sister's life mattered, and the thought of other people going through what she had with the loss made her equally unhappy.

She quickly filled two small plastic dishes with a vegetable salad and makings for a sandwich.

Not having the time to take a shower, she combed her hair and twisted it in an up-do, and searched for something to wear. She opted for a simple beige suit with a pink camisole to wear underneath. The days were becoming warmer and she could get some sun in the park if it was warm enough.

Making sure that she turned off all the lights, Tess gathered her purse, food, and jacket, deciding to leave the house through the garage. Opening the door, the garage was dark and smelled like motor oil. The doorknob was loose and appeared to have been vandalized at some point. She took a quick photo with her phone to send to the landlord later.

Tess turned around to head back inside the house and was instantly overpowered from behind, causing her to drop her purse, cell phone, and jacket. Her food hit the ground and scattered all around. She tried to scream, but her mouth was pressed hard with duct tape. Strong hands and arms kept her immobile. Terrified and panicked, she tried to fight back but her face was pushed down onto the cold cement floor and held hard there to keep her immobile while her attacker expertly tied her wrists and ankles.

She tried to twist her body and head to see who was behind her, but she only saw dark pants and heavy hiking boots.

The more she wriggled and tried to move, the more pressure her assailant placed against her spine. The cold cement against her right cheek numbed her face and sent tingling pains through her teeth and gums. There was a prick on the back of her right arm. Before she could move again and try to fight back, an overwhelming tiredness floated throughout her body.

She tried to fight it, but eventually succumbed to sleep and blacked out.

CHAPTER 23

Monday 1145 hours

Katie and McGaven spent some time moving the furniture around in her office so that both desks were offset enough for them to easily move around. They organized the boxes out of the way, so they wouldn't be running into them every time they got up from their desks. Katie wanted to ask John if they could use the empty office across the hall to store the other cold-case boxes. It was already empty, larger, and had its own security code.

Katie leaned against her desk and let out a sigh. She knew that a lot of work needed to be accomplished. "Sorry that I put you to work doing physical labor right away, but this feels much better," she said.

"I agree. I felt a bit like a bull in a china shop the way it was before."

Katie pulled together everything that she had on Amanda's case and sat down at her desk facing McGaven. "Okay, this is what we have so far." She had made another copy of Amanda's file and the first-week update she'd given the sheriff.

McGaven began reading and looked up in surprise. "When have you had a chance to sleep?"

Katie laughed. "Basically, just yesterday. I'm actually feeling quite rested."

"It's a waiting game with forensics and the autopsy report," he said. "What's this?" He pushed the file forward, referring to the clothing Amanda wore when she was first found.

"I don't know why Detective Petersen, the investigator originally assigned to the case, didn't have it tested, but he claimed that it wasn't necessary. At least it wasn't misfiled or lost. It's getting tested now."

"Petersen is an interesting guy," McGaven mused, without elaborating. "So you've spoken to Detective Petersen, Deputy Windham, Dr. Smith at the psychiatric hospital, and Marco Ellis at the First Memorial Hospital." He quickly read the result of the interviews and the notes that had been written by Petersen.

"What do you think?" she said.

"You haven't been able to contact anyone from Amanda's family?"

"I looked into it. I spoke with two cousins out of state—otherwise Amanda had no family. I don't think there's anything that needs to be followed up on with them."

"That just leaves the boss, girlfriend, and the ex-boyfriend."

"Yes, but there are so many possible suspects at the hospital. But my gut tells me that the killer either works there or has business there. At this point we can't rule anyone out."

"This is interesting about Jane Doe. Do you think that link has legs?"

"Yes, I'm not sure how but I think she might be a key missing piece to this investigation."

"This takes me to these notes you've been getting."

"Yeah, I'm trying to figure them out. Both are with John to see if we can get any prints, but I'm not hopeful."

"You think it's the killer taunting you? Or someone related to the killer trying to help you?"

"I really don't know. We have to move ahead and see where all this fits."

McGaven stared at her. "Either way, you need to be careful. It may be a wacko, or not—watch your back."

"Hey, I've got Cisco."

"Still."

"I will be careful, don't worry," she said. "Okay, here's my plan."

"Shoot," he said with his eyes wide and ready to get to work.

"This is the part that most detectives hate."

"Not sure that I'm liking the sound of this," he said lightheartedly.

"We need to find out information and backgrounds on people we have so far. We also need to see if there are any security cameras leading into the park area next to Whispering Pines or near Emily Day's house. Anything we can get. See what you can do."

McGaven grabbed a yellow notepad and began writing.

"I haven't been able to get in contact with Amanda's supervisor, Dr. Jamison. The hospital seems to keep him incredibly busy. I think I want to do some checking on him as well as Emily Day."

McGaven nodded and continued to make notes.

"We need a background check on Dr. Smith from the psychiatric hospital. For due diligence. He's odd and I want to see if he has had any issues, problems, or lawsuits revolving around the hospital, patients, or personally."

"Noted," he said.

Katie paused, staring at the board. She studied her notes on the killer as well as what they knew about Amanda. "I need to rework the preliminary profile once we get the forensics and autopsy results. I'm going to do some digging for property information."

"On what?"

"First, the house in Basin Woods Development that Amanda described and the deputies searched seems strange to me."

"Strange how?"

"I'm not sure. I'm certain it's the right house, but there's nothing there. I want to find out more about the homes that were built in the development and try to obtain the building plans."

"Maybe there were building shortcuts? Payoffs? Somebody got shorted that worked the original project and the wrong person got pissed off?"

"I like the way your mind works," Katie said. She took another look at the overview maps of the area. "You bring up a good point. What about all the people who lived there? How were they relocated? Were they compensated in any way?"

McGaven shifted in his chair, making it squeak. "Someone losing their home is pretty traumatic. Would that make for a motive to kill?"

Katie stood up and stretched her back. She had tacked a county map on the wall and marked all the areas of importance including the housing area, crime scene, hospital, Amanda's apartment, and Emily's apartment. "There's no connection to Amanda or the people close to her—as of right now."

"What about Amanda's crime scene area?"

"I was thinking that too. Find out who owns the land, or what corporation does, and anything of interest."

"It's on my list now," he said and smiled.

"I don't know how good you are at spreadsheets, but we need to be organized with all this information."

"Got it," he said.

Katie picked up the internal phone, dialed extension #41 and waited. "Hey, Denise, how are you?" she asked. Denise had been invaluable helping her with background information and various searches on her last case involving a missing girl. She wanted to utilize her skills on Amanda's case.

"Katie, I'm doing great. How's the office?" Denise said.

"It's really good. We've been moving stuff around to make it more efficient."

"I heard you have McGaven working with you again."

"Wow, word travels fast."

"You know I'm plugged in around here. Nothing gets by me." She chuckled.

"I was wondering if you had a few minutes to come down."

"Sure. Give me five."

"See you in a few," Katie said and hung up.

"What's on your mind?" McGaven asked.

"Well, Denise is a lot more proficient with computer searches than I am. And some of them take a while, so she can do her other duties at the same time."

He nodded in agreement.

"Since I didn't get to talk to Dr. Jamison at the hospital, or Emily Day, I thought we could find out more about them before our next attempt."

"Background search?" he asked.

"More like social media."

"Perfect, people say and post things like the entire world can't see it."

"Exactly. I also want Denise to see if she can find out anything else about the ex-boyfriend, Marco Ellis."

"Great idea," he agreed.

McGaven studied her preliminary profile of the kidnapper, now killer, and the victimology for Amanda Payton. "You're sure that the kidnapper is the same person as the killer?"

"Of course, don't you think?" Katie asked. "I know I don't have solid proof, but I'm going to proceed as if I do."

"Are you sure? As I read your notes here, and I get what you mean, but what makes you think it's the same guy unequivocally? Okay…" He got up. "The linkage isn't here, at least not yet."

"I see where you're going with this, but—"

"And until we know for sure from John that there's linkage in these cases, shouldn't we move forward objectively and systematically by not zeroing in on one thing?" he said.

"You're right," Katie agreed. "What stands out to you?"

McGaven studied the board and the case files for a couple of minutes before he answered.

"I know there are no *typical* murder crime crimes, but this doesn't seem familiar. You know what I mean?"

"You mean like a crime of passion—from a lover or someone she might have crossed paths with. There's no overkill. Only her restraint marks on her wrists and ankles." Katie thought about the extent of the crime.

"Is that from Sherlock's ideology?" asked Denise as she stood at the doorway holding a notepad.

"It could be," said Katie smiling.

McGaven stood up to greet her and seemed to light up.

"Wow, this office is great, in an underground bunker sort of way," Denise said looking around. She was dressed more casually than normal in slacks and a short-sleeved sweater.

"Thanks. It's going to take a bit to get used to, but I think I'm really going to like it down here," Katie said.

"Now you're not completely alone," she said, referring to Deputy McGaven. She smiled at him.

"It's hard to overlook someone of my height," he said, almost embarrassed.

Katie grabbed a sheet of paper with the names of the people on their list that knew Amanda. She sat on the corner of her large desk. "I've already okayed this with the sheriff. But, if you don't want to participate or if you feel uncomfortable doing it, it's voluntary, so there's no hard feelings. Okay?"

"Okay," Denise said slowly. "You've definitely got my attention now."

McGaven perked up due to the fact he was just hearing this.

"Here's the list of people that are on the radar who knew or had contact with the victim: friends, supervisor, ex-boyfriend. I need you to make up a profile on social media that you're a single woman that's a nurse and friend some of the friends of the people on this list before you actually friend them specifically. Or however that works. It will help to make your profile look legitimate. I don't particularly like social media sites, but they can be extremely useful for information…"

"Like where they like to frequent, favorite restaurants, and even what they're doing right at any given moments," chimed in McGaven.

"Exactly," said Katie.

"Do I interact with them?" Denise asked.

"No, I don't want you to do that because there could be some legal consequences if any of this is brought into court—then it'll get messy and I don't want anything to jeopardize the case with some type of technicality. You can see what you can find before making your own profile, but you will have full access when you friend them."

"I can do that," she smiled. "I'm going in undercover—that's more exciting than *any* records work."

"Great. The best way to keep records is to keep computer files of screen grabs for documentation. Keep me updated when any movement or interaction happens from these people."

"Easy enough," she said, taking the paper from Katie and making some notes.

"Don't hesitate to text or call me with any questions."

"Will do," she said and turned to leave. "Bye."

"Bye, Denise," Katie and McGaven said in unison.

Katie felt like she was in control of the investigation and had a direction and definite plan. "Okay," she said. "Ready to continue to disseminate everything we have so far?"

McGaven sat at the computer and said, "Bring it on."

CHAPTER 24

Monday 1845 hours

After fading in and out of uneasy sleep, Tess tried to open her eyes. Everything was dark, but she thought she could detect some light in her peripheral—there was a sticky blindfold tied around her head. Licking her dry lips and taking several deep breaths, her head cleared.

She jerked her arms and legs before realizing her limbs were restrained, fully extended like a starfish. Her wrists and ankles burned from the ropes cutting into them every time she moved. She could tell that she was on a firm bed from the pressure beneath her and that there was a small pillow under her head. Her legs were cold as she realized that she didn't have her pants on—only her undergarments. A fact that frightened her all the more.

"Where am I?" she demanded. "Is anyone here?" Her voice became more hysterical as she spoke. "Who are you? Please say something to me."

Silence.

"Why am I here?" She began to cry as her anger turned to misery. "Why…"

Tess quieted her crying and strained to listen. Someone was in the room with her. She couldn't hear them, but the air around her felt heavy with someone else's breath. She took a sharp inhale and caught a hint of an exotic flower—lilac or gardenia, no, it was jasmine. She breathed deeply but the scent seemed to dissipate as quickly as it had appeared.

"Who's there?" she asked again. "I know someone is there? Say something," raising her voice louder with each plea.

She tried to quiet her own breathing, to listen carefully above the sound of her pounding heart. Her skin prickled as if someone lightly touched her.

"Who's there?"

Finally, she heard someone quietly shush her.

"What are you saying? Who are you?" Her voice wavered in alarm as her worst fears were realized. Someone was standing next to her—waiting and watching.

She felt weight next to her on the bed and jerked herself away. She felt hot breath on the side of her face and the extra weight pressing down against the mattress as they leaned in close.

"Please… Please let me go…" she wheezed.

The silence finally broke and a man whispered with a low and deep voice, "I want you to tell me the *truth…*"

CHAPTER 25

Monday evening

Katie went home exhausted. Every muscle and joint screamed with fatigue. She and McGaven had gone through every single piece of information that had been generated on Amanda Payton's investigation and Katie's mind was spinning as she left the department. She was moving forward with a plan and most of the next steps were dependent upon the results of forensics. It was too soon to feel good about the progress of the case, but tomorrow was another day.

It was going to be an early morning and a very long day for her. With a twinge of guilt, she played with Cisco in the garden for a little while longer than usual, knowing he would be cooped up in the house for most of the next day. He seemed to sense her concerns and took extra advantage of running around the yard, barking, and retrieving his favorite ball.

Every time Katie took time to walk around the large acreage, she couldn't help but think of her parents and the wonderful times they'd had at the house as she grew up. She and her dad would play hide and seek for hours, especially in the summertime. It was one of Katie's favorite games. Anything to stay outside just a little bit longer.

She watched Cisco trail something, nose down on the ground, as he made his way to the farthest perimeter of their land. Then he grew bored, losing the scent, and began zigzagging across the yard with a large stick in his mouth.

Katie slowly began to unwind from the day—if she was going to make it as a detective she was going to have to learn how to shut off and relax. She breathed in the outdoors and her muscles and the tension headache slowly began to release its grip on her body.

After spending enough time with Cisco, Katie made her rounds through the house cleaning up the kitchen and picking up anything that wasn't in its place. It made her feel better knowing that everything was in order when she began a new day. She fell into bed an hour later and within minutes was sound asleep.

A low growl woke her. She opened her eyes to the unmistakable silhouette of a German shepherd standing guard at her bedroom door listening and sniffing the air for danger. She called him over, but he remained on high alert.

Something bumped against the side of her house, causing her to sit straight up in bed and drop her feet to the floor, her hand silently reaching for the drawer to her nightstand. With a slow deliberate slide of her hand, Katie pulled out her handgun.

Wearing only a tank top and pajama shorts, she crept from her bedroom, down the hallway, and then to the sliding doors at the back of the house. It was dark, only the faintest sliver of the moon to illuminate her backyard. As she stood motionless, waiting, nothing moved or seemed out of place.

Retreating back into the kitchen, Katie picked up her cell phone from the counter and pressed the house alarm application from the main phone menu. Two cameras appeared in a window, one showing the front yard while the other displayed her backyard. Nothing moved. No alert showed itself.

Maybe it was an animal?

Glancing at the small neon kitchen clock on the stove, it was barely past 1.00 a.m. She felt as if she had slept almost the entire night, but in reality, it was only a couple of hours. However, she felt strangely alert.

Bump.

There it was again.

This time Cisco barked twice as a warning to who or whatever was outside.

"Easy, boy," she whispered, still not knowing where the thumping sound originated from.

Glancing at her security camera from her phone, it clearly showed that the yard was empty, but there were a few blind spots. One was on the farthest side of the house and the other was down the driveway.

Katie contemplated the risk for a moment, but decided to investigate, otherwise she would never get back to sleep. Flipping the lock mechanism of the sliding door, she slowly pulled it open with little sound. Cisco's nose pushed toward her and she gently signaled her hand to make him stay—to his frustration, he begrudgingly waited, staying behind.

The damp air made her shudder as she slowly made her way toward the other side of the house. Her bare feet felt the damp dirt. Directing her weapon ahead of her, she moved the barrel slightly from left to right keeping everything in prime view, inching forward until she reached the end of the house. Sucking in a deep breath and then letting it out, she moved around the corner.

Nothing.

Katie felt silly, but in the past there had been some real dangers lurking around her home. It didn't hurt to be extra cautious and not take anything for granted.

Looking down, strange indentations in the dirt caught her attention. They looked like drag marks in the soil. Katie stood her ground and looked around in a one-hundred-eighty-degree view. She strained to hear anything unusual. A soft scratching sound came from the sliding door, which she knew could only be Cisco wanting out to find a bad guy.

Lowering her weapon slightly, she continued to walk toward the front of the house when she saw a figure leaning against the outside wall. With her weapon raised, Katie ran toward him. "Put your hands up now! Sheriff's department, put your hands up!" she yelled, still keeping a solid stance in her flimsy pajamas.

Cisco's bark became rapid and louder as he raced over to the window nearest Katie.

The man slowly raised his hands. Since Katie didn't have a flashlight, she couldn't see the details of his face. The low wattage outside lights cast a shadow on the man's appearance. There was some type of duffle bag sitting next to him.

"Who are you?" demanded Katie as her breathing became shallow. "I said, who are you?"

"US Army Sergeant Nicholas Haines at your service," he replied with a slight southern drawl.

What?

Katie moved closer and could see that he was wearing army fatigues, but she still didn't believe her ears.

Nick?

"Who are you?" she demanded again, this time with less authority.

"Scotty, it's me, Nick," he said with a familiar tone and still a slight Kentucky accent. No one called Katie Scotty except her sergeant from the army.

"Nick?" she said, almost breathless.

He slowly stood up with slight difficulty, revealing one prosthetic leg. "It's really me, Scotty."

Realizing that her eyes weren't deceiving her, she lowered her gun and rushed to him. She hugged him tight. "Nick, it's so great to see you. What are you doing here at this hour? How'd you find...? What happened to your...?"

"Well are you going to ask me inside before you run out of questions?" he asked. "Is that Cisco I hear? I'd recognize that huge bark anywhere."

Katie suddenly focused on Nick with his dark wavy hair, intense green eyes, and a three-inch scar on his right cheek near his jawline. On so many missions, he had been the soldier that had her back while her attention was on Cisco's behavior—he was her cover. Their relationship grew with her time in the army. He was known as a lifer—someone who would spend his lifetime in the military until retirement. Her house was the last place she ever thought she'd find him. He would have given his life for her, and she'd have done the same for him.

"Of course, please come inside." Still with their arms around each other's waists, Katie guided him around back to enter through the sliding door. He didn't have a crutch to lean on but managed fairly well. Cisco met them with plenty of yips and happy puppy barks. Katie grabbed a robe and put it on.

"Why didn't you call?" she said and took a deep breath. "Why didn't you just knock on the front door?"

The sergeant hobbled slightly toward the kitchen and opted for a seat at the counter. "Well, first I wasn't sure if I was going to find you. I caught a ride here and it was late, so I was going to knock on the door in the morning."

Katie was taken aback but happy to see him. He had been her support and friend through so many times. Those familiar feelings, both good and bad, tumbled back into her. She thought about her team every day and especially just before she went to sleep at night. Her body trembled inside, as old memories threatened to surface.

"You know you're always welcome here," she said.

"It's great to see you, Scotty. I didn't think you could look this good, but you do."

"You woke me up, I hardly would say that." She went to brew some coffee. "What can I get for you to drink? Coffee? Tea? Soda?"

"Yeah, actually coffee sounds good."

Katie quickly set the coffee maker, her mind in a flurry as to why Nick showed up unexpectedly and how he lost his leg. Her gut told her to wait and let him tell her in his own time. She loved him like a brother, like family, all of her team was like family with a special bond that no one outside of the military would totally understand. She knew that he would tell her everything eventually, so she didn't bombard him with too many initial questions.

"I can see civilian life is agreeing with you," he said and gazed around. "This was your parents' house, right?"

"Yep. It's been mine for a while though. I've been asked to sell it, but I love it here too much."

Cisco ran around, still excited about the late-night guest.

Petting the dog, he said, "You've probably figured out that I've been honorably discharged." He patted his leg.

Katie nodded and remained silent.

"One of those damn things you couldn't plan for—you fear, but don't plan. It happened when we had some time off, would you believe? Remember when we would have those barbecues?"

"Like it was yesterday," she said.

"Yeah, well we were all drinking, more than we should have, blowing off steam. When there was a commotion going on—we thought it was just an altercation between a few guys at the restaurant." He paused for a moment, petting Cisco who sat patiently. It was clear he had relived the incident many times. He caught his breath, and said, "So, Freddy went to see what the problem was and I followed him. The rest..." His voice trailed off.

It stung Katie because by Nick's tone she instantly knew that Freddy hadn't made it. He didn't have to say it. She closed her eyes for a moment as she braced for the worst.

"... I remembered the sound and a huge bright light, then nothing; I woke up five days later at a hospital where they had removed my leg above the knee to save my life. Out of all the damn places to get hit like that… a restaurant, not the battlefield."

Katie turned to him, tears in her eyes.

"And that's when I found out that Freddy never had a chance. Bomb took down the whole restaurant. There were seven casualties in total, including Freddy."

"Nick, there are no words…"

"I'm just glad you weren't there. I know—we all know—that you would have marched in there to save everybody and it would have been you they buried and sent back to the States." He paused to keep his grief under control. "I loved Freddy too, but the thought of losing you… well…"

Katie hugged Nick for a couple of minutes, each lost in their own grief, each with their own story that they had to manage and live with every day.

With an upbeat voice, he said, "Now, I bet you're wondering why the hell such a sorry ass like me is sitting in your kitchen."

Katie laughed wiping the tears from her face, "I don't care, I'm just glad you're here. I just hope I don't wake up and find out this was a dream." She poured a cup of coffee and slid it over to Nick.

He drank a couple of sips before he continued, reaching into one of his jacket pockets and pulling out several pieces of paper. Unfolding them, he said, "Apparently, since you've been home you have already caught a serial killer. And, it's not completely clear from the articles, but you were kidnapped and still managed to beat him and save a little girl?"

"It's not exactly like that, but I did get ambushed and kidnapped."

"Damn, girl, I always knew you were tough, but that's the stuff for horror movies."

"I'm doing okay, getting better every day," she said forcing a smile.

"Well there was quite a bit of info on you, so it wasn't difficult to find you. Besides, you described this house and property perfectly. Congratulations on your promotion to police detective."

She smiled. "Thanks. It feels good, you know?" She sipped on a soda, enjoying the cold sting as it slid down her throat.

"Do I detect a bit of uneasiness?"

"It's just I've been thrown right into a current homicide barely out of my first week. It's pretty intense."

"Scotty, don't you worry. I know you, and I know that you will find the person who did it." He sipped his coffee, still eyeing her.

She pulled up a stool next to him. "Tell me what's on your mind?" she said softly as she squeezed his arm.

"Well, since I can't be in the military anymore, it's got me thinking."

"About what?"

"Family."

Katie knew that he had been estranged from his family for quite some time. "Go on."

"I have a brother, Jimmy, and well, I've lost touch with him. And it seems that no one knows where he is."

"He moved away?" she asked.

"No, he just moved out of his apartment of ten years and never went back to work. See, he loved that job, so it just doesn't make sense. None of this makes sense. But he was living in California, near here."

"When was the last time you spoke with him?"

"I hate to admit it, but it was about six years ago."

"Oh," she said, not knowing what else to say.

"We had an argument, it is stupid now, and then time passed, and I didn't know what to say… hardheaded and embarrassed… I guess…"

"It's okay. You want me to look into it?"

He sat quiet for a moment. And then, "Yeah, I would. I know it's hectic for you now, investigating a homicide, but after the explosion I just realized that life is short, that time is precious—you know? It hit me hard."

"I know. Look, I'm going to be swamped for the next several days, but, leave me all the information and a photo if you have it, and I'll see what I can do…" she said.

"Scotty, I knew I could count on you," he said, taking her hand and gently squeezing it.

It made Katie feel good that he would trust her enough with something this important. She loved him. Nick was family and she would do anything for him.

CHAPTER 26

Tuesday 0835 hours

Katie had a difficult time finding a parking place at the sheriff's department. There were more cars parked than usual, but she managed to squeeze her Jeep in the last place farthest away. Jumping out, she ran across the lot to meet McGaven. She was already more than fifteen minutes late. With the unexpected visit from her sergeant last night, she barely got four hours of sleep and almost slept through her alarm.

She and Nick had talked for almost another hour as they waited for a friend of his, Bobby, to pick him up. He was going to stay with him for a while in Bramble, a town just on the outskirts of Pine Valley, waiting until Katie got in touch with news of his brother's whereabouts.

Her boot heels clipped the pavement as she hurried toward the county morgue. She didn't have much time to prepare her questions, but it was mostly regarding a preliminary report to see if they had some type of indication or new evidence. McGaven waited patiently near the entrance, glancing at his watch as she ran around the corner and practically knocked him down.

"Where's the fire?" said McGaven partly smiling. "I've never seen you like this—basically late. You okay?"

Catching her breath, she finally said, "It isn't pretty, is it?"

"It's not about pretty. What's going on with you?"

"Sorry I'm late." She was still panting. "I had an old friend show up at my house last night and I didn't get much sleep."

"Oh, I get it," he said sarcastically. "Good for you."

"Do you ever think about anything else?"

"I thought you already had a boyfriend," he said. "Do tell."

"You know, McGaven…" she said, exasperated.

He smiled.

"Never mind. It's not important now." She straightened her jacket and checked her briefcase, trying to not look like she was rushed. "Let's go." They went inside the building.

Katie put her briefcase down on the floor, leaning it against the wall outside the examination room before entering. She hadn't seen Dr. Dean in a while and wondered if he still dressed like he was ready to board a cruise ship. She remembered the first time she met him during the autopsy of little Chelsea Compton: His unusual casualness of vacation attire followed by his directness made him an interesting medical examiner. He always took Katie's questions seriously as she learned her way around the process.

"My favorite detectives," said Dr. Dean, almost in a musical tone. "Good to see you back officially as a detective, Ms. Scott—rather, Detective Scott." He winked at her and then moved toward the last exam table where the sheet had been pulled all the way back.

"Thank you." She smiled, never knowing whether to call him Jeff, doctor, or Dr. Dean. "Your email said for us to come and see you."

"Yes, isn't it more fun this way?" he said.

Katie didn't know exactly how to respond to that and she glanced to McGaven who had a confused expression as well.

"Well, I don't know about fun," she said.

Dr. Dean looked up from the report and said, "Oh, no. I think you misunderstood my meaning. It's nice to speak with the investigating officers in person. My staff is rather introverted, not a lot of conversation around here. And the only other people I see are the grieving family members. Not a fun group. So it's nice to have a conversation."

"We understand," said Katie forcing a smile, still feeling the rushed adrenalin after running from her car.

"Okay then. Amanda Payton, thirty-one, good health, has several old minor bruises and abrasions, and also has fresh defensive wounds," the medical examiner began as he lifted her left forearm to illustrate. "Cause and manner of death: Asphyxiation by strangulation, which I'm deeming a homicide, of course. Estimated time of death I put at around 2 a.m. Thursday, give or take a half hour."

"Anything unusual? There was what looked like fibers under her nails," Katie explained.

The doctor continued reading. "Oh yes, we did a full combing of her hair and scraping under her nails, which we sent to be tested."

McGaven decided to speak up. "Do you see a lot of strangulation cases?"

Dr. Dean thought a moment, nodding as he replied, "Unfortunately, yes I do. Not all are declared homicides, some are suicides, and a few accidents from autoerotic behavior."

Katie did her best to look at Amanda's corpse directly—recalling sitting in her living room just days ago. The thought made her swallow hard. This part was never going to be easy so she had better learn to let certain things go.

Suck it up, Detective Scott.

The medical examiner continued, "However, there are a couple of things that might interest you."

That statement caught Katie's immediate attention. "Such as?"

"Would you say Ms. Payton was wealthy or had a rich boyfriend?"

Katie wasn't sure how to answer that, but nothing directed her to believe that Amanda was wealthy. "No, unless she had some great investments somewhere."

"The reason why I'm saying this is because of the contents of her stomach."

Both Katie and McGaven hung on every word.

"I've been doing this job for twenty-four years and I've seen a lot of stomach contents," he said. "Ms. Payton had, what I would say, the palate of a rich person."

"Like? Heavy French sauces and braised truffles?" chimed McGaven.

"Close," he said. "Her last meal, which I would estimate was no more than two hours before she was killed, consisted of escargot, some type of veal with saffron, and chocolate dessert."

"Okay," Katie said.

"And where in town can you order that?" McGaven countered.

"I can't think of any right off hand. You'd have to go to another town or all the way to a larger city like Sacramento," Katie said, still trying to figure out where she ate that meal. "Unless she ate at a private residence?"

"Sounds plausible," stated the medical examiner. He moved closer to Amanda, rolled her torso slightly to the right. "We've taken photos of this wound on her side and I've sent it to John to see what they could come up with, but preliminary examination," he said, "appears to be an imprint from a car door."

Katie joined him and turned her head slightly, trying to wrap her own brain around the assessment. "Oh, I see, it's the end of the interior part of the car door." Squinting her eyes a bit, she said, "You can see the distinct outline. It seems like possibly a smaller car and not an SUV." Katie looked up and refocused her eyes and then examined the imprint on the skin again. "Aren't most car doors taller? This seems too low."

"Expensive dinner and ride in a sports car," the doctor said. "You have your work cut out for you, Detective."

"Has the toxicology report come back?" asked Katie.

"Let me see," he said and flipped through a file. "Hmmm."

"What?"

"There were traces of fluoxetine and sertraline. Nothing serious. They are anxiety and depression drugs that can be prescribed by any doctor."

"You mean like Prozac?" she said, remembering the prescription bottles on the end table at Emily Day's apartment.

"Yes, Prozac and Zoloft, to be exact. Quite common."

"Thank you, Dr. Dean," Katie said.

"Jeff," he reminded.

"Yes of course, Jeff, thank you."

Katie and McGaven left the exam room, and she retrieved her briefcase, still reeling over the new information about Amanda Payton's last hours alive.

CHAPTER 27

Tuesday 0935 hours

"So you're still not going to tell me what happened last night," said McGaven with a huge Cheshire cat grin.

Katie had just ended the call with Emily Day and was still thinking about that imprint on Amanda's back and side as she drove towards Emily's house.

"Hello? Earth to Detective Scott?" he said.

"I'm not talking to you until you drop the whole 'last night' thing."

"Fine." He gave a dramatic sigh, still smiling.

Katie eased the unmarked patrol sedan into a parking place in front of the apartments where Amanda had been staying with her friend Emily Day. She cut the engine and retrieved the key. The air conditioning stopped, leaving the interior almost immediately stuffy and confining.

"Let's go," she said.

Looking at the landscaping and black wrought-iron fencing, McGaven said, "Nice place."

"This was the only time I could get to talk to Emily away from work."

Both detectives left the vehicle parked on the street and entered through the garden to ascend the stairs to apartment #10.

Katie knocked on the door. They waited only a minute before it opened and a tall blonde stared at them. Her long hair slightly curled around her shoulders and she was dressed in casual yoga clothes.

"Emily Day?" asked Katie.

"Yes," she replied, her blue eyes wide with amazement that two police officers stood at the door.

"I'm Detective Scott and this is Deputy McGaven. We spoke on the phone. I wanted to ask you a few questions."

"Please come in."

The detectives entered the small apartment. Everything looked the same as before, but Katie noted that the blanket was missing from the couch as well as the prescription bottles from the end table. Overall, the apartment was tidy and smelled of a flowery air freshener.

"I don't know what I can help you with, but please ask away."

Katie made herself comfortable on the couch; Emily sat in the chair across from her, while McGaven casually wandered around the living room.

Katie flipped open her small notebook and then focused on Emily. The woman appeared nervous. She kept rubbing her hands together and then wiping them down her thighs.

"Ms. Day, we're trying to retrace Amanda's last hours. Are you feeling up to it?"

Emily kept her focus on Katie and nodded.

"Amanda's body was found early Thursday morning at Whispering Pines, and the medical examiner puts her time of death at 2 a.m."

Emily looked confused. "She was here."

"What do you mean?"

"She was here on Wednesday night—well, she was here every night. I know because I was working at the hospital from 6 p.m. to 6 a.m."

Katie made a note just to double-check her story.

"She must've left, or maybe someone came by to visit."

Still shaking her head, Emily said, "No. No way. Amanda was terrified to go out at night. She would have never left."

"When was the last time you spoke with her?" This was the first time Katie had seen some emotion from Emily. Her voice cracked as she held back the tears.

"It was on my dinner break around 10.30 p.m. on Wednesday. She sounded fine and said that she was going to go to bed early and that I would see her in the morning. When I came home after my shift, I saw she wasn't sleeping on the couch, but I assumed that she had gone running. That was the only time she would ever leave the house, either to go running or to the grocery store."

"You're sure about that time?"

"Absolutely sure."

"Did you call her cell phone?"

"Amanda didn't have a cell phone. She got rid of hers after the... incident."

"I see. Did you notice anything different about Amanda?"

"No, she was scared but she seemed like everything was the same."

"Who else did Amanda talk to?"

"I... I really don't know," she said and looked away.

"Emily, if you know something you have to tell us."

"I don't know..."

Katie sensed her dishonesty, but she wasn't going to push. "Was she dating anyone or interested in anyone? It didn't have to be a formal date, but someone else she talked to."

Emily remained quiet. It was obvious that she was struggling with something. "I think she might have been talking to someone. I don't know who it was, but I got the feeling that it was someone from the hospital."

"What makes you say that?"

"She made a reference about doctors. That's all I know." Emily stood up now, clearly distraught. "Amanda was my best friend and I can't even help in her investigation..." She began to cry and pace back and forth.

Katie paused. "It's okay, Emily. We're done for now. But, if you remember anything, even if it doesn't seem important, call me, okay? Emily, okay?"

She nodded as she tried hard not to cry anymore.

The detectives walked to the door.

"Oh, one more question," said Katie.

Emily waited. "Yes?"

"Did Amanda cook dinner here on Wednesday night? Something fancy? A roast?"

Emily looked confused. "No, she was mostly vegetarian and only sometimes ate meat."

"Okay, thank you."

They left the apartment.

Katie waited until she heard the door close before she turned to McGaven. "Check the phone records to check her story. I think she's telling the truth, but I want to make sure she isn't covering for someone."

"Will do. Sounds like I have some desk time," he said.

"Emily Day isn't off the radar yet."

When they reached the car Katie pulled out her cell phone and dialed as McGaven climbed into the passenger seat.

"Hello," said Denise, sounding chipper as usual.

"Hi, it's me. You busy?"

"Always, but never for some real investigative work."

"Good," she laughed. "I have something for you to check out, basically some background stuff—hope I'm not piling on too much."

"Not at all—go ahead."

"First, this is unrelated to the homicide case we're working on. Is that okay?"

"I'm intrigued."

"It's a missing person case for a very special friend of mine. I promised that I would check it out. It's probably going to be an easy case where we find out he's at a new job or residence."

"No problem, Katie. I've got your back, no need to explain."

Katie almost let out a loud sigh of relief. "Okay, the name is James Samuel Haines. That's spelled H a i n e s."

"Got it."

"His brother is Army Sergeant Nick Haines. And… Wait, I need to get the rest of the info from my briefcase. Can you hang on or do you want me to call you back?"

"I'll hang on… I'm running reports, so no problem."

Katie quickly opened the vehicle and pulled out her briefcase, setting it on the hood. She had slid out several files and her notebook, when a white piece of paper dropped to the ground.

Staring at the familiar fold of paper, she slowly said, "Denise, I'm going to have to call you back. I'll text you all the information I have."

"Katie? Everything okay?"

She picked up the piece of paper, carefully holding to the edges. "I'm fine," she managed to say.

"Katie?" Denise said again.

"I'll call you later," she said slowly and ended the call.

Unfolding the paper, which was written in the same cursive blue handwriting, she read:

Don't spend too much time there.

"What? What is that?" said McGaven.

Katie instinctively looked around the car for anyone suspicious or watching her. There was no doubt someone was tailing her, shadowing her, and watching her moves before they left this note.

McGaven was at her side. "Another one?"

Her cell phone chimed with a text message from John. The sound made her twitch, adding to the uneasiness she already felt.

Linkage between Payton and Jane Doe cases—tan carpet fibers match 87%.

CHAPTER 28

Tuesday 1145 hours

The smell of diesel and exhaust fumes filled her senses and Tess woke with a dry cough, the stinging pain from her wrists and ankles a devastating reminder of where she was and everything that had happened to her.

She turned her head slightly from side to side, the tape over her eyes tugging on her hair and the skin near her ears. There it was again, the familiar smell she had recognized before—jasmine. Sweet and pungent. It was lighter than before, so she knew that the person who had been in the room with her was now gone.

She was alone.

"Anyone there?" she croaked as her throat was still exceptionally dry. "Can I have some water?" She didn't expect to hear a reply but wanted to hear someone's voice—even if it was her own.

She began working her restraints, feeling out the thin, sturdy twine and how many times it wrapped around her wrists. She tried to move her body upward on the bed to try and figure out how her hands were tied. Rocking and bouncing slightly, the bed springs groaned and squeaked until something loosened and she began to make progress with one area of the twine.

"I can almost…" she whispered to herself. "If I could just…"

A door slammed nearby making Tess start and jerk her arms down, pulling hard on her wrists. She let out a feeble cry as two strong hands pushed down hard on her upper arms as he leaned across her body, paralyzing her. Without saying a word, a man tightened her restraints, all the while breathing heavily near her ear. After he secured her, he didn't speak to her. He didn't touch her. She waited in absolute terror for what was next.

What was he waiting for?

And then, she felt a slow weight press down next to her body. Her flesh prickled as if ants were crawling all over her. She couldn't help but recoil. Any hope she had felt previously had been dashed. "Tell me, Tess... What are *your* dirty little secrets?" The eerie voice in the dark was nothing more than a whisper.

"Tell me!" He hissed like a snake.

"I... I don't know what you want from me," she stuttered in terror. "What secrets?"

"Truth," he said. "You'll give me the truth before I have no use for you anymore."

"What truth? I don't know what you want. Please... please..."

Tess felt the weight next to her face and tried to turn away. Paralyzed in fear, she shook, waiting for another taunt or strange request she couldn't answer.

His breath panted against her cheek and then in her ear, making her shoulders shudder uncontrollably. Goose bumps paraded up her arms and down the back of her neck.

"Tess..." he hissed. "Tess..." he repeated again but this time with more drama. "I know you want to tell the truth. Let it out..."

CHAPTER 29

Tuesday 1330 hours

Katie sat at her desk in her quiet office, thinking. McGaven had opted to use a computer upstairs in the detective division to run backgrounds, while obtaining a court order for phone records from Emily Day's apartment, to find out if calls came in from the hospital.

Katie finally picked up the phone and dialed the South Street Psychiatric Hospital to make an appointment to speak with Jane Doe again.

"Administration," said a woman who answered the main phone lines at the hospital.

"This is Detective Scott from the sheriff's department. I was in last Friday to visit with a patient. I was wondering if I could make another appointment to speak with her."

"Name of patient," said the woman with little voice inflection.

"Well, she hasn't given a name. It's just Jane Doe on her record," Katie said.

"One moment."

Katie could hear the pecking of a keyboard as the administrator searched for the patient.

"I'm sorry, Detective, but I don't see any patient by that name."

"Are you sure? I spoke with Dr. Smith," Katie persisted.

"Let me try something else. One moment." There was a loud click.

This time Katie could tell that the woman put her on hold. She tapped her fingernail on her desk—waiting for almost five minutes.

"Hello?" said the administrator.

"Yes, I'm still here."

"Jane Doe has been moved to another hospital—Silver Springs Hospital."

"Where is that?"

"It's near Cold Springs, about an hour from here."

"May I ask why?"

"The only notation I have is that there are larger therapy groups there that can accommodate her for an extended length of time."

"Did Dr. Smith put in for the transfer?" Katie asked, trying to pry a bit more information from the woman.

"There's no notation of that but he did sign the transfer papers."

"Thank you," said Katie and hung up the phone.

She leaned back in her chair, still not grasping why Jane Doe had been transferred. Was it because there was better therapy and care more fitting to her needs? Or was there something more sinister?

Katie didn't have time to call the other hospital, but made a mental note that she wanted to check in on Jane Doe very soon. Katie not only knew that Jane Doe had some answers about the killer, but she feared for her safety. First things first, she had an appointment with the county building and planning department in fifteen minutes. She grabbed her things and left the forensic division.

Parking at the Sequoia County Office Building, Katie walked to the entrance carrying her notebook. It had been an official county building since 1884 and still had the architectural integrity of the historical provenance to prove it. The stairs made a grand entrance to the main large double doors of the stout building. Once inside, signs directed you to the various local government areas.

Katie headed for the building and planning department. She opted for the stairs instead of the elevators and quickly climbed to the second floor. From there, it was easy to find where she needed to be. What she wasn't expecting was how busy the office would be, with people submitting blueprints and obtaining building permits. There were more than a few glances at Katie, taking in her badge and gun with wary curiosity.

"Hi, I'm Detective Scott from the sheriff's office and I'm here to see Shane?" she said when she made it to the front of the line.

The short, dark-haired man barely looked at her as he keyed up her name on the appointment computer. He clicked a couple more keys with his chunky fingers. "It'll be just a few minutes and he'll be able to help you."

"Thank you," she said.

"Next," said the man, stretching his neck along the line.

Katie stepped away from the counter and glanced around the room.

After waiting about ten minutes, a very tall thin man in his early thirties came out around the counter. He glanced around the room. His wiry, sandy hair, partial beard, and gold-rimmed glasses made him appear more like a college student or teaching assistant than an employee for the building and planning department. He caught sight of Katie waiting and smiled as he approached her.

"Detective Scott?" he said. "I'm Shane, the county researcher and archivist."

"Nice to meet you," Katie replied.

"Well, you're in for a treat. I received your request for the original plans of the Basin Woods Development and any other information we might have. Follow me," he said. There was an upbeat tone to his voice.

Katie remained quiet and followed the man as they passed several offices, some with open doors and others not, and then descended a staircase for more than two stories until they reached a basement.

Shane stopped a moment at the entrance to flip on several light switches, brightening the dark room with a slowly increasing glow. He turned to Katie and said, "I know it's a little chilly down here, but you get used to it. You're going to be okay?"

"I'm fine," she said.

"It's actually even too cool for the paper archives. I've been trying to get the county to put some money into a more climate-controlled environment down here. But, you know, there's never any leftover money in the budget to pay for such things," he explained.

Katie nodded.

The overall basement was huge. It seemed like it went on for miles and it would be easy to get lost, unable to find your way back. It felt like a crypt. Even though Katie was cool, a sickly heat began to infiltrate her body. With each step, she had to concentrate on walking a straight line. The long rows of filing cabinets seemed to close in on her. But she kept her breathing normal and walked with purpose, following Shane deeper into the basement.

Not now…

There were large metal filing cabinets stacked high all around her, each drawer labeled with numbers and letters corresponding to section and contents. Along the back wall were old roll-top desks topped with several cubbyholes with rolled-up papers inside them. Katie assumed they were blueprints and old contracts. She was intrigued with the storage of archives and wanted to know what kind of information there was about the Basin Woods Development.

"After you called, I was thinking about your request," he said, opening a tall cabinet with small square slots inside. "I had just organized some of these cabinets recently and remembered the name, Basin Woods Development."

"Are there the original blueprints?"

"Better than that," he said with a twinkle in his eye.

Katie couldn't help herself and laughed. "You must really love all of this."

"Detective, it's more than just documents, blueprints, and archived old newspaper articles. It's history. It is a part of Sequoia County—everything here is what made it what it is today."

Katie smiled, inspired by what he said. "I guess I never thought about it like that, but you're absolutely right."

Shane pulled out a large bundle of old blueprints. Pulling the rubber band from the tube, he walked to a low metal table in the corner. "Here are the original plans," he said as he carefully unrolled the package. He grabbed four plain glass paperweights to secure each of the four corners. "Okay," he said and rubbed his hands together.

Katie stood next to him reading the plans. "It says Woodland Pines Project?"

"Yes, that's what the project was supposed to be," he replied.

"I'm not completely following," she said.

"Okay." He leaned over the plans; using his right index finger to point out sections, he explained, "These were the original plans submitted in 1984—six years before the actual submission."

"Alright, now I'm following."

"This project was created by the Magna Group, and Baseland Architects did the drawings."

"How did it end up as the Basin Woods Development?" Katie asked, studying the illustrations. There were notations from the architects and builders: codes and numbers. One had a penciled-in note, barely legible, "Highland Project NP #367-44," which had been written on the lower right corner.

"Well," he began, "that's where it gets interesting. I dug up old newspaper articles, which were fairly well researched for the time. It turns out that the budget for the original project fell through and the Magna Group had its funding revoked. This company originally wanted to build more of a luxury area, but politics play a major role and so eventually it fell through."

"Did another company bid a new project?" she asked.

"You're on the right track, Detective. Simms Development swooped in and proposed more of an affordable housing project—basically a low income." He flipped the pages and it was clear that the new area was much more conservative and smaller. "Two years later, this was what was proposed, and after the permit was processed, it went into full construction mode."

"Why am I getting the feeling that there were internal issues?"

"To say the least; funds went missing, construction cut corners, and there was a man killed on the job when part of a roof caved in on him."

"Wow, I had no idea."

"Yeah, well, it was a while ago and most people forgot about the place."

Katie flipped through several pages of renderings and she began to recognize the area. "Do you have the individual house plans?"

"I thought you might ask. I've located about half of them. Was there one in particular you were looking for?" He adjusted his glasses while he stared at her, eagerly awaiting an answer.

Katie opened her file of an aerial view of the street which included the house she had searched. "Here," she pointed. "I know it's difficult to see with the trees, but you can see the side streets."

"No, I can see. Can you leave this with me? I can get you the plans and courier you a copy. Would that be okay?"

"Yes, absolutely. That would be great—thank you."

Shane took out his cell phone to write down the information. "So, Detective Scott, Pine Valley Sheriff's Department. I'll look up the address."

"Can you send copies of everything you have told me about the original project and what was actually built?"

"Yep." He made more notes on his phone.

"What were the names of the people?"

He went to a cabinet close by and pulled out a thick file folder. "The Magna Group president was Kenneth Jamison, Sr., and Simms Development president was Bradley Carter. I don't know if that helps."

"Jamison?" she asked, a little surprised.

Reading over the paperwork again, "Uh, yes. I'll send copies of this too."

"Shane, you have been absolutely amazing."

"Naw," he said as his cheeks flushed.

"One more favor," Katie said. "I need a list of all the people who owned/rented the houses before they were forced to move. Would that be the county assessor's office?"

"It would be, but I can get you that list too—if you like."

"Are you sure that you don't mind getting everything back to me?"

"Not a problem, Detective Scott. That's what I do. And... I'm assuming this is for an investigation."

Smiling, Katie said, "It is... a very important case."

Shane began to roll up the plans. "I'll get everything together and then have it couriered tomorrow some time. Would that be okay?"

"That would be great."

CHAPTER 30

Tuesday 1430 hours

The Adirondack Plaza was a special place, a park where locals loved to spend time and a place where out-of-towners always visited. It was the perfect hunting ground. He sat on a bench in the shade of several large trees, wearing dark sunglasses. No one looked at him, no one sat next to him, and he knew that no one would ever remember him. He watched a group of three women sitting at a table, obviously on a break from work by the way they were dressed. The trio wore plain beige pantsuits with their jackets off in the heat revealing sleeveless blouses in various pastel colors. The sun kissed their arms and shoulders.

Intriguing.

Exciting.

Two of the women were brunette and one a strawberry blonde, the loudest and most animated of the group. He watched her lips when she spoke, imagining what truth would come pouring out of her mouth. What she could share with him. It made his extremities tingle.

He inhaled deeply, trying to get a read of the wonderful scents of them as they passed.

A noise drew his attention away from the women suddenly as a slender young woman in jogging clothes pushing a baby carriage sat herself down next to him on the bench and gave a smile. She rocked the stroller gently back and forth.

The fragrance of baby powder, baby lotion, and something sweet, most likely orange slices, hit his senses and sent him into a frenzy. He couldn't bring himself to look into the stroller.

He was trapped. His legs felt frozen to the bench.

Terror filled him. His throat constricted.

Looking down at his hands, they looked red like blood.

He couldn't take it anymore. Leaping up, he rushed away from the park.

CHAPTER 31

Tuesday 1645 hours

Katie walked as fast as she could back down to the forensics division after the meeting at the county building, so fast that McGaven had to run to keep up.

"What's the emergency?" he asked as he jogged alongside.

"It *is* a homicide," she retorted with a tone that was out of character for her. She swiped her badge at the keypad in front of forensic services.

"Hey, I'm on your side, remember? I seem to recall you asking me if I had your back." He blocked her with his lumberjack-sized body. "What's going on?" he asked with a stern tone, and then relaxed when he saw the expression on Katie's face.

The door disengaged and Katie entered followed closely by McGaven. She kept walking to the office, down the main hallway past the examination areas, and then made a left, following another hallway until she reached the cold-case office.

Neither of them spoke until they were inside and the door shut behind them.

McGaven leaned against Katie's desk with his arms crossed. "What's up?" He had rolled up his shirtsleeves.

She put down her notes. "First of all, I'm sorry for being abrupt with you. It's wrong and unprofessional."

"I'm a big guy—I can take it," he said with a lighter tone.

Keeping her voice low in case someone could overhear, she said, "You know, I've been faced with stress before, not knowing if the bad guys were going to blow us up. You would think that would prepare me for working a homicide. Right?"

"You have worked a homicide before—those missing girls—remember?" he said.

"This is different."

"How? There's no difference except for the victims."

"I hear what you're saying, but this *is* different. I talked with Amanda; I told her that I would look out for her and keep her safe. I sent patrol by the apartment, and it still didn't save her life."

McGaven took a deep breath, choosing his words carefully. "Katie, the sheriff wouldn't put you in charge of this case unless he thought you were ready. You rocked the crime scene according to the officers that were there. They said if they didn't know better, they would have thought you'd been doing this for years. It was seamless."

Katie was taken aback for a moment.

McGaven laughed. "You know, Katie, you're hard to figure out sometimes."

"What's so funny?"

"You. You really don't know how great you are. Do you? You have a gift and a sixth sense that goes way past a gut instinct."

"McGaven, I appreciate the compliment, but I need—"

"You need to stay with this investigation and work through it your way—thorough and methodical." He gestured to the preliminary profile. "This," he emphasized, "is what is going to drive this investigation. I know you take everything to heart, too much at times, but you will get through this and *we will* find the killer."

Katie dropped her files on the desk, then went to the cabinets to search for something.

"What are you looking for?" he asked.

she doesn't know who she is keeps her safe. I can't let anything happen to her," she said, deeply concerned.

"Safety behind bars—creepy kind, but still…"

"What now?"

"Road trip."

"Road trip?"

"For me, first thing tomorrow. And it's going to be a long day."

"Darn."

"I want you to finish background checks, push the phone records for Emily Day's house, and start looking at employees working at First Memorial Hospital, in particular employees working on Amanda's floor."

"I'm on it."

"And push the search for video cameras near and around Emily Day's house the night Amanda left. Focus about an hour before 10.30 p.m. for now, until we see the phone records."

"I'll see what I can find out."

Katie stared at her board and the map of the county. The hospital seemed to be in the middle of everything. "See what you can find out at the hospital. Use your charm with the nurses," she instructed. "I can catch up with you after I finish what I have to do. I think at this point it makes more sense us splitting up for efficiency. But call or text me with *any* news."

McGaven wrote more notes down.

"I think we need to do a backdoor approach to Dr. Jamison before confronting him head on. I want to make sure that Jamison senior from the building project is actually his dad so we can ask the right questions when we have him."

He nodded. "I'll check it out."

"Denise is still gathering information on social media, so that could lend some interesting reading and maybe some new people of interest. If you like, you can check in with her."

"Where is the open road going to take you?"

"I'm going to visit Jane Doe again and see if I can get more information, but I have something personal to take care of along the way."

"Do you think you can get more information about the kidnapper from this Jane Doe?"

"I think Jane Doe is the key to this entire investigation."

CHAPTER 32

Wednesday 0745 hours

Katie made sure that she had packed the police sedan with some extra essentials: a change of clothes, snacks, and plenty of water. Cold Springs was a good hour of a scenic drive from Pine Valley. It would have been nice to have McGaven riding along but they would cover more ground going their separate ways.

She had almost let too many emotions slip out when talking with McGaven yesterday, but the truth was something in her had resurfaced after seeing Nick again. It felt too soon to have her new life as a detective intersect with her time in the army. How could she possibly balance these two huge parts of her life at once?

Her cell phone rang. Glancing down, she saw it was Chad and decided to ignore the call until later. The last thing she needed right now was more complications. She accelerated and sped along the main roads for almost half an hour until she took the cutoff towards Cold Springs.

Pressing the button to lower her window, she took in the magnificent fragrance of the California pines. It was such a picturesque area with trees and intermittent open meadows and slightly sloping valleys. Taking a deep breath she felt herself relax.

Katie had a gap of time before visiting hours to see Jane Doe, so she decided to make the most out of her trip. Her mind continued to run through her perp and victim lists. She desperately wanted to zero in on a suspect soon. Things were moving along, but not fast enough.

In less than forty minutes, Katie turned onto a freeway leading to Cold Springs only five miles ahead. Glancing at her notebook, she'd written down a street called Chanticleer, which was the last known address for Nick's missing brother, James Haines. Nick had given her a photo taken about ten years ago of a handsome man, clean-shaven, brown hair, and a crooked smile; just like Nick, but younger.

The area of town was old and run-down with junked cars parked in front of most houses and barns. She saw two men sitting in old beach chairs drinking beer and playing cards and slowed the sedan until she saw a dilapidated mailbox leaning to one side that read 545.

The thought never occurred to Katie that she might be entering into a hostile environment, but she was confident that she wasn't going to assume anything without proof first. She pulled to the side of the road and parked—it was the best place she could leave her vehicle and the easiest location to make a quick departure.

She opened the driver's door and was immediately hit with the heavy smell of marijuana, legal in the state of California, but nauseating. Everything would smell like pot smoke by the time she left and that annoyed her. She sighed, but exited her car anyway and quickly shut the door. It appeared to be an area where they grew the large plant harvests. That changed a few things a bit; it might make some of the locals around the area suspicious by her presence—even make her visit seem a bit dicey.

Katie made sure that her weapon was concealed properly and she had her cell phone tucked securely in her pocket and walked up to the cabin. The front area was entirely dirt with a few rocks tossed to the side. Large trees grew behind the cabin with looming branches draped over the rooftop. The chimney puffed ringlets of smoke into the tree branches.

Katie walked up the two steps to a small lopsided porch and knocked on the door. There was no answer and no sound of any movement inside. She knocked again—this time more assertively. Still no one answered.

She stepped down from the broken porch and walked around the cabin. There were all types of tools and wood, some organized, while other pieces were strewn all over. She heard the sound of someone chopping wood.

Thud... clack... bump...

The repetition was distinct and rhythmic, but made her cautious. She was stepping onto someone's private property, without an invitation, trying to locate someone's lost brother. Not the best idea, but there was no other way.

Thud... clack... bump...

Katie moved slowly and kept her balance as well as her wits. Rounding the corner of the house, she saw a large, bear-like man swinging an oversized ax splitting wood. He slowly reset another log. He was dressed in a heavy lumberjack shirt and dark blue jeans tucked into waterproof boots. He grunted now as he wielded the ax and slammed down onto the log. She stood for a moment, not entirely sure how to alert the man to her presence. Should she introduce herself as a police officer, or just a woman looking for a friend's brother?

The man continued to work through his routine, each time getting a little bit slower as exhaustion began to take over.

Thud... clack... bump....

Katie decided it was now or never.

"Hello? I was looking for James Haines. Does he still live here?" she said in her most casual voice.

The burly man stopped what he was doing and froze, not looking up.

"James Haines? Does he live here?" she repeated and walked toward the man.

The man slowly looked up and then straightened—even taller than Katie had anticipated. He lifted the ax and seemed he was about to attack.

"Stop!" Katie yelled and drew her weapon in one swift action. "Stay right there! Now, drop your weapon."

The man didn't move, the ax still above his head.

"Take it easy. I'm just looking for James Haines. He's not in trouble. I'm a friend of his brother."

"Who are you?" he said.

"I'm Detective Katie Scott with the PV Sheriff's Department. Now, please put the ax down."

A few tense seconds passed.

"I'm not going to ask you again," she said, holding firm and inching closer to the man.

In one awkward moment, the man dropped the axe, turned and ran in the opposite direction.

Crap.

Katie took off after him. "Stop!" she yelled.

His weighty footfalls and labored breathing echoed in the forest making it easy to follow him. Gaining distance, jumping over low-lying logs and pivoting around branches, she ran with swift speed. Taking a lower path, she managed to easily pass the large man and doubled back.

At the last second, she jumped out in front of him and yelled, "Stop!"

He stopped and dropped to his knees, trying to catch his breath, face red, and chest heaving. Weakly, he raised his hands, giving up in defeat.

"What's your name?" she asked, still training her gun on his torso.

"Bear," he gasped.

"Bear?"

He nodded.

"Bear what?"

"Ham… Hamlin."

"Okay, Bear Hamlin. Get up."

It took him a moment and then he managed to stand up and face her. Even though he was a big man, he looked sheepishly at her and seemed to be ashamed of what he had done.

"Why did you run?"

"I thought you were them."

"Them who?"

"Those guys who were looking for Jimmy."

"Are you talking about James Haines?" she said.

He nodded.

"Does he live here?"

"He moved out a couple of months ago."

"Why were those guys looking for him?" She relaxed her gun and lowered it by her side, but still prepared to use it.

"I'm not sure."

"Guess."

"He owed some people money. I know he gambled and mixed with certain kinds of people that don't like it if you don't pay them back."

"I see. Do you know where he moved to?"

Bear shook his head. "I don't know."

"Again, take a guess."

"He liked this girl."

"Now we're getting somewhere. What's her name?"

"Gaby or Nady, I think."

"Last name?"

"I don't know."

"Where does she live?"

"I don't know."

"Did he visit her when he was living here?"

"Yeah. Somewhere in town."

"If I put this away are you going to behave like a gentleman?" she asked, drawing attention to her gun.

"Yes."

"Okay," she said and holstered her Glock. "C'mon, let's go."

Katie walked back to the cabin with Bear and neither spoke until they were back at the wood chopping area.

"Mr. Hamlin, thank you for your time," she said, not knowing what else to say.

"Ms?"

"Detective," she corrected.

"Detective, when you find him let him know that he was a great roommate and it's not the same around here."

Katie smiled. "Will do. And sorry about the misunderstanding. Please take my card. Call me anytime if Mr. Haines contacts you or comes back."

Bear smiled, took her card, and shyly turned away from her.

Katie hurried back to her car and didn't waste time in case there were more misunderstandings with locals with an ax to grind against the cops.

Quickly maneuvering her vehicle around and away from the cabin, Katie retraced her route and made it back to the freeway. There was still time before the visiting window at the psychiatric ward. She headed toward James Haines's last known job in the special effects department at the California Studios and Amusement Park.

CHAPTER 33

Wednesday 0840 hours

After he got off the phone with Katie and they had confirmed the duties for the day, McGaven decided that he would take a few moments to find out who worked at the First Memorial Hospital before barging in and asking questions. There was always information about any work employees on social media, through team sports, and the hospital roster.

He didn't have to search the Internet long. There was a social media page that highlighted several hospital employees and first responders that had league baseball teams. McGaven looked up at the closed office door and realized that it was extremely quiet. He sighed just to hear a noise.

At first, hearing about the new cold-case office in the forensic basement, it sounded like the best thing ever, but in reality, it was isolating and lonely. He wasn't sure if he could work case after case in solitude—even though it was probably just a one-case assignment. At least in the detective division there were other detectives coming and going, phones ringing, and people coming in for interviews and polygraph testing. There was something going on at all times—it made it seem like you were part of a team.

He looked around the large space, still amazed at how Katie was so at ease and able to put together comprehensive lists and observant deductions from such a difficult case file. Not wanting to admit it to anyone, but the first day they had met, which was under unusual, if not stressful conditions, he liked Katie right away. He may not have shown it, but he respected her tenacity and being able to stand up to people. She was the kind of partner that every police officer hoped for.

McGaven was able to find out a couple of the nurses' names, Abigail Sorenson and Lisa Lambert, who both worked on the same floor as Amanda. There was a longstanding security officer by the name of Randy Drake who seemed most likely to have a good overview of all the staff. All of them were on social media, so he decided to memorize some of their interests before leaving.

As McGaven entered the hospital main entrance and made his way to the elevator, he realized that this was his first official assignment as a detective. He was proud that the sheriff thought enough of his abilities to assign him to the Payton homicide case with Katie.

The elevator doors closed and it climbed to the next floor. When the doors opened an orderly wheeled a gurney inside with a semi-conscious man on it. Usually people gave him a once-over due to his height, but so many things happen at a hospital that no one cared that there was an armed six-foot-six plain-clothes cop standing next them.

The doors opened again and the gurney was wheeled out and they disappeared down the hallway. McGaven stepped out and looked in both directions, not quite sure where to go, but he decided to take his time and walk down the hallway, bypassing the nurses' station.

He wasn't sure how he ended up in the maternity wing, but he found himself standing in the middle of it, nonetheless. The realization hit him hard and he felt a lump in his throat. Sadness overtook him. Seeing newborn babies, so innocent, so tiny, brought back stinging memories. He remembered when he was five years old and his mom had come home from the hospital with his new sister—Isabella. He had been so excited that he was going to be a big brother. He loved everything about being the older sibling—playing, feeding, and telling stories to his little sister. Less than a year later, Isabella became extremely ill and was in the hospital for a long time. She never came home. His parents told him that she was with God now and he would see her again someday. He had learned later that Isabella contracted a rare heart defect and that she was unable to survive the operation to try to correct it.

On patrol, whenever he was called to a family disturbance and there were infants involved, it would pull at his heart remembering his little sister. He would always make sure that they were safe first, before anything else. He often wondered what his sister would have become if she had grown up.

McGaven gathered his emotions and quickly moved on. There were different sections to the hospital and he wanted to stay within the main areas, where he would most likely find the nurses he'd identified on social media.

A tall brunette with her hair fixed in a ponytail hurried out of a patient's room and then entered another one. She moved with ease as she kept a stethoscope looped around her neck. McGaven immediately recognized her as Abigail Sorensen. According to her personal page, she was recently engaged to her high school sweetheart, an avid runner, and had two small rescue dogs.

McGaven set himself in position, estimating that she was doing typical rounds, checking in on patients, and would soon jet out of another room in about three or four minutes.

He didn't have to wait long as the nurse came out of the room and was headed for the next when McGaven stepped in front of her.

"Oh, excuse me," he said and gave his best smile looking down at her.

She began to say something rude, when she gave him a double look. "I'm sorry. Are you lost?" she said.

"Hi, I was looking for Abigail Sorensen. Would you know where I could find her?"

"That's me. What can I do for you?" She gave him a complete once-over this time and raised an eyebrow in interest.

"My name is Sean McGaven from the sheriff's department," he said carefully. "I'm part of the homicide investigation for Amanda Payton. Would you have a few minutes to answer some questions?"

"Homicide?" she said and looked confused.

"Yes, I'm sorry to say that Ms. Payton was found murdered a week ago. I'm here to just get some background information." McGaven casually showed his badge.

Nurse Sorensen looked pale and she seemed honestly shocked at the news of Amanda's death.

"Ms. Sorensen, you okay?" He watched her carefully.

"I... I... didn't know." She caught her breath. "When? How?"

"The case is currently under investigation. Do you have a moment?"

"Of course."

"Can we go somewhere less public?" he said.

She nodded and made a gesture to follow her. They walked down the hallway, took a left and went into a lunchroom. There was only one other person inside drinking a soda and reading a paperback novel.

"Please call me Abigail," she said and sat at a table.

"Of course. I'm sorry to give you the terrible news like that, but I figured everyone knew by now."

"I don't hang out with most nurses and I stay away from most media news."

"Did you know Amanda?"

"Yes, of course. We both were hired at about the same time and trained together."

"Did you know her well?"

"At work—yes. Plus a couple of casual evenings out mostly to blow off steam and complain about some of the doctors." She looked down at her hands.

"Did you notice any changes with Amanda?"

"I'm not sure what you mean."

"Did she seem edgy? Angry? Withdrawn? Anything like that before she left?" McGaven watched the nurse closely as she averted her eyes.

"Well…"

"Ms. Sorensen, whatever you tell me is kept confidential—for now. This is just a casual interview. We really don't want to bring everyone down to the police department for questioning," he explained, trying to sound firm but still friendly.

"Something happened to her before: she just didn't show up one day. According to the supervisor, she just quit. No notice. Nothing. And that wasn't like her. If you knew her and how hard she worked, everything was done by the book. And if she noticed something that you missed—she let you know about it in a nice way."

Two people dressed in green hospital scrubs and carrying food entered the room and sat in the corner.

"Do you know what happened?" he asked.

"She didn't tell me in so many words, but I guessed that she was attacked, or worse."

"Would you say that Amanda was well known and well liked around the hospital?"

The nurse thought about his question. "I'm not sure if she was well known, but she did have some secrets and wasn't likely to tell anyone about who she might have dated."

"Was she dating anyone?"

"I'm not totally sure, but there was someone from the morgue; I think his name is Marco. She seemed smitten."

McGaven waited a few moments before he continued, "If there is anything that you think is important for us to know about Amanda, will you please not hesitate to tell us. It could mean the difference in finding her killer and having her case go cold." McGaven hoped that he didn't sound too dramatic.

The nurse sat silent.

"Thank you, Ms. Sorensen, for your time." He dropped his card on the table and stood up.

"Wait," she said.

McGaven sat back down—curious.

"The only time she acted different, even a bit weird, was when she talked about some guy that she was involved with from time to time."

"Someone here?"

"No, I got the feeling it was someone she had met somewhere else or even in a bar. But she said to me on one especially rough shift: 'Any more days like today, I'm going to have him take me away from it all,' and then she clammed up and wouldn't say anymore."

"Did she say a name? Or a reference of any kind?"

"No, I asked her, but she refused to say anymore."

McGaven waited for her to drop more information, and he made sure he remembered what she quoted from Amanda exactly.

Again, the deputy rose from his chair, glancing at the three other people in the break room who appeared to not pay any attention to the conversation. "Thank you, Ms. Sorensen, please give me a call if you remember anything else."

She forced a smile and gave a weak nod.

McGaven managed to find his way to the security area, which wasn't easy without a map and a personal direction from a managing nurse. The deputy saw a lot of things walking through the wards he wished he could un-see; all types of procedures, gravely ill patients, and verbal confrontations, in the various rooms and emergency areas to make him never want to visit the hospital again. He wasn't so sure how clean everything was either—it made him shiver thinking about all the diseases and germs whirling about.

He finally reached the area where the patrolling guards would change, receive their equipment, and monitor the security cameras. The hospital security guard was the equivalent, at least in duties, to a police officer roaming the halls. They kept a watchful eye on everything that went on and helped to protect patients as well as the staff.

As McGaven approached, he heard loud voices, not heated, but an entertaining conversation underway. Two security guards were laughing about something that happened the evening before about a patient that wandered out of their room and was found hiding in the nurses' break room.

He saw a medium height, slightly overweight man with receding, close-cropped hair. He looked to be in his mid to late thirties. He stood like a cop, wider stance, hands every so often on his belt, and his eyes seemed to shift back and forth while being watchful. McGaven knew it was the guy he spied on social media that bragged about fishing and hot girls he met with his new boat.

The security guard immediately spotted McGaven as he approached.

"Randy Drake?" asked McGaven.

The guard nodded to his friend who quickly left. "Yeah, I'm Randy." He eyed the tall deputy and spotted the badge and gun.

"I'm Sean McGaven from the sheriff's department. I'm working the Amanda Payton homicide. Would you have a moment for a few questions?" he asked, keeping his authority to a minimum, not wanting to put Randy on the defensive. He had known the type and wouldn't be surprised if Randy had tried to become a police officer and didn't make the cut.

"Oh yeah, I heard about that. That's terrible. Amanda was a really nice girl."

"Is this a good time?" McGaven persisted.

"Sure, c'mon in."

McGaven followed the security guard into a small office. Randy closed the door and began to straighten up the messy desk, then gave up.

He plopped down in an adjustable office chair. "What would you like to know?" he said, now eyeing McGaven's police issued firearm. It was quite common for people to keep glancing at his gun.

"How well did you know Amanda Payton?"

He thought about it, shaking his head in a strange manner as if trying to recall his relationship. "Not well, she and several other nurses from her floor were just the kind of people you said hello to in passing. We just knew each other at work."

"Did you want it to be anything more?"

"With Amanda? Nah, she really wasn't my type."

"Your type?" McGaven asked.

Randy leaned forward and said in a quieter tone, "I like 'em kind of dirty, if you know what I mean? Amanda was a nice-looking girl, don't get me wrong, but she was too clean and conservative for me." He smiled and leaned back in the chair smiling broadly. He then broke out in a creepy laugh as if imagining what it would be like being with her.

"As far as you knew, did she date anyone here?"

"I'm not sure. I actually wouldn't know… Oh, wait…" The security guard spun around in his chair and opened a laptop computer. He turned it on. Opening a desk drawer, there were several CDs and he pulled one out. "Okay, this might blow your mind." He inserted the CD and waited to play the image. "Wait, I'm not going to get in trouble, am I?"

"I don't think so," McGaven replied.

The CD spun in the computer as they both waited.

McGaven didn't say anything, but he hoped it wasn't some personal home movie.

"I actually almost forgot all about this. There are, how shall I say, interesting things that go on in the hospital. Us guards have seen quite an eyeful, if you know what I mean. This might help you."

McGaven waited, but he wasn't entirely convinced until he saw the footage.

There was a black-and-white security image of a long hallway. McGaven didn't recognize the area even though he'd walked through much of the large, rambling hospital. The area looked narrower than he had been through, with swinging doors all the way along. There was a woman walking down the hallway, back to the camera, and she seemed to be waiting for someone.

As she paced, the camera caught a shot of her face and it clearly identified Amanda Payton. She nervously chewed her thumbnail as if contemplating whether or not she should leave. Within a minute, a dark-haired man appeared and they proceeded to have a conversation. Their body movements were restrained at first, but then they let go of their inhibitions and embraced in a passionate kiss.

"Yeah, you see. Amanda could be a tiger, I guess," said Randy holding back a laugh as he viewed the screen.

McGaven watched and had to agree with the security guard as the couple burst through one of the doors, their bodies locked together, their hands exploring hungrily.

"When was this taken?" asked McGaven. There were no identifying dates on the video itself.

Randy opened the CD holder where there were pencil markings. "It was nine months ago."

"Who is that with Ms. Payton?"

"That's Marco Ellis, he's a morgue technician," said Randy.

According to Katie's interview with Marco Ellis, he had said that they hadn't been together but went out casually a few times. The video clearly showed that there was more going on between them.

"Can you burn me a copy?"

"Yeah, of course," he said and proceeded to duplicate the footage.

"If you see any other recording that might help the case, call me."

"You got it."

McGaven left the hospital with a little bit more knowledge about Amanda Payton, but no closer to a suspect from what they already had. However, the investigation was beginning to show more about Amanda, things that she had conveniently kept to herself.

He walked across the parking lot to his car and got inside. Before starting the engine, he sent a text message to Katie:

Amanda was involved with someone secretly. Her relationship with Marco was more than she had said. Video footage to prove it.

CHAPTER 34
Wednesday 1105 hours

Katie flashed her badge at the gate to the amusement park featuring the world famous ScareFest. The security guard waved her through and directed her to the employee area. The parking lots were huge and she had a difficult time believing that so many people wanted to be scared to death for pure entertainment.

Three large warehouses formed part of the creative and special effects department for the festival of horrors. She had been directed to building A and parked accordingly.

Katie's cell phone buzzed and she saw that McGaven had sent a brief text about the video footage of Amanda and Marco. She couldn't wait to meet with him for an update. As she stepped out of her vehicle, the hot sun beat down on her, making her directly aware that she was still wearing a suit jacket. She quickly took it off, tossed it into the car, unbuttoned her blouse cuffs, and rolled up her sleeves. It made her badge and gun visible, but she had no choice. The heat was insufferable.

Katie followed the painted outline showing the way to go for artists, technicians, or models for makeup and fittings.

Interesting.

She followed the obvious path for the special effects personnel and searched for the overseeing director of special effects, Tim Durango. He had barely spoken to her on the phone and seemed to speak in hashtags with social media lingo. At least she got the opportunity to visit the area where James Haines had worked. There had to be something that she could use to find him—or at least learn more about him.

Standing at the entrance where the gigantic metal sliding door was opened wide enough for a person to squeeze through, Katie straightened her blouse and entered.

Inside, the cool breeze of large air conditioners working overtime was a welcome change, but she was more mesmerized by all of the high-tech gadgetry and robotics around her; the hum and clicking of technicians testing out their creations that would soon become every evil or fantastical character you could imagine.

Metal arms moved around her while large beast heads surged and snapped their teeth with a scary tenacity as she walked past a couple of computer operators. She stopped and asked, "Excuse me. Where can I find Tim Durango?"

"Down that way." The man gestured across the warehouse. "Keep going until you see makeup effects. You can't miss his office," he said and smiled.

"Thanks."

Katie followed his instructions, and the noise lessened as she came through another area where there were numerous artists working on masks, makeup, and creating other add-on items like bumpy horns, pointed ears, and odd tails.

She kept moving and felt like she was walking into another world, unsure if she would ever find her way back to reality. Finally she reached a door that read: "Director of F/X."

Pushing the door open, she peered inside. There was no one there, but she decided to say, "Hello? I'm looking for Tim Durango."

The small office was crowded with everything to make a monster: fabric, plastics, fabricated body parts, two human heads, metal gadgets, paints, drawings, boxes, heavy makeup cases, and a desk covered with more unusual items. It was difficult to see the size of the desk or if there was even a chair.

"Hello?" Katie said again. This time, her voice pushed her words with a harsher tone. She surveyed the room, very slowly taking in each item carefully before moving on. Something wasn't right.

She took another step inside.

Several chatting people hurried by outside, but no one seemed interested that a cop was standing in the director's office.

Then Katie saw it.

Movement.

"Oh damn," said a voice with a distinct British accent. "You're good, Detective." One of the mannequin-looking heads stood up; beneath was a regular body. "You're the first newcomer that didn't fall for it." He came out from the cramped area.

Katie still didn't quite know what to think about the entire situation. She definitely felt like she had stepped into another dimension. "Tim Durango?" she finally said.

"Well of course, who else would I be?"

Katie couldn't help but laugh. "They told you I was coming in, right?"

"Of course. We have to try out our newest innovations on someone unsuspecting. It's marvelous usually."

"It's amazing. I wouldn't have thought it was real, but I felt something wasn't right."

"Most people dismiss so much of what goes on around them. You are one of those rare people that don't rely just on what you're seeing, but you allow your gut to tell you otherwise." He sat on the edge of the desk, dressed in jeans and a tie-dye T-shirt showing off his impressive tattoos of various superheroes. He carefully peeled away the silicone mask pieces that had dramatically altered his cheeks, forehead and chin.

"Well, it's my job actually. I think proper introductions are in order. I'm Detective Katie Scott with PV Sheriff's Department."

"Very nice to meet you. Everyone calls me Tim." He used a towel to wipe his face; he was a nice-looking man with very expressive eyes and slightly sharp features.

"Well then, Tim, can I ask you a few questions about a previous employee of yours?"

"Shoot."

"James Haines," she said, and watched his reaction.

He let out a sigh. "James was one of my best new creators. He was green when he started, but then he caught the inspiration bug and really became a great artist. One of my best, in fact. I was sad that he just left, no word, no phone call, and not even a text message. It was like he just vanished."

"How long did he work here?"

"About two years, give or take a month or two."

"Did he ever speak about a brother?"

"He didn't talk much about his personal life. Every once in a while he'd tell a funny story from when he was young, but other than that, he was totally into his work."

"His brother has asked me to look into his whereabouts. It's very important that I find him. Do you know where he could've gone? Moved to? Anything?" she asked.

Tim shook his head and said, "I know he had a roommate. A guy he called Bear, if I remember correctly."

"Yeah, I've already talked with him," she said. Hesitating and then asking, "Did he seem to change? Become depressed? Angry? Anything unusual that would make him leave so abruptly."

Tim cocked his head to one side as if thinking back. "Now that you mention it, he was a little moody, even for him, and seemed to have something weighing heavy on his mind."

"Do you know what it might have been?"

He shook his head.

"Could you wager a guess?"

"Detective, I really don't know. The only thing that sticks in my mind is that he did like to place bets on sports teams like the rest of us. Maybe he had debt? I really don't know."

"His brother is his only living relative. It's so important that I find him. Some things… have changed and I think it's so important for the brothers to get back in touch."

Tim let out a sigh. He seemed to understand the importance of Katie's trip. "I really can't think of anything, but his workstation might give you some clues."

"Is it still available?"

"I haven't had the heart to clear it and give it to someone else." He forced a smile. "I was thinking, maybe, he might return."

"May I see it?" she asked.

Standing up and joining Katie at the doorway, he said, "Sure, follow me."

Katie followed the special effects director down another hallway where there were open rooms on both sides. She saw people working on models and robotic monsters.

Tim stopped at one of the rooms toward the end. "This is it. Look around as long as you like. It was nice meeting you and I hope you find him," he said, pausing a moment before he left. "Oh, if, or rather when you find him, tell him he always has a job here." Tim left.

Katie stood looking around at all the unusual equipment and materials used to make special effects. There was a large table in the middle of the room with smaller work areas around the walls. Two silicone dragon masks were in one corner and pieces to some hideous red monster lay on one of the other work areas. A tall stand with special small drawers and cubbyholes stood in the farthest corner. A blue rolling suitcase, partially open, revealed a variety of heavy makeup colors from every skin shade to a vast array of rainbow shades.

She looked out the door and down the hall. Loud voices were coming from another area. Otherwise, it was mostly quiet and no one seemed to be near. She waited another few moments in case someone wanted to come forward and give her any information— but no one did.

Beginning from left to right, similar to searching a crime scene, Katie looked through James's stuff to see if she could find anything that might give new information to where he might have gone—or who he might be with.

She opened every tiny drawer, where she found props from huge false eyelashes to glass eyeballs. Systematically searching, she only came up with things that were work related. Sticky materials and various shapes of clay, silicone, and other substances adhered to her fingertips, making her hands feel oily.

She kept examining every item.

She stopped at a mechanical monster still in the early stages of a head, torso, and arms. Stuck between an intricate jawbone in the face was a small torn section of paper, obviously tucked securely so that he wouldn't lose it. Written in pencil was the name "Nadine" and a phone number in the same local area code.

Katie tucked the paper in her pocket. She finished the pursuit of finding anything that would lead to James, but there was nothing else.

Feeling somewhat disappointed, Katie quickly dialed the phone number and it immediately went to voicemail with a computerized voice. She would keep trying and do a search in phone records when she got back to her desk.

Katie retraced her way through the building and finally back to the parking lot; leaving the area, she headed toward Silver Springs Hospital to meet with Jane Doe with just enough time during the allotted afternoon visiting hours.

Her cell phone buzzed. There was a text from Nadine's number:

Who is this?

CHAPTER 35

Wednesday 1330 hours

McGaven was still on an emotional high after leaving the hospital and felt like he was actually a fully sworn police detective running down clues. He tried not to dwell on the fact that it took a woman being murdered for him to get a chance to show that he could contribute to an investigation.

When he returned to the office, several CDs had been forwarded to the department from multiple businesses and the state transportation department along the route between Emily Day's apartment and the Whispering Pines area. McGaven began the painstaking task of trawling through all the footage.

He stretched his arms over his head, rubbed his eyes, and tried to make himself more comfortable in the chair. It was quiet. Too quiet. Even the chairs didn't squeak loud enough down here. He thought you actually could hear a pin drop if he decided to test that theory.

He stood up as the videos were still running and moved around the room examining everything closely—especially the notes Katie posted on the board.

Sitting back down, he tried to make a game out of watching the boring surveillance footage. There were more women featured than men. Men seemed to walk slower and take their time to get into their vehicles, while women hurried, sometimes dropping their keys, before getting into their cars. There were dogs with their owners, usually small dogs. He noted there was one Labrador and a German shepherd too.

Two hours had passed and he was finally approaching the time that Amanda must've left the apartment. He looked at the timestamp and it read 11.05 p.m. She was walking down her road and waited at the corner of Forest Avenue and Spruce Street. The video was taken by a nearby convenience store and gas station. She appeared to be waiting for someone and it didn't take long before a dark, high-end sedan pulled up next to her. She bent over and talked to the person driving. Amanda blocked the view of the driver, but she seemed relaxed and chatted a moment with the unknown person.

McGaven then saw the car pull to the side of the road near the store. The vehicle was barely in range of the surveillance camera, but McGaven could still see a man get out of the car and open the passenger door for Amanda. It was all cordial and there wasn't anything that suggested there wasn't a mutual friendly trust between them.

Interesting.

Doesn't match her story.

McGaven watched the footage several times, but he couldn't get a clear photo of the driver. The videos were blurry and the resolution was extremely poor. He made several stills, but the man in question could be twenty or sixty. It was hazy to be able to tell what kind of hair he had, but he was wearing some type of dark jacket and pants. There was no way to properly identify him. The video was a tool to begin to retrace the timeline of Amanda's last moments.

One thing was for sure, Amanda wasn't under duress or kidnapped—she went willingly.

CHAPTER 36

Wednesday 1445 hours

Katie sat in the parking lot at Silver Springs Psychiatric Hospital. She tried to respond to the text she received from Nadine, but she got no reply. She tried a couple of more times. No answer.

Damn.

Katie must've spooked her.

Readying herself, she knew that her prime directive was to find out more information from Jane Doe, to see if there was actual linkage between her and Amanda's homicide. As much as she wanted to follow up on this mysterious phone number and message, she had to keep her top priority on Amanda.

The new psychiatric hospital was much different than the last place due to the exceptionally well-tended landscaping and the style of the building. It appeared more like an upscale condominium or vacation spot, except for the chain-link fencing with barbwire along one entire side.

Before Katie exited her vehicle, she quickly ate a protein bar and drank some water. Her stomach had been rumbling, so she needed something to tide her over before she got back home.

Readying herself, she got out of her vehicle and headed to the main entrance. Tucked in her briefcase was a beautiful book about growing and cultivating roses, which she was going to give to Jane Doe.

She couldn't help but remember the message that waited for her when she left the previous psychiatric hospital. Would that person leave another note? Could they have been following her today without her knowing? Katie didn't think so—she was cautious and watched her mirrors in case anyone was following or showing up in more than one place.

Before she reached the door, she was hit with the most wonderful aroma of blooming flowers: honeysuckle and orange blossoms. The smell of a garden lifted her mood as she pulled open the door and approached the main desk. The setup was different from the last mental health facility—casual and friendly with bright artwork on the walls.

Katie stood at the main desk and announced herself, "Hi, I'm Detective Katie Scott and I called about visiting a new patient here—Jane Doe." She flashed her badge.

The young receptionist, with extremely long nails, tapped quickly over the keyboard. "I'm sorry, Detective, but no one called you?"

"No, called me for what?"

"Jane Doe isn't receiving any visitors today."

"When did this happen?"

The receptionist clicked on another screen and said, "I'm not seeing that information. It just says that there are to be no visitors for her today—and until otherwise noted."

Katie was disappointed and even a bit aggravated. "Was it ordered by Dr. Trent Smith?"

She shook her head, "No, I don't see that name."

"And you can't give me any more information than that," Katie said.

"I'm afraid not, Detective. I'm very sorry you drove here for nothing." She forced a professional smile.

"Can I leave this book for her?"

"I'm sorry, no, hospital policy."

Katie was going to say something else, but realized it was futile. "Thank you."

Hurrying to her car, she looked to see if another note had been neatly folded and stuck in her window frame, but there wasn't one.

Why were they not allowing Jane Doe to see any visitors?

What had changed?

I'm not giving up on you, Jane…

CHAPTER 37

Wednesday 1645 hours

He watched her as she lay motionless on the bed, straining to listen. For what, he didn't exactly know. It wouldn't help her escape. No one was within earshot. No one would hear her pathetic screams. She could cry out all she wanted, but no one was going to rescue her.

His interest in her grew weary. She wouldn't tell him what he wanted to hear, but she was special. There was something deep inside her that she really needed to express—tell someone—but she wouldn't divulge any of it. She held strong. He could see from the way she squirmed that she thought she could still escape. That was a mistake he'd made before, but he wasn't ever going to make it again.

As he left the house, he saw the fire again—flames inching out the windows. Smoke everywhere.

Stop it… stop it…

Exhausted, he leaned against the front of the house, gasping for air, still trying to catch his breath. He tasted the burn and smelled the smoke.

No…

Nothing was going to take away from his mission…

The truth.

Nothing.

CHAPTER 38
Wednesday 1800 hours

Katie was beyond tired and felt ready to sleep even though it was still early. The two strong cups of black coffee had worn off; even though she had new information to shed some light on the case, she was too tired to contemplate it now. As her energy waned, poisonous self-doubts crept into her mind. Was she wasting time following up with Jane Doe? Was she moving the investigation in the right direction? Her gut told her that there was an important piece of evidence associated with Jane Doe and time would have to play that card sooner or later.

As she eased her police sedan onto her property—she'd been too tired to pick up her Jeep at the department—she saw her uncle's white SUV parked in the driveway. She had called him to check in on Cisco, which he always loved to do, but she was surprised that he was still here.

Katie slowly got out of the car and walked towards the house. The door opened just as Cisco jetted outside and ran around her three times, wiggling his rear end and tail.

"Hey, boy," she said wearily, giving him a quick pat.

Her uncle opened the door wider. "Long day?" he said.

"Really long, but productive," she said, closing the door. "What are you still doing here?"

"I wanted to see you and make sure everything was okay."

"I'm fine," she assured him as she dropped her briefcase and shed her jacket. Usually she was particular about putting everything in its place, but tonight she just didn't care. "Just really, really tired…"

"I wanted to hang out with Cisco and we watched the game together."

Katie laughed. "That's good. I know he enjoys a good game and some guy time."

Cisco grumbled and ran to the couch, jumping up on it and making a spectacle.

She walked into the kitchen and opened the refrigerator. Staring at the contents, nothing looked good to her.

"There's a plate with foil over the top. That's for you," her uncle said from the living room.

She grabbed the plate and curled back the foil to find a chicken breast, wild rice, and a fresh vegetable medley. "Yum. Did you make this?"

The dog made a beeline for the kitchen and was immediately next to Katie's side, nose sniffing at the open fridge.

"Hardly. Claire did. She's really an amazing cook. You don't know how lucky I am finding her."

Katie pulled the plate out, tossed the foil, and put it into the microwave for a couple of minutes. She walked into the living room, kicked off her boots, and sat down next to her uncle.

Letting out a sigh, she said, "What's up?"

"What do you mean?" He tried to sound casual.

"I mean, why are you here at this hour?" She leaned against him and asked, "What did I do?"

"Nothing. I'm just a bit worried."

"Alright, who said what?" She knew someone must have made a comment about her working hard that made her uncle worry and stay up this late.

He laughed and put his arm around her. "No one said anything. It's just that Chad mentioned…"

"Chad talked to you? What? Are you guys best friends now?"

"Now take it easy. I want to make sure that you're not working too hard and that everything is okay," he said softly.

Katie yawned and found it difficult to keep her eyes open.

The microwave dinged.

She slowly got up and went to the kitchen.

"I'm going to hear about it in your report," he said. "So you might as well tell me now."

Pulling the plate out and setting it on the bar counter, she grabbed knife, fork and napkin. It wasn't until after she made herself comfortable that she began to explain, "I had a few places to go today." She sliced a piece of chicken breast and popped it into her mouth. "Wow, this is heaven. So, so good. Tell Claire thank you. I'll call her tomorrow too."

"Okay, everything out on the table," he stated.

"Uh-oh, here comes the sheriff."

"It's not about your job performance; it's about how much work you're taking on yourself."

"What do you mean? I have McGaven doing half the work— maybe even more with all the background checks and videos. I even have Denise running down information. I think that I'm *delegating* work just fine and we're making progress."

"That may be true, but you're taking on too much," he insisted. "I need all my officers and detectives balanced in their workloads—including you—especially you," he said softening. "You've been through more than a lifetime of trauma and stress at such an early point in your life—in your career." He moved to the counter and sat across from her.

Katie listened and she appreciated his sentiments, but she had noticed her anxiety and panic episodes had subsided quite a bit. "I know what you're really saying. You're afraid that I might go over the edge emotionally, psychologically, because of my stress and undiagnosed PTSD." She put down her fork and moved to the living room and sat down next to her uncle. "I love you, Uncle Wayne and I cannot imagine if I didn't have you and Aunt Claire as my family—I'd be so lost. But work is my therapy and whether you want to believe it or not—it's helping."

"Have you…?" He trailed off.

"Have I what?"

"Have you ever thought about seeing someone—just to get some things straight and having someone to talk to on your terms? An unbiased person."

"No—well yes, I have, but I'm fine the way things are right now."

"You know, your dad and I used to try and scare each other as kids," he said, recalling a fond memory.

"Dad never told me about that," she said.

"Well one time I went too far and I had him believing that I was going to die. Stupid kid stuff and without any thought, just thinking it would be funny getting something over on my big brother. I guess I was pretty convincing."

"What happened?" she asked.

"When I saw how scared he was at the thought of me dying, we made a pact that we would always be there for each other. We were less than two years apart, but we had a bond like we were twins. So from then on whenever either of us had a difficult decision or something serious was bothering us—we were there for each other."

Listening to her uncle talk about her dad as she slowly ate made Katie sad but at the same time she loved to hear stories. It made it seem as if he was still here—in the room with them. She missed him dearly every single day. Her parents were killed in a car accident when they were coming home from vacation from the coast. It stung deep every time she thought about it. They never got to see her graduate from college or the police academy. There were many times that she needed her mom to talk to and those opportunities were now lost.

"Katie?" he asked.

"Oh, I was just thinking."

"I know, I think about them a lot too," he said as if he had heard her thoughts. "So you have to understand why I take it so personally and why I'm protective of you. I don't want every case of yours be a life or death incident like the Chelsea Compton case."

"I know."

"Just do me a favor. Don't take on too much. Don't think I don't know about your army sergeant visiting you."

"He's staying with a friend in Watkins and he's doing fine—in case you wanted to know. I'm helping him find his brother—that's the only family he has."

"You can't help everyone," he said.

"No, but I can help family. Nick is like a brother to me."

The sheriff hesitated as he understood her point. "Just be careful with your workload."

"Wow, am I under a twenty-four hour watch now?" she said playfully.

"I mean it, Katie."

"I know. Even though my parents are gone, I'm still the luckiest girl in the world to have you," she said, and squeezed his arm.

CHAPTER 39

Wednesday 2330 hours

"Hello?" answered a very sleepy voice.

"Hey, McGaven, you weren't in bed, were you?" said Katie. She couldn't fall asleep right away still thinking about the case and her uncle's visit.

"Katie?"

"You sound surprised. Sorry it's so late. Got home a while ago and my uncle was here. I've found out some stuff. It's been interesting to say the least."

"Some of us do have lives, you know."

"I have so much to tell you, but that can wait until the morning. I've been thinking..." she began.

"Oh no, here it comes," he said, sounding more like his usual chipper self.

Katie adjusted her cell phone's speaker. "So I want you to pull up everything about Dr. Kenneth Jamison that you can find—everything. Get anything from Denise that she has from social media."

"Couldn't you have waited until morning to ask me to do that?" he said. There was a soft giggle in the background.

"Oh." Katie realized that he wasn't alone. "Sorry, you're with your girlfriend. Please apologize to her. Hopefully, she won't hate me too much before I get a chance to meet her."

McGaven laughed. "She knows all about you and she still wants to meet you."

"I guess it can wait until tomorrow," she said slowly.

"Go ahead, finish your thought—otherwise it will bug the crap out of you."

"Well, you seem to have more to share with me from today."

"Don't change the focus to me. What do you have?"

"Jane Doe has been put on lockdown—no visitors—and there's no indication of when she will have them."

"Interesting."

"I'm worried for her safety. She must be terrified. I don't want—"

"Don't psyche yourself out thinking that what happened to Amanda will happen to Jane Doe."

"I guess things can wait until tomorrow."

"Well, I've found video footage of Amanda getting into a high-end car with an unknown man."

"What? Are you kidding? What time?"

"A little bit after 11 p.m. the night before she was found at Whispering Pines. You can't identify the man or even get a good description of him; the video is too far away and very low resolution. It's beginning to look like Amanda hadn't been entirely truthful."

"Could still be a doctor?" she said.

"You think the man in the video was the kidnapper too?"

"Maybe, but I think he fits into this somewhere or he has information we need. And I want to see who this guy is, study him without him knowing it."

"How are we going to do that?" he asked now with more enthusiasm in his voice.

"I'll tell you tomorrow."

"Dammit, Katie. Why do you do that? Now I'm not going to be able to sleep."

"Go back to your girlfriend, and don't forget to wear something nice tomorrow. Maybe a change of shirt too."

"Katie, what the hell are—"

"I'll see you tomorrow."

"Hey, Katie, lay off the heavy caffeine at this time of night. Otherwise, you're going to be paying more for psyche fees."

"Will do." She ended the call.

CHAPTER 40
Thursday 0745 hours

Katie drove to work early, eager to get back to the investigation. She felt surprisingly rested and alert after a long day yesterday; perhaps it was the pep talk from her uncle. She fully understood where he was coming from, but sometimes you just had to let baby birds fly on their own. She would give serious thought to speaking with a counselor—but for now she forged ahead.

She pulled into the parking lot at the sheriff's office and drove around the building to her usual parking area. There was some kind of commotion going on. As she slowed to take a closer look, she saw the familiar crime scene tape cordoned off a section with John dusting for prints—from *her* Jeep.

"What the hell is going on?" she said to herself.

Pulling over, she was out of the car in seconds and by John's side as he dusted print powder along the rear windows of her car. "What the hell is going on, John?"

He looked up from his work and said with a smile, "I was leaving late last night and caught a guy scoping out your Jeep. I called him out and he ran before I could catch him."

"He touched my car?"

"Yep."

"I don't keep anything in there besides some training stuff for Cisco. What was he looking for? You think he was just a thief?"

"Don't know. It was hard to tell."

"What did he look like?"

"That's the thing, I couldn't see his face clearly."

Katie frowned—it wasn't what she wanted to hear. She thought of the person leaving her messages and wondered if it was the same person here last night.

"Sorry, that's just how it goes sometimes," he said, concentrating back on his work.

"So he actually touched the Jeep?"

"You already asked me that. We're checking cameras too."

"I'm just trying to figure out why he would want to do that."

"I only saw him for a moment. I'm hoping that I'll get a good set of prints and we can find out who he is so you can ask him what he was doing."

"I hope so."

"It may be nothing, but I'll be thorough." John tried to reassure her.

"Yeah, it could be nothing," Katie said, but she wasn't so sure. "Could you…?"

"I'll let you know immediately if the prints get a hit," he said, still concentrating on his task.

Katie smiled. She knew that John was methodical at his job. "Thanks, John."

Back in her office, it was clear McGaven had been busy. On the board, he had written:

> *"You're on the right track": Left on car at psychiatric hospital*
> *"You're closer, red hot now": Left at abandoned house*
> *"Don't spend too much time there": Left inside briefcase—at morgue or apartment?*

McGaven looked up from his work as Katie put down her things. "You thinking what I'm thinking? That the guy messing with your car last night was the same one leaving you notes?"

Katie sat down in her chair still looking at the messages. "I cannot worry about it right now; if John gets a hit then we'll see if it fits into the investigation. Otherwise, it's just on the back burner."

"I agree."

"I read your overview report from yesterday while I had breakfast," she said. "Very interesting. I'll watch the video from the hospital later if need be, but I trust your assessment."

"I think we should really take a look at these messages you've been receiving."

"I thought we were going to leave it on the back burner?" she said.

"I'm looking at them and I'm thinking…"

"Obviously, someone is trying to tell me, guide me, or throw me off track on this investigation," she said.

"The killer?"

"I don't think so. The statements are too straightforward, not playing games, not dramatic enough, and it seems like they are *really* trying to help me. A concerned person? Maybe someone who knows the killer?"

"It's strange like…" McGaven said as he reread the messages. "It reads like a…"

"Story? Or a list of instructions?" Katie added.

"Exactly."

Katie let out a sigh. "What bothers me is that the person got close enough to slip the note into my briefcase."

"Did you notice anyone following you yesterday? Someone staring at you or making notes?"

"I've had some weird experiences, that's for sure, but no, I haven't seen anyone watching me."

McGaven looked concerned.

"Don't worry about me. My uncle has already played that card. I'm fine. Really," she stressed her point. "I'm not a kindergarten teacher; I'm an army vet, *and* a police officer."

He laughed. "You're right."

"What's so funny?"

"I could just imagine you as the drill sergeant for a bunch of four-year-olds."

"Is that how you see me?"

"Sure," he said still laughing. "Well, not quite."

"I think you should put five bucks in that coffee can."

"Hey," McGaven said, back to his serious mode looking at the computer. "Have you checked your email?"

"Not this morning yet."

"John has some preliminary stuff for us. There's a match for a carpet fiber found under Amanda's nail."

Katie had risen from her chair and peered over McGaven's shoulder, reading the reports on the computer screen. "The fiber was from inside a high-end vehicle."

McGaven read the report. "It states there's a high probability it was from a Mercedes, Lexus, or possibly some of the BMW models. But the company that supplied these carpets, Trevvo, is no longer in business. Now all three of these makes of car use a new company, Brenalin Works." He moved to his notes and took a CD and inserted it into a laptop. "Check this out." He smiled.

The video played showing Amanda walking toward the convenience store and the entire interplay with the unknown man.

"Can't quite see the type of vehicle. BMW maybe?" she said. "Hand it over to John and see what he says."

"Done."

"Okay, we have a carpet fiber from a high-end car; Amanda was seen getting into a high-end car with an unknown man at 11 p.m. on the evening before her body was found. Time of death was 2 a.m. within a half hour. So between 11 p.m. and 2 a.m. Amanda ate a rich dinner and then was killed, driven to Whispering Pines and her body dumped." She sat back. "It's beginning to tell a story," she said. "But why would Amanda not tell me that she was seeing someone?"

"Maybe she wasn't seeing that person?" McGaven suggested. "And maybe the killer was taking extra precautions?"

Katie browsed her lists and tried to zero in more specifically, but they just didn't have enough information. Her thoughts returned to Jane Doe.

"What's going on in that brain of yours?" said McGaven.

"I keep going back to Amanda and her original story about being kidnapped, why I couldn't find anything to prove she had been held, but her description of how to get to the house seemed accurate—and the deputies didn't find anything either. Something isn't right, and I just can't see it—yet." She let out a frustrated sigh.

"Maybe she just lied."

"It's possible—but we have to keep running down more evidence before settling on a definitive fact."

"Yeah well, someone is trying to give you some intel," he said and gestured to the notes. "And they've gotten really close to you in order to leave those messages. Seems pretty risky."

"You're starting to sound like my uncle."

"Well, great minds *do* think alike," he said, smiling. "Seriously, please be careful."

"Noted," Katie said. She tried not to sound like it bothered her, but in truth, it made her a little uneasy.

There was a sudden knock at the office door. Katie and McGaven looked at each other. It was strange to have visitors to their office.

"Come in," Katie said.

The door opened; it was Sissy the upstairs receptionist. She carried a large bundle and put it on Katie's desk. "Hi, this just came for you, Detective Scott, special courier from the county."

"Oh great," Katie said. "Thank you."

"You're welcome," the receptionist said as she hurried out of the office.

"Gifts," McGaven said.

Katie was already unrolling it. "This is great."

"Great, more paperwork," he said with a low tone.

"No, here's all the information for the housing project—architectural drawings—*and* a list of residents before they were given notices to vacate." She began sorting through the papers, separating them into piles. "I love this guy."

"Who?"

"Oh, this researcher, Shane, at the county. He knows how to find anything."

"Sounds like you're smitten with him."

"It's not like that… I think he will be very helpful in future investigations." Katie took her attention away from the new paperwork and asked McGaven, "First impression—what do you think of the notes—friend, killer, or someone else."

"My first thought, honestly, it's someone who's trying to help us but doesn't want their identity known—maybe they have a record or maybe they are related to the killer."

Katie thought about that and said, "Maybe someone who has a reputation or a job to lose?"

"Like a doctor? Someone like Dr. Jamison?" he said.

"It would make some sense, Amanda's supervisor. Maybe she was having an affair with him?" Katie speculated. "But we're talking about two different things—the notes and the killer."

"I bet the doc has a high-end vehicle and likes expensive dinners."

"I bet most doctors at the hospital would fit that description too." Katie thought that Dr. Jamison had some information they needed, but he was most likely not the killer. "The hours they keep. How would he have the time to hold someone hostage, plan out the ambush, and dispose of the body?"

"More questions than answers," he said. "Should we bring in Dr. Jamison to find out? We can also ask him about his dad and the original Basin Woods Project."

Katie reread her preliminary profile of the killer. "I've called the hospital, Dr. Jamison's voicemail, his personal cell phone, and left messages. Nothing. He's busy, I'll give him that. The hospital told me that he's working back-to-back surgeries—but they also told me that he promised to call me back, but hasn't made any attempt."

"Do we bring him in or go to the hospital?"

"No."

"No?" he said surprised.

"No. I want to go on a little field trip first before we bring him in," she said. "I don't want to spook him if he's hiding more than infidelities, or anything else for that matter. Once we bring him in then he'll be prepared and there's a chance he'll request a lawyer. I want to see him in his comfort zone first. Find out what makes him tick."

"Great, another field trip," he said disappointed.

"What?" she asked.

"You get all the fun."

"Don't worry. You're coming too." She smiled. The more she thought about it, the more she thought it might shed some light on things. It was a little unorthodox for a criminal investigation, but she wasn't breaking any rules or doing anything compromising to the case. "Hope you're ready for this…"

McGaven gave her a silly thumbs up sign. "I'm ready."

CHAPTER 41

Thursday 0945 hours

The room was quiet—unnerving and frightening. Just waiting. Tess thought that she heard breathing coming from the corner to her right. Straining to hear, she was sure she could detect a soft inhale and exhale. Slow and long.

"I can't keep you anymore," he finally whispered in a low forced tone.

Tess startled. He usually leaned on the mattress before he spoke. Even if it was mere seconds, she knew his voice was coming. But this time, there was nothing. Just his disturbing whisper in her ear, as if coming from inside her own head.

Leaning in close, the man's sour breath wet her face. "I'm not getting what I *need*, Tess. Tell me the truth…"

CHAPTER 42

Thursday 1245 hours

That afternoon Katie and McGaven arrived at the hospital fifteen minutes before Dr. Jamison was scheduled to leave his twelve-hour shift. They found a parking spot with a good view of the area where the employees exited to walk out to their cars. It had been easy for McGaven to find out schedules of doctors and nurses from his new contact in security, Randy, who had come through with the shift information they needed.

"Do we know what he looks like?" asked McGaven.

Katie showed a current photo from the doctor's social media page on her cell phone. "This was taken last week." He was a tall man, medium build, with dark hair, wearing a navy polo shirt and white shorts, standing on the deck of a sleek sailboat. He had an import beer in his right hand.

"Nice tan. When does he have the time to hang out outside?" he asked.

"Must be a tanning salon," she said sarcastically. "He's a cardiothoracic surgeon, and loves to travel and meet new people. That's according to the bio he wrote."

"Isn't he married?"

"Separated—according to his public page. He made some postings about trying to work things out, but if you look at all of his 'friends' they are mostly women—gorgeous too."

"Makes you wonder," said McGaven, watching for the doctor.

"Denise said it was easy to get added as a friend, just as long as you have a pretty face."

"And Denise certainly does. Did she use her own photo?" he said.

"No. I wanted her to use a free stock photo to keep her identity safe. But I agree, Denise is cute, but the more I get to know her she's such a beautiful person. A bit corny, I know."

McGaven lifted a pair of mini binoculars to his eyes and said, "She's very cool. Most of the deputies like her too."

"Where did you get those?" Katie referred to his binoculars.

"From my stash for possible stakeouts."

Katie laughed, not meaning to be rude.

"What?" he lowered the binoculars and looked directly at her.

"What else do you have in your *stash*?"

"Stuff."

"Like what?"

"SLR camera, flashlights of all sizes, change of clothes, thermos, plain clothes, baseball caps, windbreaker, the usual stuff."

"Do you have a Swiss army knife?"

"You're a riot, Detective."

"Wait," she said, straining to see. "I think that's him. Over there." She pointed.

"Yep, that's him." He studied the doctor through the binoculars. "His hair doesn't look as combed as it did in the photo. There's some gray speckled through his hairline as well. He's getting into a black Mercedes sedan, four doors; it needs a wash. The plate begins with DM5… and then 4…"

"I see him," she said and started the engine.

Katie eased their car closer to the doctor and watched him slowly pull out into traffic. She followed him with two cars in between. Maneuvering on the road, she managed to pass one car, leaving the other blocking in between, but she decided to stay in her current position.

"Where's he going?" McGaven asked.

"I'm not sure but I believe his residence is the other direction and he's heading downtown."

They continued to follow the doctor; he drove conservatively and made it easy to keep the Mercedes in view.

"Aha, he's going into the Parsons Hotel," said McGaven.

"I'm not surprised. That's a very pricey place; a grand a night for a suite." Katie slowly passed the doctor's car and headed to another parking area. Dr. Jamison went to the valet parking. "Put your cell phone on and go follow him casually. Make sure your badge and gun are concealed under your jacket. I'll catch up," she said and dropped McGaven near the entrance.

CHAPTER 43

Katie quickly found a parking place on the street so that they didn't have to pay and leaving would be quick and easy. She knew that the doctor didn't know what she or McGaven looked like—it would work in their favor. They wanted to see what the good doctor was up to and study his habits before contacting him officially again—this time it wouldn't be a request.

Katie shed her jacket, revealing a nice sleeveless top, something that she would never wear to work but it would suffice for entering the hotel. She was glad that she chose wisely for a potential outing. She didn't know for sure he wouldn't immediately go home, but trusted her instincts and was ready. She put her regular firearm in the trunk and made sure her backup weapon was secured in her ankle holster. It was uncomfortable but she didn't want to be without any protection.

She shut the trunk and secured the car as she dropped her keys and cell phone in her pocket. One last touch, she let her hair down and quickly combed her fingertips through it. She looked more casual and less uptight; nothing like a cop.

She walked through the parking lot and arrived at the hotel main entrance. Her cell phone buzzed and she answered it with a smile on her face as she passed a few people.

"Hi," she said. "Where are you?"

"The bar," McGaven answered with a strange inflection to his voice.

"Be right there." She hung up.

Katie walked through the grand entrance, which was adorned with two-story-high plants, luxurious couches, and a water feature too big for a normal house or mansion. The carpet even felt expensive under her feet, and she was relieved that her boots wouldn't make a sound.

Following the signs, she found her way to the bar area. There was piped-in jazz music, which was at the perfect volume—not too loud or soft. The large room was only partially occupied with two groups of people at tables and five people sitting at the bar. Dr. Jamison sat alone at the far end with his back to her. And then there was McGaven casually leaning against the bar as he ordered a drink—it was a seltzer drink with a lime in it. He looked over to see Katie entering the room—a few others noticed her too.

Katie forced a smile as she moved toward McGaven. She became slightly self-conscious with so many eyes staring at her, but glided through her discomfort. It was doubtful that anyone would suspect that she was a cop.

"Hi, honey," she said to McGaven, raising her eyebrows—meaning play along.

"You look amazing," he said and leaned in to kiss her on the cheek to keep up the charade. Most onlookers had already gone back to their conversations and cocktails.

"Let's go to a table," Katie said.

"Sure."

They went to a small cocktail table so that Katie had a perfect view of Dr. Jamison. After they were seated, a waitress came to their table.

"May I take your order?" she asked.

"I'll have what he's having," said Katie.

"Another for me, thank you."

The waitress left.

Leaning forward, she said, "That is non-alcoholic right?"

"Of course," he said, shaking the ice. "What's he doing?"

Katie leaned on the table as if she was telling him something personal. "He just downed another drink. I believe it was a whisky something…"

"Did you tell your uncle, uh the sheriff, what you were going to do?" he asked.

"We're not doing anything but watching a subject, simple as that."

"But did you include it in your report?"

"Not yet." She smiled. "Looks like he has company."

McGaven started to turn.

"Don't," she said and reached out and grabbed his arm. "A woman," she whispered.

"What does she look like?"

"Simmer down. She's tall, running clothes, her back is to us, but she's wearing a hoodie so I can't see her hair color and I only saw her profile quickly, and she's wearing sunglasses…" Still keeping her voice low. "She seems familiar, but I can't get an ID on her."

"Interesting," McGaven stated. It was quite clear that he was excited to be a part of their pretext.

"It's obviously someone he knows very well by the way he's moving his hand around her body. She's standing up now."

The waitress dropped off their drinks.

"It looks like they are going to leave," she said. "I'll follow and you pay for the drinks and then follow me. Got it?" she said as she readied herself and stood. "I'll send a text so you know where I am." She leaned over, kissing his cheek, and whispered in his ear, "Just keeping up the pretense. See you shortly."

CHAPTER 44

Walking quickly trying to catch up to Dr. Jamison, Katie didn't want to run or look suspicious, so she pretended to be looking for something in her small purse as she slowed and casually continued. The closer she neared the couple it was obvious they were getting friendly with one another and could barely wait to be alone.

They waited for one of the elevator doors to open. One arrived emitting a bell tone and when the doors opened, the couple moved inside. Before the silver doors had slid shut, they had their hands underneath each other's clothes.

Katie stood and watched the floor numbers tick by, climbing upwards until the fifteenth floor, which was really the fourteenth as, like most hotels, the Parsons Hotel had superstitiously skipped the number thirteen. Another elevator opened and Katie stepped in—luckily, she was alone. Quickly retrieving her cell phone, she spoke into it to send a text to McGaven.

"Going to the fifteenth floor," she said and returned her phone to her pocket.

McGaven arrived beside her suddenly, breathless from the sprint from the bar.

"Honey, you made it," said Katie.

The elevator doors finally closed.

"Thought I'd join you," he said, still winded. "What floor?"

"Fifteen."

"Ah, a penthouse suite."

"What is it they say?"

"The more the merrier?" he replied.

"Why haven't we moved?" she said, looking up.

Katie pressed the button to open the doors but still nothing happened. She pressed the fifteenth floor again, hoping to initiate her exit—but it remained stalled. "Crap," she muttered.

"What's the deal?" McGaven eyed the listing of floors.

"I don't know. The door won't open and it won't go up either."

She was just about to press the emergency button when the door slowly began to open a few inches and paused. "What the hell…" she said. Now she pressed everything she could to release the doors.

The elevator climbed several floors. Then it stopped abruptly, knocking Katie and McGaven off balance.

"Nice elevator," McGaven managed to say.

After pushing every button possible, Katie leaned back and sighed. "It's official, we're stuck." She tried her cell phone, but the signal was sketchy. "No cell signal."

"Great."

Katie pressed the emergency button. After a moment of static she heard a voice, "What's your emergency?"

"We're stuck in an elevator at the Parsons Hotel on Eighth Street."

"How many occupants?"

"Two."

"Any health issues?"

"No."

"The hotel's security and maintenance department have been contacted. Please remain calm while they assess the situation."

Katie interrupted, "Is there a reset button that we could push?"

"I'm sorry but that doesn't follow proper protocol and safety precautions. Please remain calm and I will update you shortly." There was a loud *click*.

"Hello? Hello?" Katie repeated.

No response.

"How rude," said McGaven.

"Great, now what?" she said.

"I'm sure it's not a big deal. It probably won't take more than a half hour, don't you think?"

Katie took her shoes off.

"What are you doing?"

"I'm not going to wait around while a couple of lazy security guards decide when to get us out."

She tested the metal handrail around the car to make sure it was sturdy. Estimating the height of the ceiling, she figured that she could reach it—with McGaven's help. She made sure that her ankle holster was secure.

"Okay, hoist me up," she said, gesturing to the ceiling, where there was a small access.

"What?"

"C'mon, hoist me," she said.

"I hope you know what you're doing."

"I've jumped out of helicopters before. I think I can handle this…"

McGaven gave her a surprised look. "Yes, ma'am."

Katie used the wall and the handrail as a guide to balance herself, while McGaven lifted her up. She pushed the access opening with ease, popping the covering off. It made a metal sound as it hit the roof of the car.

"Got it?" McGaven grimaced.

"Almost… don't let go yet."

Katie grasped the opening and pulled her body upward. It occurred to her that the elevator might start ascending with her on top of the compartment. She hurried.

"Be careful," said McGaven as if the thought of the elevator moving had occurred to him too.

Katie balanced on top of the elevator car. She peered down. It appeared higher than it really was. She swallowed hard and refocused her eyes.

"You okay?"

"Yeah, I'm fine." She looked around and saw that there was an access ladder that led to a maintenance door. "I see an escape."

"Then what?"

"I'll make my way to Dr. Jamison's penthouse."

McGaven gave her a look of concern. "What's the hurry?"

"Instinct."

"Oh, that."

"It may be nothing, so I'll make sure they get you out."

"It's getting warm in here."

"Don't worry, I'll be back," she said with a half-smile.

"Don't worry, I'll be here."

Katie began to climb across the top of the car and then made her way to the ladder. She felt the circulating air from outside whirl around her. There was a distinct hint of car exhaust mixed with heavy machinery grease that seemed to pollute the air. She tried not to breathe too deep.

Her bare feet hit the ladder rungs and chilled her body. Feeling every indentation and smoothness of the ladder, she quickly made her way to the maintenance door. The number ten was stenciled in paint, identifying the floor.

A loud engine shift echoed throughout the elevator shaft. First Katie froze, then she looked to see if McGaven was jetting up to the fifteenth floor, but the cab remained frozen. It was the other elevators moving, causing the area to feel like a small earthquake had erupted. The noise rose in decibels, making her cringe and her head to ache from the sound.

As Katie hurried upward toward the maintenance door her foot slipped from the ladder rung twice. She stopped—daring to look down into the shaft abyss. Heights didn't scare her; it was the fear of the unknown that terrified her the most.

Her hand reached the lever as a rush of wind pushed up her backside. The entrance opened and she jumped inside and slammed the door behind her. Finding herself in a darkened closet with maintenance supplies as well as a power grid with fuses, she hurried through the obscurity blindly with her arms outstretched to find another door leading into the hallway.

CHAPTER 45

Katie quickly climbed the stairwell to the fifteenth floor feeling the cold tiles beneath her shoeless feet, and then she had the choice of left or right. She moved right toward the larger suites along the carpeted area, which seemed like the most logical choice for a heart doctor to have a luxury accommodation.

She heard voices talking—no, they were arguing—and it sounded like it was becoming increasingly heated. The voice inflections were more pronounced and rapid. She moved tentatively, not sure if it were someone else or the doctor and his friend. If it were someone else, she waited to make sure there wasn't anyone in jeopardy.

Moving down the hallway, she passed a few outside windows in between the suites and realized how high she was. For a moment, it made her stop and a tingling anxious energy tried to make tracks up her arms and down her legs.

Go ahead and try it…

Her cell phone buzzed with a message from McGaven:

Elevator opened, making my way up by stairs.

The arguing had stopped, leaving the hallway strangely silent. She could hear her own breathing—which had become shallow and rapid—slowing with each breath.

Katie shifted her focus back to her job and kept moving down the hallway. She noticed dirty dishes on a tray outside one of the doors for the maid service to pick up. All of the doors had a gold emblem with different initials indicating the type of room, like STE for suite, QN for queen, PH for Penthouse.

She kept moving, not quite sure what she was going to do when she got to the correct room. There were no easy hiding places and she hadn't come up with a plan as to why she was wandering around at the top of the hotel.

Katie moved her hands and arms slightly to shake off any lingering anxiety. She eyed the set of double doors that were open about ten inches. It was one of the penthouse suites and she thought it was odd the doors were open and no one was around.

Standing a foot from the doors, she leaned in and listened. It was quiet. No voices. No movement detected. She hesitated whether or not to peek inside. After a moment of contemplation, she decided to walk back down the hallway.

She was just turning when a piercing scream rang out.

Without hesitation, Katie ran to the doors and burst through the entrance into the large living space and instinctively headed toward the balcony. The scream sounded as if it came from outside. As she reached the heavy railing, she saw a dark hoodie caught there, blowing slightly in the wind.

Looking all around her, Katie didn't see anyone so she carefully moved to the railing and peered down. The outline of a woman was smashed against the cement surrounding the pool. A few horrified bystanders rushed to her aid and then retreated, realizing that there was nothing they could do for her. The people automatically looked upward.

Katie gasped and quickly turned back. She was moving through the large patio door, running toward the doorway, when she was hit against the back of her head. She catapulted forward and hit the floor with force.

CHAPTER 46

"Katie, Katie," repeated McGaven. "You okay?" His voice was filled with distress. "Can you hear me? Katie?"

Katie heard him talking to her and she gradually began to stir. "Yeah," she managed to say, rolling to her side. A horrendous headache gripped her, making it difficult to think clearly. She slowly sat up and then stood. "My head."

"What happened?" he asked.

Her memory flooded back. "I was outside in the hallway… I heard a scream…" she managed to say while rubbing her temples to try to stop the pulsating pain.

"Who was here?"

"I don't know… didn't see anyone."

"You didn't see anyone?" he asked.

"No. The woman fell."

"We know, the first responders are on their way. We need to get you checked out."

"No," she said adamantly. "I'm okay—just a bump. I want to go down there."

"No way, you need to see the paramedic at least."

"After," she said and headed out the door. Her balance became steady and her headache lessened.

As they both exited the room, Dr. Jamison headed down the hall toward them.

McGaven pulled his weapon and aimed it directly at the doctor. "Sheriff's office. Stay right there. Put your hands in the air. Now!"

"What's going on?" he said. "I don't understand."

Katie had retrieved her small weapon from her ankle holster and took aim. "Do as he says! Now!" Her headache pulsed, making it difficult to keep her focus steady.

"Okay, okay," he said and put his hands in the air.

McGaven holstered his gun and took his handcuffs out, restraining the doctor.

Again, the doctor repeated, "What's going on? Where's Emily?"

"Emily?" Katie said.

"Yes," he said and appeared distraught.

"Emily Day?" she asked.

"Yes. Who are you?"

"I'm Detective Katie Scott from the sheriff's office and this is Deputy McGaven. We haven't formally met yet—just played phone tag."

The doctor had a look of acknowledgment as he studied both of them.

McGaven guided the doctor back into the main room and sat him on the sofa.

Dr. Jamison looked confused and genuinely concerned. "Where's Emily?"

"Interesting question, since someone pushed her off the balcony and assaulted a police detective on their way out," said McGaven.

"What do you mean? I was down at the spa. I left my wallet down there the other day and I was retrieving it but—"

"Convenient timing."

"You mean Emily fell? She's…" Jamison couldn't finish his sentence.

"You have an answer for everything," said McGaven.

Two deputies entered the room and looked around. One of them said, "Everything okay?"

"Yeah, we're fine," said Katie. "Watch him, we're going downstairs. Don't touch anything and don't let anyone in until forensics gets here."

The deputies nodded, one taking watch at the door while the other one took a position next to Dr. Jamison.

Katie and McGaven hurried to an elevator.

She hesitated.

"What?" said McGaven.

"The elevator."

"C'mon, let's go," he said. "It's not the same one. No way getting stuck in an elevator would happen twice in one day."

Katie made a sour face.

They rode all the way to the main level without any trouble. Katie was relieved there wasn't a glitch this time and quickly moved to the doors opening into the pool area. There were several guests and hotel employees huddled in small groups, recounting the horror of what they had seen.

Katie burst through the doors and wasn't quite prepared to see the carnage of what happened to a body when it hit the ground from fifteen floors up. It was beyond gruesome. She grabbed a white towel from a beach chair and laid it over Emily's broken body, covering what was left of her head. It stung Katie deep. This was the second woman she had spoken with who had met their death. She couldn't think about it now, only the facts.

"It's beginning to look even more like Dr. Jamison has some serious explaining to do," said McGaven.

"Maybe there's a reason he's been avoiding me," she said.

McGaven remained quiet.

Some people began inching toward the pool area. "Please stay back," ordered Katie.

She heard sirens coming into the hotel parking lot.

"Something bothering you?" asked McGaven.

"One, I need to go find my shoes. And two, make sure that John and his crew dust for prints all around the balcony and entrance—and bag Emily's hoodie for examination."

"You okay?"

Katie nodded.

He pulled out his cell phone and dialed John.

Katie's cell phone vibrated and alerted her to a text message from Denise:

Hi, don't know where you are but found out that James Haines just got out of jail (drunk and disorderly) a few weeks ago. His two known associates are Craig Porter and Nadine McMillian. Mean anything?

CHAPTER 47

Thursday 1525 hours

Dr. Kenneth Jamison had been brought back to the sheriff's department for questioning. He hadn't been officially charged yet—he was merely a person of interest until his charges were upgraded and forensics tests concluded. The police wanted to know what he had to say about Emily Day and her fall—and the homicide of Amanda Payton. There was a fine line for any investigator to walk when the interrogation teetered on a full confession or complete denial.

Katie had gone back to her office to change back into her work clothes and pull her hair back. She tried not to think about how important this interview was to the investigation. When she was a patrol officer, her interviews were casual and usually undertaken behind her patrol car. This was a whole new territory for her.

Interrogation wasn't something that was taught; it was about knowing a case and gathering information beforehand in hopes of catching the suspect in a lie—and then another lie. It was a chess game she knew her fellow detectives, and her uncle, would be following closely.

The pressure mounted, but she made sure to keep a level head and not become so nervous that she would derail the interrogation. Breathing steadily, she headed upstairs to the interview rooms in the detective division, where McGaven was already waiting for her.

As Katie walked into the area, a few of the detectives, including Detective Hamilton, nodded at her with acknowledgment. She exchanged a nod and slight smile and hurried through.

McGaven greeted her. "You ready?"

"As ready as I'll ever be," she said softly.

"Don't worry, I've got your back."

Both detectives entered the interview room and McGaven shut the door behind them. The room was small with no windows, a square table set up and moved toward one corner to give the suspect a feeling of claustrophobia, and two empty chairs for the cops—one on one side of the table and the other next to the person of interest.

The air in the room was kept warmer than the rest of the offices, making interviewees drowsy and more likely to start talking just to get out of the room. According to psychologists, it was a proven fact from many studies that most people want to tell the truth and even feel better after doing so.

"Dr. Jamison, we met briefly at your suite. Again, I'm Detective Scott and this is Deputy McGaven," she began and made sure her voice sounded matter of fact with the right amount of authority. She had learned how from her uncle's example on so many occasions.

The doctor sat in the uncomfortable chair with his hands on the table, fingers intertwined. He stared straight ahead with a solemn expression, but it was clear that he was terrified and trying to hide behind his privilege. His dark eyes were dilated and he held his hands together to keep them from shaking—not a good trait for a heart surgeon.

McGaven took a seat, silently watching every move the doctor made.

Katie pulled out the remaining chair and made herself comfortable. "Doctor, you know that you're not under arrest, correct?"

"Yes."

"Whenever there is an accident or suicide, we are obligated to talk to everyone that was in the vicinity," she explained.

"Of course," he said, trying to make his voice steady.

"Where were you when Ms. Day fell?"

"I went downstairs to the spa to get my wallet. I had left it there from last Tuesday."

"We talked to the spa associates and no one talked to you and they said they weren't aware of your lost wallet."

"No, there wasn't anyone there. I lost my wallet and that was the only place I could figure that I had misplaced it."

"So you never actually retrieved your wallet?" Katie pressed.

"No."

"How long had you known Ms. Day?"

"Several years at the hospital."

"Was the hotel suite one of your regular—get-togethers?"

"Sometimes."

"Was Ms. Day aware that you are married?"

"Separated."

"Was Ms. Day aware of your separation?"

"Yes."

"Did you and Ms. Day argue before her fall?"

He hesitated. "Yes. Earlier, but everything was fine."

"Did you hit her?"

"No, I would never do that."

"Did you push her over the railing?"

"No, God no." He began to unravel, his hands moved strangely and he kept putting them up to his face and the sides of his head.

"Dr. Jamison, is there any reason to believe that Ms. Day took her own life?"

"I've been trying to think of a reason, but no, she would never do that—ever. This doesn't make any sense."

"What do you expect me to believe? Put yourself in my shoes."

"I… I don't know…"

"Someone pushed Ms. Day over the railing and someone hit me on the back of the head as they fled. Who? Tell me who would do that just at the same time that you went downstairs to see if your wallet was at the spa?"

Dr. Jamison's frustration revealed itself as he pounded his fists once on the table. "I told you… I don't know…"

"You were the only one there—so you're trying to tell me that you didn't do it? And that we won't find your prints on the railings?" Katie leaned in, keeping his gaze. "Maybe it was an accident and you ran because you were afraid. Was it an accident?"

"I didn't do it!" he yelled.

"Please calm down, Dr. Jamison. We're trying to figure out what happened. A woman is dead. There was barely enough of her left to perform any type of autopsy," Katie stated, still holding her alpha position as the interrogator.

The doctor looked away from her, obviously trying to get that terrible image out his mind.

"Let me ask another question. How well did you know Amanda Payton?"

He looked directly at Katie and said, "I worked with her."

"So when did you begin an intimate relationship with her?"

"What?"

"You heard me, Doctor. Don't play games with us. You're in enough trouble right now. How long was your intimate relationship with Amanda Payton?" Katie watched him closely as he appeared to get his story straight in his mind before he answered her directly. She wanted to see a glimmer of recognition or even a look of dread.

"Answer the question," said McGaven. His voice almost startled Katie because she was so focused on Dr. Jamison that nothing, or nobody else, was in the room with her.

He must have thought better and decided to answer the question. "We went out for drinks a few times. We flirted at work, but that was all. We didn't have a relationship." He emphasized the word *relationship*.

"Is that so?" she said. "So we're not going to find any of your DNA at Amanda's crime scene?"

The doctor remained quiet. It wasn't clear if he was trying to remember where he might've left some DNA or if he just didn't want to dignify that question with an answer.

"Dr. Jamison, we have a serious problem," she said. "More specifically, *you* have a serious problem. Attractive young women seem to die around you—two women in one week."

He looked away, obviously trying to pretend he was somewhere else—anywhere.

Finally he said, "Are you going to arrest me?" He looked defeated.

Katie studied his face and mannerisms—especially his hands, which told quite a bit about people and how they held or released their stress levels.

McGaven looked at Katie with a calm demeanor, waiting for her answer.

"Dr. Jamison, is your father's name Kenneth Jamison senior?" Katie changed tack, trying to knock the doctor off balance.

"What?"

"Kenneth Jamison senior?"

"Yes."

"What does your father do?"

"He died two years ago. What does this have to do with…?"

"What did he do for a living?"

He hesitated, clearly confused. "He was a real estate developer."

"Here in this county?" she said.

"Yes."

"The Magna Group?"

"Yes, that's right."

"Have you heard of the Woodland Pines Project, which is now the Basin Woods Development—what's left of it."

"I don't understand what this has to do with Emily's death."

"Did you know that Amanda Payton was kidnapped, taken hostage, and held in one of the abandoned houses in Basin Woods?"

Dr. Jamison still seemed confused, but he knew what Katie was talking about. "You're talking about a project of my father's when I was a kid."

"But you are aware of the area, correct?"

"Yes."

"Had Emily had any problems lately? Anything she was upset about?"

"No, I don't think so."

"Did Amanda ever come to you, or confide in you, about anything that was bothering her?"

"I don't know... maybe... like what?" He began to let his frustration show.

Not missing a beat, she said: "Anything that happened to her that she was upset about?"

"Amanda? I don't know. She was moody, you can ask anyone at the hospital," he replied.

"C'mon, Doctor, what was the gossip around the hospital?"

"What I heard was she was attacked and there was talk about an old boyfriend. But we had not had any relations way before all that happened, then she quit. I never saw her again." He shifted in his chair, not looking at Katie or McGaven.

McGaven budged his chair closer to the doctor. It was an old technique when interviewing suspects, when a detective would take away space around them—giving the person of interest the squeeze. It was doubly effective because McGaven was a big officer.

Katie stood up and sat on the edge of the table. "Did you care about Emily?"

"Of course."

"Did you have the same affection for Amanda?"

"I cared about her. She was actually a great nurse—better than most."

"Are you seeing anyone now, well, except for Emily?"

"No, no one."

"Are you sure?"

"Yes."

"Okay, give us a minute," said Katie and she motioned for McGaven to leave the room with her.

They shut the interview room door and walked down the hallway a little ways to have a quiet conference.

Katie quickly reread her text message from Denise and was relieved that there were leads to track down Nick's brother. She switched back to the doctor's interview.

"What do you think?" she asked.

"I think he's telling the truth but holding back on something."

"I agree. There's nothing we can officially hold him on. We have to cut him loose and wait for what comes back from forensics before we can obtain an arrest warrant." Katie shifted her weight, thinking, biting her thumbnail. "I have a difficult time seeing him as the killer—"

"A little too convenient?" said McGaven.

"Just what I was thinking."

CHAPTER 48

Thursday 1635 hours

Katie and McGaven sat in Katie's favorite diner grabbing a quick late lunch after Dr. Jamison's interview before returning to the department. Since it was in between lunch and dinner, the restaurant was empty except for a group of four at a nearby table.

Katie was lost in thought, picking at her turkey sandwich. She reran Dr. Jamison's answers and his reactions to her questions, but nothing seemed to indicate that he was lying. He appeared shocked by Emily's death and hadn't become increasingly agitated. His mood was more scared and confused, but there were hesitations, perhaps of something he didn't want her to know.

"Katie?" said McGaven.

She looked up. "Oh, I'm sorry."

"Is anything wrong?"

"No, just thinking about the interview with Dr. Jamison."

"And?"

"We just seem to have a lot of information and it doesn't seem to zero in on anyone specific. The evidence we have so far, his father's real estate development business, the now abandoned area, and now Emily falling to her death. There's too many... It seems..." She sighed and took another bite of her sandwich, washing it down with a drink of soda.

"Like it's too convenient?" McGaven stated.

"It's as if these vague things are to blind us from the truth. What I mean is, it's weak evidence, but somehow done on purpose."

"Someone is making it look like he's guilty."

Katie's phone alerted her to an incoming text from John:

Linkage evidence found.

"What is it?" McGaven asked.

"John. More linkage. We need to get back to the lab." She glanced at her phone and saw that she had missed three phone calls from Chad. Unfortunately, he would have to wait a little longer. She felt a twinge of guilt, but would make it up to him.

They quickly paid for their lunches and rushed back to the forensic lab. Katie kept concentrating on linkage and all the different scenarios it could pertain to.

She needed hard evidence to narrow the suspect pool. In her gut, she knew it had to somehow revolve around the hospital, but she needed to find how these women were connected to one another. There had to be a connection.

McGaven sped into the parking lot and took the first available space.

"Let's go," he said as he got out of the car, but Katie was already ahead of him.

It was barely minutes after the text arrived when they entered the large examination and forensic computer room, and they found John hard at work with evidence from another case. He looked up and smiled. "I think that was record time."

"When have I ever dawdled when it comes to evidence," she laughed.

"Did you really just say *dawdled*?" said McGaven.

"What do you have for us?" she said, ignoring her partner. She remembered to take a breath as she waited in anticipation. She felt a slight tingling in her arms.

John took a seat at a computer and pulled up images with specific graphs. "Each woman, Amanda Payton and Jane Doe, had unidentified stains on their garments that I thought were initially nothing, but we had them analyzed. What I found was very interesting. A combination of chemicals of different amounts were found to have made the stains, and though different, they were consistent with one another."

"Don't keep us in suspense," she said, barely keeping herself calm.

"There were traces of ethylene oxide, formaldehyde, glutaraldehyde, peracetic acid in combination with hydrogen peroxide and latex."

"What is all that?" asked McGaven.

"Latex gloves?" said Katie taking a guess.

"Mostly these are substances used in disinfectants, sterilizing, and embalming. Basically, all of these things are easily found in and around hospitals and morgues," John said.

"These two women had a low level of these chemical combinations on their clothes? Their undergarments?" she asked.

"Yes, without a doubt. But I don't think you're fully understanding the significance." He pointed to the screen which showed a graph. "The combination of these chemicals, the amounts and proportions, are nearly identical on both sets of garments."

"How could that be?" she asked.

"It would mean that both women were exposed to the same combination, from the same source. These chemicals aren't part of a single product including them; they are a random combination of chemicals. To have this random combination twice would be highly unlikely."

"Would you be able to know if it was transferred, say from another person who had contact with those chemicals? Or, was it transferred from the victim onto themselves?" Katie's attention went from Dr. Jamison to Marco Ellis, the morgue technician, and even Dr. Smith.

"It's possible. The levels were slightly higher on Amanda Payton's clothes than on Jane Doe, but then she worked at the hospital. More likely, someone else had this combination of chemicals on their clothes, or person, and then somehow they were transferred to each of the women."

What about Amanda's hair smelling like sulfur?"

"It's most likely from a contaminated water source," he said.

"Meaning?"

"Sometimes you can get that rotten egg smell from drains or old water heaters that have been sealed off and allows bacteria to grow—hydrogen sulfide."

Katie thought about that for a moment. "The killer rinsed her body, or at least hair, with bacteria contaminated water." She really wasn't waiting for an answer, but merely making a statement. "What about Amanda's body?

"Nothing," he stated. "She'd been wiped down with some type of alcohol, except they forgot to check her nails."

"So wait a minute," she said. "What are the odds of these two women having close to the same amount of a chemical combination on their clothes *and* contact with the same contaminated person who attacked them?"

"That would be highly unlikely to be a coincidence," said McGaven.

John nodded in agreement. "True. I have more."

"More?" Katie said in disbelief.

"As I was beginning the examination of the evidence from Emily Day's crime scene, I saw something unusual on her hoodie left on the balcony."

Katie waited barely breathing.

"This same chemical combination was also on Emily Day's hoodie," he said. "I haven't completed it yet, but it seems to be consistent."

"Well, she was a nurse at the same hospital as Amanda."

"Someone had contact with all three women—or they were all in the same place. It would make sense with Amanda and Emily, but where does Jane Doe come in? There's linkage," said McGaven. He looked as eager as Katie looking at the computer screen.

This was the first big break in the investigation. Katie was running on adrenalin now and could barely contain her excitement. She forgot all about John in the room as her mind raced.

"Do you have a list of employees at the First Memorial Hospital?" Katie asked McGaven.

"Yes, but it's not a complete list."

"Get it, but for now, we need to eliminate female personnel and non-medical personnel. Unless they would have regular access to the operating rooms, patient rooms, maintenance, or morgue as part of their job. This is the first pass for background checks. I need to see who is on that list."

"Got it," McGaven said. "This is going to take a bit of time."

"Something else has been bothering me for a while, but I want to look into Dr. Smith from the psychiatric hospital."

"And the employees?" McGaven asked.

"Yes and—" she said almost breathlessly.

"I have one more thing," interrupted John.

Katie and McGaven looked at him with questioning expressions.

John laughed at their reactions. "I do have one more thing—trust me, it's a good one."

"I'm sorry, John," said Katie, slightly embarrassed by her excitement, because she was thinking about the hospital employees and the possibility that the killer was among them.

He turned to another computer that ran the Integrated Automatic Fingerprint Identification System (IAFIS). "We found

a match from the beautiful right index fingerprint lifted from your watch. It came back to a Madeline Jean Thomas, thirty-four, and she lives not far from here in the brick district."

Katie was excited as she leaned forward. "Can you pull up a photo?"

"Already ahead of you," he said as he made a few mouse clicks, bringing another window open.

Madeline's photo and identification from her driver's license appeared. She was an attractive brunette with dark green eyes. Her smile was friendly, much different from her pathetic condition at the mental health facility.

"That's her," Katie said.

"Do we identify her officially?" McGaven asked.

"For right now, unfortunately, she's safer in there than out. We can at least begin a background on her." She turned to the forensic supervisor. "John, you've done an incredible job as always. Thank you."

"Still working on the prints from your Jeep… something should hit soon."

Katie and McGaven turned to leave and head to their office when Katie's cell phone buzzed. The text was from Detective Ames from Missing Persons. Katie had contacted him a few days earlier, asking that if any woman fitting the description and age of Amanda went missing to please forward the information to her. It read:

Tess Regan reported missing, kidnapped by force from her home. See report in email.

"It can. We've had some problems, but it usually has to do with employees or a difficult patient. We've had more than our fair share of those. The stories I could tell…"

"Well, I thought I would ask anyway," McGaven said.

"I'll ask the other guys and if I hear anything, I'll give you a buzz."

"Great. Appreciate it." McGaven thought more and decided to ask. "Oh, speaking along the same lines, do you recall any issue with the doctors and nurses? Like an exacerbated argument, someone accusing someone else of something…"

"There was a doctor who flipped out one time. It turned out that he was addicted to some pharmaceutical drugs he was helping himself to here—some kind of painkiller, I think."

"Do you remember the doctor's name?"

"I had just started here and I think his name was Darren something… Darren Patterson… that's it, Dr. Patterson. He no longer works here—not even sure if he still has his medical license."

"Anything else?"

"I'm sorry, I don't think so."

"Okay, thanks."

"I'll call you if I remember something," Randy said before he hung up.

*

After Katie had read the full missing person report for Tess Regan, fear squeezed her chest and soured her stomach.

"I think we have another problem," she said as she saw McGaven hang up the phone.

McGaven looked away from his computer. "What's up?"

"I've just read the missing person's report for Tess Regan. It appeared that Tess had been taken from her home by force—apparently the perp had entered through a broken lock to the garage. Her purse, jacket, and cell phone were found on the garage

CHAPTER 49
Thursday 1735 hours

Back in the office, McGaven hung up the phone from talking with the First Memorial Hospital administrator with the promise that they would email over the complete list of employees in a spreadsheet. As he waited for the information, he thought that he would put a call in to Randy, the security guard, to ask him a couple of follow-up questions.

He dialed the number and waited, unsure if he was still on shift.

"You got Randy," was the greeting.

"Hi, Randy, this is Deputy McGaven from the sheriff's office."

"Hey, what's up?"

"Glad I caught you. Just have a couple of questions."

"Shoot," he said.

"Do you recall anytime that there's been a problem with employees or patients?"

"What do you mean?"

"Oh, you know, being difficult, loud, harassing employees, anything that might attract some attention."

"Let me think," Randy said and paused. "I can't think of anything right off. There's so much that goes on around here every day, people coming and going."

"I've noticed. It must make your job more difficult."

floor. Tess had called in to work earlier in the morning letting them know she would be late due to a dental appointment—according to the dental office she never made an appointment. The information reported from friends and family described her personality as conservative and kind. She lived alone, no current boyfriend, and worked for an insurance company as a medical billing associate."

"A *medical* billing associate?" he said.

"Wait, there's more," Katie said, trying to keep her voice steady. "According to her friends and family, they were worried about her because she had been distraught after the death of her sister who had committed suicide. Tess blamed herself, but she mostly blamed the hospital that they didn't do enough to save her. Apparently, she made quite a scene there."

"The hospital was First Memorial?"

Katie nodded. "Yep."

"Coincidence?"

"We now have three women connected to the hospital: Amanda, Emily, and a missing woman."

"What about Jane Doe—Madeline Thomas?"

"Don't know yet. We need to do a background, but my gut is telling me that she's somehow crossed paths with the hospital in some way."

Katie leaned back. The information was overwhelming. She stood up and stared at her preliminary perp board. "The killer is picking women he has had contact with, maybe even befriended, and seen at the hospital…"

"The hospital is his hunting grounds," McGaven stated seriously.

Katie thought it and McGaven stated it—it seemed that way.

"I believe Tess is another unsuspecting victim. It's more than possible. The killer has made mistakes, two women have escaped… he's not going to make any more mistakes now." She studied the map of the areas where the women lived in comparison to the hospital.

"I know that look," he said.

"You're right, it's his hunting grounds. I believe it's possible he follows them home and if it's within his comfort zone, that's when he abducts them." She continued to study the map and make notations.

Both Madeline and Tess lived within two miles of one another and their companies were in the same business district, which meant that they lived, shopped, and worked in close proximity of each other. The First Memorial Hospital was within five miles of where all the women lived and worked—including Amanda.

"A killer's hunting ground is almost always an area where they feel comfortable, an area they know well and don't have to worry about unknowns and variables in their searches or their body dumping grounds," she said.

"Just got the hospital employee list," said McGaven.

"Once you omit women and anyone who wouldn't normally have access to operating rooms and the morgue, put everyone in alphabetical order," she instructed. Then she began to sort out the packet from the county. "I'm going to make a list of all the last residents and anyone working on the Basin Woods Development. Let's see what we get and then we can compare. I know that the hospital and the abandoned development connect a killer. He didn't just pick that area on a whim."

"We got a plan," said McGaven.

The only sound in the office was the hurried flurry of keystrokes.

Katie rattled off an additional assessment of the killer: "The killer abducts and holds these women where he feels comfortable—safe—protected. Something happened to him, a deep scar, a defining moment in his life that cuts so deep, and it revolves around the hospital."

Katie and McGaven worked for almost two hours, immersed in their lists and background checks.

"Here's a little background on Madeline: She was the assistant to the CEO at a financial company called Brown & Donner

Financial, which is close to where Tess works just in the next building. Nothing in her background seemed unusual or out of the ordinary. She is thirty-four years old, MBA from a prestigious college, lived alone; no boyfriend," Katie said.

"Finally," said McGaven.

"What?" Katie asked.

"Just got the phone records for Emily Day's land line. And…" he said, reading down the report, "a call came in from the hospital at 10.17 p.m., so it seems that Emily was telling the truth about when she called Amanda."

"Fair enough."

"But…"

Katie looked away from her computer and at McGaven.

"It seems that there was another call from the hospital from a different extension at 10.49 p.m.," he explained.

"Emily could have called back for a number of reasons."

"The phone extension belongs to Dr. Jamison."

CHAPTER 50

Thursday 2005 hours

It was just after 8 p.m. when Katie drove up her driveway. She was completely exhausted from the events of the day; her eyes were blurry from looking at names on the computer all evening. She needed some food and a good night's sleep, but her mind was still whirling from all of the information they had received.

As she neared the top of the driveway, her headlights caught Nick standing at her porch holding two bags. He smiled, which caught her off-guard. In khakis and black T-shirt his prosthetic leg wasn't as noticeable, and he seemed to be moving on it a little better.

Katie cut the engine and got out. "Hey, I don't remember ordering take-out."

"Private delivery."

"What are you doing here?" she asked walking up to the porch. She noticed that he looked more rested and cleaner than he did the first night.

"I wanted to bring you dinner. I'm sure you're not eating enough investigating a homicide."

Cisco barked several times in greeting.

"Well, thank you. And yes, you don't eat enough when working." She unlocked the door and made her way to the alarm to disarm it.

Cisco ran from one end of the room to another.

"I'm sorry, I should have called."

"No, that's fine. I'm actually starved and would love to have a conversation that didn't revolve around forensics, autopsies, or suspect lists."

"That's a mouthful."

"Make yourself at home. Grab some plates in the kitchen. I need to let Cisco out and quickly change," she said, opening the sliding door as Cisco bolted outside.

Katie went to her bedroom and took off her holster and badge. She quickly slipped out of her work clothes and opted for yoga pants and a hoodie.

There was a knock at the front door.

"Nick, can you see who that is?" she hollered, zipping up her sweatshirt and letting her hair down.

Glancing at herself in the mirror, she saw how tired she looked with dark circles under her eyes and dull skin. She splashed water on her face and then brushed her hair. She hurried out of her bedroom.

"Nick, who was that?" she asked as she entered the living room. Then "Hi," when she saw who was standing there.

"Hey," said Chad.

"I didn't know you were coming."

"I made plenty of food for everyone," hollered Nick from the kitchen, pushing more of his Kentucky accent than usual. The sound of plates rattling followed.

"I tried calling a few times, but I knew you were busy," he said.

"Oh, I'm sorry. Chad, this is Nick, my sergeant from the army," she said. "Nick, Chad."

"We met at the door," said Nick. "It's nice to meet you, Chad."

"I can see that I caught you at a bad time," Chad said.

"No, no, come have dinner."

"There's plenty," chimed Nick.

"C'mon," she said and took Chad's hand.

Chad wasn't his usual energetic self and it was clear that he was surprised and a little bit hurt that there was another guy in the kitchen with dinner for Katie.

"C'mon," she said again. This time with a big smile.

"Do you really have enough food?" he asked.

"I brought enough for an army—no pun intended."

Katie walked to the slider where Cisco had been fogging up the glass and let him back in. The dog immediately made his rounds with the two men. He then lingered in the kitchen smelling the food.

Katie and Chad took a seat at the counter.

"What's on the menu?" she asked.

"Ribs, fried chicken, salad, garlic bread, and of course, beer," he said, holding up a bottle.

"Wow, this looks fantastic."

"I agree," said Chad.

They served up their plates and began eating.

"So," began Nick, "what do you do, Chad?"

"Firefighter."

"He just signed on with Sequoia County the same time I started my new position as detective," said Katie, trying to lighten the awkward conversation.

"Fighting fires is an honorable profession—being a first responder," Nick said.

"I'd like to think so. So, how long had you been in the army before, well, you know," he said.

"You know, guys, this is supposed to be a pleasant dinner. I've had a difficult day," Katie replied.

"No, it's okay, Scotty," Nick said. "If I can't talk about it, then how am I going to cope? I lost my leg, I served my country, and if I had it to do over again, I wouldn't change a thing."

A stiff silence ensued.

Katie got up to get herself another beer. Normally she didn't drink much, but tonight seemed to call for one. She sat back down. "Look. We all have jobs that at any time we could be killed or maimed. Let's just leave it at that, okay?" She hated being so blunt, but it needed to be said otherwise the guys would just keep escalating and end up saying things they don't mean.

Chad and Nick nodded.

"So, Nick, I have a records' specialist running down some leads where James might be. It'll take some time."

"Scotty, I can't thank you enough. I've been giving it a lot of thought. Family is what is important now."

"This is really, really good, Nick."

"Thanks. It's one of the things I enjoy doing—cooking. It takes my mind off things."

Katie systematically turned to Chad and asked, "How's the firehouse treating you?"

"Everything is going great. Long hours, but it's a great group of guys to work with."

Katie continued to act as a referee of sorts. She loved them both—Nick as a brother and Chad as... There was no argument that she loved Chad deeply, but her hesitation stemmed from her private war with PTSD and all the demons she carried around in her soul. She didn't know if she could handle everything that went along with having a serious relationship, but she wanted to give it a try.

With Katie on high alert, the three of them continued to eat and partake in small talk until all the food was gone. Exhausted, Katie's eyes began to droop and Nick and Chad made their excuses. She was asleep on the sofa before she even heard the door close behind them.

CHAPTER 51

Friday 1145 hours

"Life comes around full circle, the beginning and the end," Katie stated. "Haven't you ever heard that before?" She looked up from her computer.

"Like from a fortune cookie?" replied McGaven with a smirk on his face. "Like yin and yang?"

Katie laughed. "Put five bucks into the Psych Out can for that remark."

"What do you mean?"

"Take five dollars from your pocket and put it into the can."

"No, I mean about the full circle." He smiled but searched his pockets for a few dollar bills.

"I read this great article written by a profiler, criminalist guy. I think his name was Dr. Chip Palmer—some crime scene genius that lives near the coast, I think. Well, basically, he claims that by working a crime scene backwards it will take you full circle. He also stressed the importance and attention needed at the physical crime scenes, claiming so much about the perpetrator gets overlooked. Everything investigators need to know is at the scene, just secondary to the body," she explained.

"Don't most investigators do that?"

"I think the author of the article means really study the crime scene area—whether it's primary or secondary—it's the beginning and the end for the murder. Don't overlook anything. And I love one of his points about *not* finding anything at a crime scene is a big clue and not to be dismissed. Everything fits together if you know where to look."

Gesturing to the overcrowded board and map, he said, "I think you're covering every base."

"Okay, got it," she said and pressed print. "Let's take a look at your list and see what we have," she said with a hopeful tone.

McGaven rolled his chair closer to Katie's desk. He gave one set of copies to her and took one set himself.

"Cross your fingers," she said.

Katie used her right index finger and slowly dragged it down the page, comparing the alphabetized names. She found one name and wrote it down, and continued to scan the list. When she finished, she had three names. She got up from her desk as she waited for McGaven to finish. She wrote the three names that were on both lists on the board—hospital worker and residents of Basin Woods Development.

Robert Glen Sykes – custodian at hospital, worked on construction crew to tear down a few of the houses at the Basin Woods Development.
Sebastian Harding – part-time intern at the morgue – resident at Basin Woods Development.
Chris D. Randall – resident at Basin Woods Development – maintenance trainee from eight years ago.

"You beat me, but yeah, I have those three names too."

"There could be other connections," she said, still studying the board.

"Like Dr. Jamison?"

"We don't rule him out." She put his name on the list with an asterisk next to it. "I couldn't find anything that connected Marco Ellis to the Basin Woods Development. I'm going to add him to the suspect list with an asterisk."

"He definitely should be considered, since he was Amanda's last known boyfriend."

"Okay, here's our list," she said.

"I haven't heard you state the obvious," he said.

"What do you mean?"

"We could be looking at the name of a serial killer."

The reality of another serial killer hit Katie with a vengeance. She swallowed hard. They had to stop him before he killed another woman.

She tried to block out of her mind the memory of the desperate expression Jane Doe—Madeline—had on her face. And Amanda's fearful declaration: *He will come for me. And I know that he will eventually kill me.*

The reality that woke her up was the abduction of Tess Regan. From everything they had so far, it led to the extreme possibility that she had been taken by a serial killer.

Tess, we will find you…

CHAPTER 52

Friday 1645 hours

Katie made a quick stop at her house to change into jeans and hiking shoes. Of course, Cisco wanted to come along. She left McGaven back at the office to try and find out more information and continue background checks. She kept the concept of working the crime scene backwards running through her head.

As Katie drove back into town and toward the vacant lot in Whispering Pines, where Amanda's body had been found, she still thought about how all the women were connected. It still wasn't clear if the women came into contact with the hospital chemicals when they were alive, or if the killer transferred it to them accidentally. She contemplated that theory until she reached the vacant land.

The automatic headlights turned on just before she found an appropriate place to park. The fall evening was getting darker and cooler. She should really come back when the light was better—and with McGaven. She quickly sent a text to him:

Where are you?

He sent a reply:

At the office admiring your map.

Katie laughed in spite of herself. She typed:

What do you think?

He answered her:

Taking it all in.

Can you meet me at Whispering Pines?

Give me fifteen.

See you then.

Katie turned her focus back to the property as she got out of the car, now better prepared with a flashlight, and followed closely by Cisco. This time he gave a high-pitch whine followed by a low chuff.

"What's up, Cisco?" she said softly.

The dog circled her in one of his protection techniques, where he watched everything all around her in order to keep her safe. He had obviously caught wind of something he wasn't sure of or didn't like. Either way, he was cautious, and that was fine with her.

Katie always carried her police firearm no matter how she was dressed, but especially on any investigation. There were too many variables to calculate when dealing with a killer on the loose, and someone following her and leaving her notes. She knew that McGaven would catch up with her soon, which lessened some of her apprehension.

She glanced at Cisco who seemed to be edgy with his hackles slightly bristled, which could mean anything from the scent of vermin to something he couldn't identify in the wind.

Katie stepped up her pace to the crime scene with her flashlight directing the way. It wasn't completely dark, but she used the extra light to illuminate her surroundings. It wasn't difficult to remember exactly where Amanda's body was found.

Katie stood still and closed her eyes so she could envision the crime scene. What story did the killer have to tell? What was so important to him? She had already been here to investigate and there were photographs, but it was important for her to remember what had first struck her when she had arrived. The body was facedown, naked, posed in a very modest way. There was no drama in her positioning, nothing carved into the body, or even anything missing. This killer wasn't taunting the police: He wanted the crime scene to reenact what should have happened if Amanda had not escaped—that was why there were ligature marks post mortem.

Why?

Katie stood at the exact spot where Amanda Payton's body had lain, the reality giving her pause, remembering their last conversation; the sound of Amanda's voice and the terror in her eyes. The last thing she said to Katie was: *He said that I would never be without him. That he would come for me. And I know that he will eventually kill me.*

There was a sound like the noise of muffled footsteps, or the stamping of something against the earth, above her near the parking lot. Katie hadn't heard any car enter or leave the area since she had been there.

McGaven?

Katie stayed quiet and listened, using hand signals to keep Cisco close until she knew what was going on—not wanting to frighten some hikers or teenagers with her gun drawn and Cisco's bark.

"Cisco, *bleib*." She softly instructed the dog to stay until she released him from his position.

Katie decided to check out where the noise came from and who might be there—an inkling that someone was following her.

She hurried up the hill and down a well-traveled path. Deciding to turn off the flashlight, she stopped and listened in the partial darkness. She saw the outline of the trees, bushes, and the paths. There was nothing indicating that there was a person waiting and watching.

The sound of human footsteps hurried right next to her—so close that she thought she could reach out and touch them. Turning, she followed the noise as quietly as she could. A line of heavy bushes and evergreens crowded between the trails, making it difficult to see over to the other side.

There was someone there—a figure moving stealthily, watching her—there was no doubt in her mind. They appeared to be lean, wearing dark clothes, a hoodie, and had the build of a man.

Katie kept up the brisk pace and when she couldn't wait any longer, she yelled, "Identify yourself!"

The figure took off running at a fast pace, but she kept up with him. Breaks in the foliage gave her glimpses as she gave chase.

"Stop! Sheriff's Department!" she yelled again.

She knew it wouldn't stop them but she wanted this guy to know she was on to him. The forest barrier would soon end as the path spilled into a parking lot.

She pumped her arms faster to get to the parking lot first. By her calculations, she would run right into the guy. That was her plan anyway. However, it was becoming increasingly difficult to keep up, much less be able to pass him. With every ounce of energy she had left, she pushed her stride and pace as hard as she could, praying she didn't trip. Seeing the outline of the parking lot up ahead, Katie thought that she could just make it in time.

As soon as her feet reached the parking lot asphalt, she turned to her immediate left and was about to confront the person when he collided directly into her. He weighed more than she did, so she took the brunt of the impact. Katie slammed to the ground—and the person barely slowed, regaining their balance once again, and then continued on their run.

She could hear Cisco's bark echoing around the park.

Winded, Katie rolled to her side in agony. A strangled sound escaped her lips as she tried to breathe. In the distance, she watched the unknown assailant enter a storage building at the side of the parking lot.

Still gasping for air, Katie felt her lungs begin to function again. She managed to get her legs and feet underneath her and stood up.

She took off at a full run until she reached the entrance to the building. She stood still, readying herself, gun drawn, in case the unknown man decided to suddenly exit.

"Come on out!" she said. "You have nowhere to go. Come out slowly with your hands up!" she insisted.

She heard a muffled clunk sound from inside.

Katie made a quick decision and slowly pushed the door open, with her flashlight shining inside. There were shelves and equipment, but no sign of the man. She took a few seconds to assess where he was. "C'mon, quit playing games and come out now." She moved deeper into the storage building.

That's when she heard the door slam behind her.

Dammit!

Katie was angry that she had fallen for the trap. She tried the door, but something was jamming it. She walked deeper into the storage area and knew that there had to be a way out—that was how the man had escaped. Behind the stacks of compost, she saw the window. She felt the cool air blow inside. Climbing up on the large plastic bags filled with redwood chips, Katie managed to get through the window and jump down. She ran around the building and saw that there was a long handle of a broom that had been wedged under the door. She continued to run toward the parking lot.

Nothing.

There was no sign of the man.

She directed the flashlight beam at the ground and could vaguely see the track of a single tire mark—a bicycle.

Of course.

A bike was how he was able to get away so quickly and quietly from the Basin Woods Development.

Defeated and mad at herself for falling for the ruse, Katie began to walk back to where she had left Cisco, her breathing becoming normal again. As she turned the corner and headed down the hill toward the crime scene area, she ran into McGaven and Cisco.

"What's going on?" said McGaven.

"I ran after a guy that had been following me," she said, still slightly winded. Her pitch sounded higher than usual.

"Who was it?"

"I couldn't see him."

"What did he look like?"

"Average, slender, hoodie, and fast as hell. Remind me to add an extra workout at the gym this week."

Cisco barked and circled around Katie again.

"Good boy, Cisco," she said.

"Why did you leave him here?" McGaven asked.

"I couldn't release the dog into an unknown situation—he's not officially a sheriff's department K9. I kept him here to keep him safe—he would have heard me yell and responded if there was a problem."

Eying Katie suspiciously and noticing the dirt smeared across her jacket, he asked, "You okay?"

"Yeah, just my pride is suffering right now." She laughed softly, brushing the dust off her jeans and jacket.

"You think that was the guy that has been following you and leaving messages?"

"Yeah."

"Think he's the killer?"

"No."

"You seem sure about that," McGaven said.

"He had several opportunities to kill me and he didn't. He seemed curious as to what I'm doing more than trying to figure out how to kill me."

They walked back to the cars with Cisco trotting behind them.

"You know what I think?" she finally said. "I think we're right where we need to be. We know that all the women have some things in common—we have the forensic evidence. Everything circles back to the locations—*all* the locations—the hospital, the crime scene, and the abandoned house. It's where we're going to find the missing puzzle pieces."

CHAPTER 53
Monday 0945 hours

"This is that part of being a detective that they refer to as ninety percent desk work as opposed to the ten percent getting your butt out of the chair work," sighed McGaven.

"So *they* say. Need some help?" she asked as she read through the reports for Emily Day's death. There was no need to visit the medical examiner in person—no use seeing the remains of the poor woman if everything was in the report.

"No. I'm still running backgrounds on the suspects. It's been slow, the system is not cooperating again."

Both detectives remained quiet, lost in their own mountain of paperwork.

Katie quickly outlined the investigation's progress report for the previous week that would be forwarded to the sheriff—she had been keeping thorough notes. She was surprised that her uncle hadn't been hovering about complaining that she was taking too many chances or not getting enough sleep. Though he should know better than anyone that a detective on an active homicide rarely got enough sleep.

The internal office phone rang.

Katie picked it up. "Detective Scott."

"Hey, Katie, I'm surprised I caught you in your office," said Denise.

"We're both here doing paperwork."

"Yuck."

"My sentiments exactly. What's up?"

"I have an active address for James Haines. The person he's staying with is Nadine McMillian. She's the one on the apartment rental paperwork. According to various sources and the rental management company, they have been seen together on a regular basis."

Katie was excited that something had broken in her investigations into the whereabouts of Nick's brother and she hoped that the brothers could reconnect their bond. "You are nothing less than amazing—lunch on me next week. Thank you so much."

"Maybe a double date for dinner? I want to meet that handsome firefighter of yours."

"Uh, of course," Katie said, realizing that she hadn't returned Chad's calls again after the uncomfortable dinner with Nick.

"I'll text the address to you. Be safe," she said and hung up.

Katie slowly hung up the phone.

"What did she find?" McGaven asked with some excitement to his voice.

"An address for me," she slowly said. "It's for a friend, some personal business." She got up from her chair, searching for her keys. "I'm going to have to run out for about an hour and half. You okay?"

"Of course. I don't need a babysitter."

"McGaven, you're a funny guy. Call or text me if anything comes in from forensics or you find something that hits from your background checks… I mean *anything*. Got it?"

He made a silly salute gesture. "You got it, Detective."

"I'm going to have to teach you how to salute properly, the army way," she said as she dashed from the office and hurried out of the sheriff's department building.

*

After Katie got into the car, she punched in the address coordinates on the GPS for James Haines. She drove as fast as she dared to try to catch him at home. She thought about calling first but decided that might work against her if he didn't want anything to do with his brother.

As she drove, she reflected on the fact that she didn't know what it was like to have a sibling, a brother or sister, someone as close as that where you share DNA. She often felt lonely, especially with her parents gone. Her Uncle Wayne was her rock and just as close as her parents had been to her, but she couldn't help but experience a twinge of jealousy from people who had a sibling to confide in through the tough as well as the wonderful times.

Ever since she had come home from her two-tour in the army, Katie thought that she would be odd person out and that everyone would think she was different. Basically, she thought that she was destined to be alone. To her surprise, she had managed to engage with a work team of wonderful, supportive, and intelligent people. It was more than she thought she would ever be involved in—police patrol work can be extremely solitary even though you are part of an overall team—it was the nature of a subculture. But now with investigations, it was a whole new world to her.

Katie knew her personal life could really use some help, but she also knew that she was the only one responsible for keeping Chad at arm's length. He was someone she had known her entire life—she couldn't think of a time growing up that he wasn't in it. The problem was that she was holding too tight to the reins of her army time, the belief that she somehow was different and didn't deserve a happy, healthy and intimate civilian life. That was the crack in her mindset where her anxiety and depression seeped in.

She gritted her teeth, avoiding the truth about her psyche and how she needed to deal with these past issues head on. It was true that she needed someone objective to talk to—a therapist maybe. She didn't know if she had the guts to pursue that avenue yet.

Her GPS alerted her that the street designated as the location for her destination was near. She snapped back to the present, unsure of the correct approach to take with Nick's brother.

Katie saw the apartments consisting of six units, which were run-down and in desperate need of maintenance and repair. The tan paint peeled from around the windows and doors, highlighting the filthy glass. No front door mats or welcome signs inviting you to show up at the front door—just a few pieces of garbage that blew out of a nearby trash can across the weeds.

She slowly drove by and saw #4 that belonged to Nadine McMillian. It was difficult to ascertain if anyone was home or they were inside not wanting to be disturbed. There were frilly white curtains covering the front windows, which appeared to be the living room and kitchen areas. Katie deduced that the bedroom was most likely in the back away from the road.

Two vehicles were parked in two of the six parking places—one older model pickup truck and a small SUV. Katie drove ahead about a block before she decided to park. Even though it was a personal visit as a favor to Nick, she wasn't going into a situation without being prepared. Not wanting to draw attention, she made sure her weapon and badge were out of sight underneath her jacket. She took another quick look at the photograph Nick had supplied of his brother, making sure that she was meeting up with the correct person. She also had a photocopied picture of Nadine who had long dark hair, and a serious expression, with dark brown eyes, and was age twenty-nine but she looked older.

With the images ingrained in her memory, Katie got out of her car and walked to the apartment complex. No cars had passed by and no voices filtered throughout the area. It was a ghost town.

She walked assertively toward apartment #4 and couldn't shake the sense that there were eyes watching her. It was obvious that she wasn't just an average person. She knew that she acted and looked like a cop—so she didn't try to hide it.

Standing at the door, she knocked three times then took a step back so that she wasn't right up in someone's personal space. There was no doorbell, so after waiting a while she rapped on the door once again. This time she heard movement and what sounded like hurried whispers.

Finally, a woman's voice announced, "Who is it?"

"Katie Scott," she said and hoped that would be enough for the woman to open the door.

"I don't know you," was the woman's reply.

"Nadine?" Katie wanted to see if she indeed had the right location.

There was a pause and she heard a couple of locks disengage. Another brief moment before the door opened about two inches. Katie saw a pretty woman without makeup and resembling the photograph peer out. "What do you want?" She eyed Katie suspiciously, looking her up and down.

"Nadine?" she said again.

"Yes," the woman replied hesitantly.

"My name is Katie Scott and I'm a close friend of Nick Haines. I'm looking for James Haines—his brother. This was the last known address for him." She tried to sound casual and not come across like a cop or in some other official capacity.

"I… I don't know any James Haines…" She was about to close the door.

Katie used her boot to stop the door from closing. "Please. I'm here to talk to him—just to talk to him about his brother."

"I know nothing about brothers." Her face clouded and she became angry. "Go away. Just go away!"

Katie heard a door slam from around back and she didn't waste any more time talking to Nadine, she took off running and managed to make her way around the building dodging large trash items, overgrown weeds, and what was left of a retaining wall.

She saw a dark-haired man trying to put on a shirt running from the apartment.

"Hey! James. Stop!"

Katie scaled the crumbling wall of concrete blocks and various-sized smooth rocks. Slinging her leg over the last obstacle, she ran to meet up with him.

"Please stop!" she yelled again.

To her shock, the man turned around to face her and grabbed hold of her, practically lifting her off her feet. He performed a smooth move that Katie wasn't prepared for as he turned her torso, causing her to fall back and land on her backside.

She knew the man was James Haines by his appearance, facial structure, and the fact that he looked just like Nick.

Recovering from the attack, Katie kicked his legs from under him. As he fell toward her, he grabbed her right arm, pinning it underneath her stomach. Somewhat out of breath, she worked her body to gain a better position. She felt like she was in self-defense class, so she went full throttle and used a wrestling move, garnering the upper hand by pinning him facedown holding his wrist up behind his back, her knee in his kidney.

"Sheriff's department," she said breathlessly. "I would suggest you stop moving if you're smart. I'm here about your brother."

"What?" he said, surprised, and tried to spin around to attack again.

"Can I trust you?" she asked, still holding his arm up behind him. She cinched it higher.

James yelled out, "Okay, okay."

"Relax," she insisted.

"Okay, okay," he said, quieter.

Katie slowly released the grip and stood up, still not convinced that he wasn't going to bolt or attack again.

He rolled over and sat up staring at her. "Where did you learn that?"

"Army."

"Should have known."

"What about you?" she asked.

"My big brother."

Katie offered a hand to help him up. "That's why I'm here."

He got to his feet and said, "Has something happened to Nick?"

"Are you James Haines; your brother is Nick Haines?" She wanted to make sure, but the more she talked with James it was obvious, at least to her, that he was Nick's brother. His voice inflection, slight southern accent, and even some of his mannerisms mimicked his brother.

"Yes." He paused. "Are you going to arrest me?"

"For what?"

He looked down and didn't respond.

"Look, I was asked by Nick to locate you—as a favor. Whatever you've done or whatever you think you're in trouble for—it's not my call or concern at this moment. Understand?"

"Then what do you want?"

Katie softened her tone. "It's not what I want. Your brother has been honorably discharged from the army and he wants to reconnect—with family. From what I understand, it's just the two of you." She watched his response and sensed that he had some issues that had hurt him, perhaps deeply, but if there was love and hope for the two of them to reconnect—they each needed to reach out.

"I thought for sure he was a lifer. The army is his family, his life." He looked away, not wanting to meet Katie's gaze.

"You know, there are all kinds of families. And I swear as I'm standing here, Nick is more like family to me. Like a brother I never had. We went through a lot together over there and I don't think I would've done two tours if it wasn't for him. Believe me, he's family. But you're blood, and there's nothing closer than that." Katie was surprised at herself for being so open and forthright with someone she had never met before. Maybe it was because they shared someone or maybe it was because both of them were hurting—still hurting from the past.

James studied her for a moment. "So you're a cop now?"

"Detective," she said.

"Nick really asked you to find me?" he said with some disbelief.

"Look, I don't know what caused your rift and why you two haven't talked. But I do know Nick, and I think you owe it to him, and yourself, to meet and talk." Katie took her business card from her pocket and handed it to James. "Think about it and give me a call. I know you'll make the right choice. Okay?"

Taking the card, he said, "Thank you, Detective."

"I know that Nick has had a hole in his life for not talking with you."

He nodded and seemed to be lost in memories.

"Whatever you're running from right now is not as bad as you think it is. There's always a way to work it out. And it's a lot easier with family on your side," Katie said.

He nodded.

Nadine came out of the back door with a worried expression. She wore a loose dress but it was easy to see that she was pregnant.

"Everything is okay," he said to her.

Katie watched the couple interact. It was clear that they were more than just a casual thing. "James, don't forget what I said. From what I see, you have a family. Don't let time or bad feelings let it slip away."

The couple watched her walk away.

Katie reached her car just as her cell phone rang. Pulling it out of her pocket, she was relieved that it hadn't been crushed during the altercation.

"Detective Scott."

"There's a match," McGaven stated with excitement to his voice.

"To what?" Katie felt goose bumps rise on her arms.

"There was a fingerprint match from IAFIS from your car to a First Memorial Hospital employee named Robert (Bobby) Sykes. And the best part, he's a maintenance worker that cleans the surgery rooms *and* comes in contact on a regular basis with the chemicals found on all three victims. And… he was on our suspect list."

"Do you know where he is now?"

"According to HR—he is on shift right now."

"Pick him up. I'm on my way back now," she said.

"I thought you'd never ask."

CHAPTER 54

Monday 1205 hours

Katie drove at warp speed back to the sheriff's department, a million questions running through her mind. Was this the person who was following her and writing notes? Was it the killer? Was this going to be the break in the case they were waiting for? She felt a surge of excitement.

After finding a parking place and turning the car off, before she exited Katie gathered her thoughts of how she was going to proceed with the interview—it was her quiet time away from the department. She didn't want to scare off Mr. Sykes, but she would press him as hard as she needed to get some answers. With some luck, he might just confess.

Someone tapped on her window, causing her to jump. She looked out her driver's window to see Chad standing there.

He smiled and beckoned with his index finger for her to get out of the vehicle. Dressed in his work clothes for the fire department, he looked extremely handsome. She noticed that he had cut his hair shorter since the other night.

Opening the car door, Katie said, "Hi, how'd you know where to find me?"

"McGaven."

"It's good to see you. I'm sorry for not getting a hold of you."

"It's okay. I know you're working that homicide. I wanted to stop by so you wouldn't forget what I looked like."

"That would be *highly* unlikely. But…"

"I know," he said softly, squeezing her hand. "Maybe a drink later?"

"I have to interview a suspect right now. I don't know how long that will be, and then I'm going home."

"Okay."

Katie moved toward the building. "It will be late. Can I call you on my way home?"

"Sure," he said, and smiled, but it was clear he was a little disappointed.

"I'll talk to you soon," Katie said, then hesitated. There was so much she wanted to share with him and there was so much she wanted to say. The Haines brothers made her think about family and those people who were close to her—how precious life was, and the people who were in her life. She didn't want to ruin the chance with Chad, because she knew that he wasn't going to wait for her forever.

CHAPTER 55

Monday 1300 hours

Katie and McGaven walked into the interrogation room not saying a word. Katie carried an electronic device, yellow steno notepad, and a pen. She had requested this particular room because it was the smallest and the lack of airflow made it smell like an old basement. Most detectives opted not to use it, but for some situations, it helped to push the person of interest into a confession.

The truth.

Bobby Sykes sat in the chair across from the detectives. His nerves were obvious as he moved his right leg in a jangled tapping motion. He was slight in build and looked athletic, like he could run fast and ride a mountain bike. His sandy hair was almost shoulder length and he pushed it out of his face out of habit—and uneasiness.

"Mr. Robert Sykes," Katie began. "Bobby?"

"Why am I here?" he asked, his voice a bit shaky.

"Do I look stupid to you?" she said.

"What?"

"Answer the question." McGaven ordered.

"Do you look stupid? No. Why are you asking that?"

Katie thought she'd jump right in. She tossed the steno pad and pen onto the table. "Write your name and where you live and work."

Robert Sykes did as he was told without complaining. He picked up the pen with his right hand and began to write.

Katie looked at her device and pulled up a copy of the three notes left for her. She watched with interest as Sykes finished his writing assignment.

McGaven picked up the notepad and he turned to show it to Katie. His expression revealed what she had hoped.

She compared the handwriting and stared at Sykes. "Would you mind explaining this?" She turned the notepad and device so that he could see them both—it was obvious that the writing was from the same person.

"I… don't…"

"You can do better than that," she said. "Explain this to me."

"Okay, fine. I wrote those notes," he blurted out. His attitude changed from the weak and unsure man to a guy with an attitude. "There's no law against it. I haven't done anything wrong."

"Why are you writing these notes and leaving them for me?"

"Just insight."

"Insight? You want to go to jail?" she pressed.

He leaned forward and spat out, "For what?"

"Homicide. Kidnapping. Terrorist threats. Breaking into a police officer's car. You want me to go on?"

"No way! I didn't kill anybody. You're nuts." He slammed his fists on the table and pushed his chair back. "I was trying to help you. Is this what I get for trying to help?"

"Where were you when Amanda Payton was murdered?"

"I was working a twelve-hour shift—and I never left the hospital. You can call my supervisor."

Katie waited a few moments to let Sykes settle down. "Why were you trying to help me?" she said in a less aggressive tone.

"I've watched you."

The thought chilled Katie. It was the way he'd said it. "And?"

"Man, you cops are dense sometimes. I've seen things."

McGaven interjected, "If you've seen things, then why the cryptic notes? Just come in and talk to us."

Sykes looked at Katie and then McGaven, and then back to Katie again. "I didn't want anyone to know."

"You mean at the hospital?" she said.

"Yeah. I need that job. Pay's crappy but the benefits are good."

Katie lightened up and said, "You know something, then spit it out."

He hesitated, looking away. His leg tapped faster. He finally said, "There's some weird stuff going on there, you know?"

"Like what?"

"It's stuff. Weird stuff. Like she was being harassed."

"You mean Amanda Payton?"

"Yeah. I guess she was dating several guys, you know."

"Who?" Katie asked.

"The doctor, Jamison, and that creepy guy in the morgue."

"Okay. What makes you think that she was being harassed?"

"Talk. Nurses talk all the time about shit. Mostly gossip, but people air their grievances. I'm cleaning and mopping floors after blood has been spilled all over an operating room. No one pays any attention to me. It's like I'm not there. I'm totally invisible. But they talk… believe me…"

Katie remained quiet and gave him the look, raising her eyebrows to continue.

"She was talking to a couple other nurses, or nurse's aides, and told them that she had been followed and she felt paranoid and scared. Like someone was going to get her. She looked like she was going to jump out of her skin half the time."

"When was this?" she said.

"It started over a year ago."

"What do you know about the abandoned houses at the Basin Woods Development?"

"Nothing."

"What do you mean nothing? You were there. You were lucky that my dog didn't catch you and take you down."

"I followed you. It's not that hard, you know."

"What do you know about the Basin Woods Development?"

"Nothing."

"Now," she said leaning forward. "I know you've had some involvement with the development. We know. Why don't you tell us?"

He clenched his jaw tight fighting to give any information. "I worked with a demolition crew a few years back. We were hired by the original development company to tear out certain things from the houses."

"Like what?" she pressed.

"There were some problems with the wiring in the kitchen and laundry areas. Me and a bunch of guys were hired temporarily to do the job."

"Why?"

"There were some lawsuits and stuff with the state—I don't know all—but I did the job and moved on, finally getting the gig at the hospital."

Katie studied him, not sure if he was telling the truth. It was too convenient.

"I'm telling you the truth," he snapped.

"How do you know Madeline Thomas?"

"Who? I don't know her. Whoever told you I did is lying."

"Calm down."

"I don't know anything…" He looked away.

"Do you know Tess Regan?"

"No. I told you I don't know who those people are!"

"Are you working with the killer? Are you willing to be an accomplice? Just throw your life away."

"It's…"

"What, Bobby?"

"There's just something weird going on at the hospital… I think whoever killed Amanda is watching me too."

"Why?"

"What do you mean? I'm the guy no one ever notices, so people talk about stuff. I'm all over that hospital. There's someone watching everyone, even me."

"You think the person who killed Amanda is at the hospital?" she pushed.

He nodded.

"What else, Bobby?"

"I've found weird things, symbols and sayings. Things where they shouldn't be."

"Where?"

"Around. I saw some weird stuff written in blood on the floor in one of the operating rooms, and then another time an 'X' written in some heavy marker on my locker. Like I said, weird stuff I can't explain."

"Why would you make this stuff up?"

"I told you—I'm not making anything up! There's something going on."

"Is there anything else?"

Bobby looked away but he became agitated, holding his frustration back—his fists clenched.

"What else?"

He shook his head.

"What else are you not telling me?"

He pushed his chair back as far as he could and crossed his arms.

"What else!" Katie stood up and leaned across the table. "Tell us!"

"I…"

"What?"

"I… think I'm going to be next."

"What do you mean?" she said.

"Killed. I think I'm going to be next."

CHAPTER 56

Monday 2015 hours

Katie was already beat and it was only Monday. Every waking moment she stressed over the investigation—with thoughts that another woman might be the next homicide victim. Her anxiety constantly tried to beat her down and take her out of the game, but the overlapping adrenalin pump with each new lead and bit of evidence kept her going. She tried to stay one step in front of it during the day, but sometimes at night, when her strength and wherewithal were sapped, she couldn't hold up a strong front anymore.

She curled herself into a fetal position on the couch as her senses assailed her with flashbacks from the battlefield. She squeezed her eyes tightly shut, Cisco snug at her side, waiting for her to get through the next shock.

Crawling on her stomach keeping her head down, she moved through the heavy dust cloud on her elbows and knees. She felt the heat of Cisco's body crawling next to her. He stayed next to her torso. She felt his heart beating—rapidly. She knew that the old building ahead was shelter but there were rocks and pieces of cement she had to navigate around without blowing her cover—bruising and scraping her arms, legs, and face. Cisco made these detours with ease as he waited every few feet for her to catch up. Shouts broke out all around her. Smoke obscured her vision. Katie couldn't see her team but knew that a few were following her. She thought she could hear Nick shouting orders to move somewhere ahead but wasn't sure. Her ears buzzed. She tried to speak but her mouth was strangely wet.

Finally the dust cloud cleared and she saw an entrance. She heard Nick's voice, "Move, move, move!" So she moved faster. Crawling over a threshold, she entered a safe haven out of direct exposure. Cisco pushed his way in and sat next to her thrusting his wet nose against her face. He began to lick her. She looked at him and realized he was bleeding, but upon closer inspection, the blood was coming from her mouth and face, dripping on the dog. Katie looked down at the front of her heavy uniform and saw that it was dark red, soaked with fresh blood. To Katie's horror, it wasn't hers or Cisco's blood, it was a soldier in her platoon. Her friend Jack, funny, strong, had lost his life. Katie was now saturated in his blood—alive because of him. A joy and burden she would carry close to her heart for the rest of her life.

Katie opened her eyes through the streams of tears, her arms wrapped around her torso. Her body trembled as she let the surges of grief and fear take over her. She thought that she could see that same cloud of dust swirling in her living room, but it was only her imagination. Cisco remained close, keeping his keen attention on her—comforting her the best way he could until the episode ended.

Worn out. Feeling lost. Alone. She had new burdens to bear and she didn't want to lose someone else on her watch. She stood up, gathering her emotions as best she could and burying them until she was forced to release them again. She made it to the shower and turned it up as high as it would go, the cascading water punishing her and cleansing her in equal measure. She imagined her memory disappearing down the drain and felt a little better.

In yoga pants and a loose sweatshirt Katie did some stretches and tried to just breathe and relax. Cisco had decided that the day was over and climbed into her bed—his curled-up body pressed up close to Katie's pillows. She didn't have the heart to move him.

She breezed through the house restoring order and picking up anything that was out of place, just in time to see headlights approaching up the driveway. Cisco barked and scurried across the hardwood floors, taking a tight corner sliding into the living room, and then stood strong at the front door.

Katie opened the front door and Cisco shot out to greet Chad. "You're such a good boy. A handsome boy," he cooed several times, leaning down to pet the dog.

He walked up to Katie and gave her a quick kiss on the cheek. "It's nice to see you." He studied her and by his expression he knew that she was hurting.

"You too. I'm sorry we haven't gotten together sooner." She waited until Cisco followed Chad inside before closing the front door. In truth, she had forgotten about Chad coming over.

"It's okay, I've been settling into those twelve-hour shifts at the fire house. They are brutal and take some time to get used to."

"Do you just love it?" she asked.

"You know, I absolutely do love it. It's been my dream job since I was a kid."

"Are they hazing you yet?" She forced a laugh, trying to keep her full attention on Chad and not her own problems.

"No. And don't give them any ideas."

"It's coming… watch your back. I know how cops are and firefighters can be just as bad."

"I'm watching my back now. You've got me scared!"

Cisco ran around the room after drinking water and decided he wanted to stand on the couch looking from Katie to Chad, and back to Katie again.

"Off, Cisco," she said. "He was sound asleep before you got here."

"You hungry?"

"I've missed a few meals because of this case—actually, cases. And yeah, I am hungry."

"Let's see what you got." He headed into the kitchen, opening the refrigerator and checking out what was in the cupboards.

Katie watched him with interest as she sat on the counter stool. "Verdict?"

"Not as bad as I initially thought. What sounds good? Let's see… leftover pasta, some kind of veggie dish, eggs, or comfort food like…."

"Pancakes?"

He turned around and his expression reminded Katie of when they were kids—eager and wanting to get into some trouble. "I think we have a winner. And that is one thing I definitely know how to make."

"My kitchen is all yours."

Cisco padded around the kitchen as if he wanted to make sure he wasn't forgotten.

"What you think, Cisco?" he asked and received a combination grumble whine. "I agree."

For the next fifteen minutes, Chad managed to dirty more dishes than necessary to create a bowl of pancake batter.

Katie laughed quite a few times and actually didn't think about the case, allowing her body and mind to begin to re-energize. She realized, watching Chad fumble once or twice in the kitchen, giggling in the process, that she had missed him much more than she realized. She thought that some things in life are experiences that are a part of life's history, but when those people in the past are back in your life and you cannot imagine ever being without them again—cherish every moment.

Before she knew it, they were both enjoying pancakes with heated syrup.

"Oh my…" Katie managed to say, "this is the best ever," and she stuffed another forkful into her mouth. "You need to make these for the guys at the firehouse."

"It's a thought. We have an awesome cook right now. It's one of those great perks. I've never seen so many excited guys looking at the menu for the week before."

"I'm glad that you're enjoying the job. It sounds like it was worth waiting for."

He nodded. "The best things are." He stared at her.

Katie didn't know what to say and it was an awkward moment. They didn't speak about Nick or the other night. Her heart felt a tugging, but she wasn't sure how to respond. She wondered if it was because of her experiences and being a cop had jaded her somehow. But she didn't want to lose a great thing—maybe even the best thing to ever happen to her. She wanted to spend as much time with Chad as possible.

"You know what would make this perfect?" Chad finally blurted out.

"What?" she said.

"Bacon. And more pancakes."

"I'm totally in."

CHAPTER 57

Tuesday 1345 hours

After spending most of the day doing background checks on hospital employees and waiting for anything else to materialize from forensics, Katie was going stir-crazy.

"That's it, I'm done with this for the day," she announced. "I'm not getting anywhere." Her eyes were tired but she still had quite a bit of excess energy. She was itching to get out.

"What?" said McGaven, looking up from the lengthy list he was working on. Sticky notes and pieces of paper with his small handwriting were stuck all over his desk.

"I'm so disappointed that the search warrant we served for Sykes turned up absolutely nothing… nothing… I still can't believe it."

"He's not out of the loop yet."

"I know… I need to do something more. I can't look at these useless background checks anymore."

"I second that," he said.

"Wait a minute." Katie began searching furiously through paperwork.

"What are you doing?"

She sorted through two stacks of papers until she found it. "Okay, I need the aerial view." She searched until she found it.

McGaven watched her with curiosity.

"I had almost forgotten all about this." She put the pieces of paper on her desk side by side.

"What is it?"

"This was the original architectural drawing of the houses in what is now called the Basin Woods Development. I'm trying to find the house where Amanda said she was held captive on here. Where I didn't find anything, but…"

McGaven helped her move the maps, smoothing out the corners.

Katie studied the neighborhood, streets, and zeroed in on an area where she had previously searched for the house based on Amanda's description. Looking back and forth from the plans, she exclaimed, "There's the house." She referred to the floor plan with the two bedrooms. "Wait. See, these bedrooms aren't situated like that. There's a portion missing in the structure—at a weird angle. Why would they cut the plan like that?"

"That could've been changed due to budget, or whatever."

"True."

"We need to start at the beginning—where everything started."

"What do you want to do?"

"Road trip," she said.

"Let's go."

"Everything for these cases is simmering right now. We need more…"

"Let's go then."

"Can we pick up Cisco?"

Katie laughed, knowing the dog would love the company. "Sure, it's on the way."

"I'm game."

Cisco was more excited than usual, emitting whines every so often, as he rode in the backseat of the police sedan. His regal face, alert ears, and attention focused on the road. It was impossible to ignore his enthusiasm as he looked out between Katie and McGaven.

"Are you going to let me drive—ever?" McGaven asked.

"What do you mean? You can drive whenever you want to." She looked at her partner. "Oh, no, you're not one of those, are you?"

"One of what?"

"Just because you're a man you feel the need to drive all the time. I'm driving now because I know exactly where we are going."

He sighed, trying to hide his smile. "I suppose."

"Just sit back and enjoy the ride," she said, partially laughing.

They both remained quiet, lost in their own thoughts about the investigation. The only audible sound in the car besides the revving engine was the sound of Cisco panting. It was not because he was hot. It was because he was excited, as working dogs become, when they instinctively know they are going to work or into unknown conditions with their handler.

Once again, Katie turned the car into the Basin Woods area. Maybe it was because she knew that the houses were empty or it was due to the fact that it conjured up creepy images, but she felt instantly uncomfortable. It was silly, she realized, but it still didn't change her reaction. She had Cisco and McGaven with her but that still didn't deter the slight chill she felt, driving down the streets littered with overgrown bushes and tree limbs along with tattered pieces of garbage rolling along like tumbleweeds.

"This is where Amanda referred to as the 'big box'." Katie gestured to the old phone box used for the housing area.

McGaven surveyed the area. He didn't say anything but his body tensed as if he was being gripped by something unpleasant.

"She told Deputy Windham that it was a house with a blue door and white trim. And she knew how far it was with the landmarks. Windham adamantly believes that Amanda had told the truth—and I believe him. I think she *was* held here."

"But there was no evidence in the house at that time to corroborate her story."

"I know… this is what bothers me about this entire case—this house. Everything hinges on this house—the beginning—this is what set everything in motion. Now, after looking at those blueprints, I think there's something weird about it."

McGaven studied the houses around the old neighborhoods.

"At least it's still daytime," she said, trying to convince herself that it was just a routine search.

"What does the county plan to do with this area?"

"According to the planning department, they are going to demolish everything and build more affordable housing," she explained.

"Great. It'll take, what? Another ten or fifteen years to look like this again…"

"Here is the house Amanda described and even the bushes she landed on while escaping. There's a small area of the open window that someone her size could fit through. So, it's possible."

Katie parked in the same area in front that she did before, lowering the windows slightly for Cisco while she and McGaven got out of the car.

"Don't you want to take him?" he asked.

"No, he's watching our backs. Anything or anyone moves within the neighborhood, he'll bark like a banshee. No one can sneak up on us. And, I have a backdoor release just in case of an emergency."

Following Katie up to the front blue door, he said, "Works for me."

Katie didn't want McGaven to see her hesitation, so she plowed forward and burst through the door, pushing it wide open. As before, the immediate stink accosted her senses with a mixture of urine and decomposing garbage.

"Nice smell. Smells like my first dorm room," said McGaven partially covering his nose and mouth.

"You get used to it. Leave the door open for some air. What I don't get is that Amanda said something about flowers, that she got the distinct fragrance, but it stinks like hell in here."

Katie made sure her weapon was ready to use at a moment's notice by unsnapping the guard on her holster. "I'll go this way; you check out the kitchen area."

McGaven moved through the house, carefully looking for anything that might prove to be a clue or evidence that Amanda had been in that house.

Katie continued toward the bedroom, easing her body down the hallway. Something appeared out of place. She pulled a copy of the blueprint out of her pocket—tracing her steps. The bedroom looked too small for the rest of the house and the layout was awkward. She wasn't expecting a perfect house plan flow, but there was indeed a structural aspect that didn't match the rest of the building.

She peeked into each bedroom and realized that there weren't any closets. Odd. She hadn't noticed it before. The house wasn't that old—as a home built in the 1920s might have had little or no closets—but this house should have had ample storage space—at least something. There were none. Looking at the plan, she saw that the closets should be on the far side of the room. She oriented herself. The plans didn't match what she saw.

Standing back in the hallway she heard McGaven moving around in the opposite area, but the sound didn't resonate inside the bedrooms. She moved back to the hallway and she distinctly heard McGaven opening cupboards and even his heavy footsteps.

Katie remained quiet, not wanting to alert her partner just yet to the strange sound difference. What did all this mean?

Digging her hands into her pockets, she pulled out the small piece of adhesive she put there the last time she was inside the house. She squeezed the small piece of rubberized plastic between her fingers and straightaway the image of the special effects warehouse came to mind with the amazing, realistic masks and piecework—the building blocks that could transform people, places and things into something else.

"Could it be?" she whispered.

Katie ran her fingers along the edges of the wall and down to where the baseboards should have been. The walls went to the floor but she could feel a faint breeze.

Just like the monsters at ScareFest, nothing was as it seemed.

Taking a step back, centering her balance with her arms up, gripped fists, she then attacked the wall with a high stomp kick. It barely made a dent, merely chipping some drywall that littered the floor. She repeated her technique two more times until she had made a hole the size of a dinner plate with her foot. Adhesive, similar to foam used on construction jobs, filled the makeshift wall and acted as a soundproof barrier.

McGaven ran into the room. "What the hell is going on?"

"Look." She gestured to the wall.

He walked up to the hole and peered inside. Even without a flashlight, he could see into the small hidden room; to an old box-spring bed with a headboard, magenta sheet, rope, and two small air vents above. "What in the...?" he uttered.

"We just found where Amanda was being held. She was telling the truth. She *was* here. Everything she described."

Katie ran out of the house to the car; opening the trunk she retrieved the tire iron and ran back inside. Using all her anxious energy and frustration, she managed to wind up and execute several well-placed swings, hitting the wall, opening it farther for them to enter.

McGaven searched the perimeter of the wall and found cleverly disguised hinges and a finger hold to release and slide a narrow portion to open the room—just wide enough for a person. "Here it is. Tricky." He showed Katie.

"We need forensics in here right now. But what if Tess Regan is here somewhere?"

"Let's go," McGaven agreed.

"We're going to need help searching *all* the houses on this block," she said.

CHAPTER 58

Tuesday 1545 hours

Tess awoke with a jerk, still weak and disoriented. Her vision was still blacked out but her hearing was acute. Her chest ached and her neck and throat felt tight, making it difficult to breathe. Her energy was dwindling at an alarming rate and she didn't think she could muster enough energy to try to loosen the restraints again.

Moving her wrists in any direction made a sharp excruciating pain shoot down her arms. There was warmth enveloping around her wrists and slow blood droplets dappled her forearms. The restraints felt different. They cut immediately into her flesh like razor wire. If she kept working her wrists or hands, the wire would no doubt cut a major vein causing her to bleed out.

"No, no, no," she said, moving her head from side to side. It was the only thing she could do that didn't cause her to cry out in pain. Her voice faded. "Why…?"

The sound of a motor caught her attention. The engine gunned and gears shifted several times.

"Please, help me, I'm in here… please…" Her voice petered out and was too low for anyone to hear her.

The vehicle sat nearby in idle for a while before she heard it leave—slowly driving away. She listened for as long as she could until silence returned once again.

Sleep overwhelmed her and pushed her to submit, the disappointment too heavy to bear.

Tess thought she heard voices talking and more cars approached, but she soon dropped into a semi-conscious state.

She tried to speak, but it only came out as a faint whisper—her last whisper.

She could only wait—to die—alone.

CHAPTER 59

Forensics arrived thirty-five minutes later as several deputies including K9 teams were dispatched to help search for further evidence or victims in the abandoned neighborhood.

Katie had called Sheriff Scott to make sure they had permission to trash the houses to search for potential crime scenes or victims. She wanted to make sure that she was doing everything within police protocol and following the appropriate chain of evidence. She didn't want anything to hinder an arrest or prosecution of the perpetrator once they were found.

"Great work," said Sheriff Scott to both Katie and McGaven. He made three calls to the developers, the county, and the district attorney's office to make sure they were within their rights.

"What bothers me is that I was here previously and I didn't connect the dots," replied Katie.

"Most people wouldn't have put it together," the sheriff said.

"Even with the plans, it didn't look like there was a secret room when I walked into the house," said McGaven.

"Now we have to wait," she said.

"We've got everything under control here. I want you and McGaven to go back to the station and keep working on your suspect lists. I'm sure this search is going to go into the night."

"But…" Katie began.

"I'm sure both of you are exhausted. Get some food and keep working. Keep me updated," the sheriff ordered.

CHAPTER 60

Tuesday 1905 hours

A new awakened life rushed through Katie's body, which was something she had so desperately needed during the investigation. She also needed sleep and food, but was too focused on the new break in the case and what was going to happen after the searches were over.

Katie pored over the massive amounts of paperwork and her notes to try and find some cohesive connection between the hospital and Basin Woods—the person who was responsible. Glancing back and forth from her cell phone to the desk phone, she knew that at any moment they would call and announce that they had found someone alive. Maybe even Tess Regan.

"What's the whereabouts for Dr. Jamison?" she asked McGaven, who had been bombarded with numerous phone calls ever since they arrived back at the department.

"He was at the hospital and now he's back at his hotel suite," he said.

"The entire time?"

"There were about forty minutes where he was unaccounted for."

"Shit."

Katie was impatient as she tapped her index finger on her desk. "What about Robert Sykes and Marco Ellis?"

"Ellis has been working a twelve-hour shift and hasn't left the hospital." McGaven made notes and conversed with a few of his fellow deputies who had been assigned special details on the case. "Okay, thanks," he said and hung up.

"Well?" she asked impatiently.

"Sykes took a dinner break. The deputy assigned to him said he's still at the hospital, but he doesn't have eyes on him."

"Tell him to go and actually lay eyes on Sykes. That guy is really slippery. The way he was able to get those messages to me without me knowing. He's like a ghost."

"How many cups of coffee have you had?" asked McGaven.

"None. This is just me. I know we're close—really close—and I can't rest now."

The phone rang.

Katie snatched the receiver up. "Scott."

"I know you must be chomping at the bit," said the sheriff.

"That's an understatement," she said.

"I wanted to update you—we haven't found anything else since you were here."

Katie remained quiet.

"I'm sorry, but we're about to wrap things up as far as the searches are concerned. John and the forensic crew are still finishing up processing the scene. It will take a while, most of the night," he said.

"Okay, thank you."

The sheriff ended the call. Katie still held the receiver and slowly hung up.

"Nothing?" McGaven asked.

"No."

"It seems like the perfect area for a killer to keep his victims hidden. He could've had all kinds of victims scattered throughout that abandoned neighborhood and nobody would have ever known."

"That's it," Katie said with urgency.

"What?"

"When I was at the county planning department, I noticed that when Shane pulled out these drawings there were notations about another area. There were notes that said something about a non-profit. It seemed strange that this would be written on those particular blueprints. I didn't think anything of it."

"Where is it?"

Katie rolled out the blueprint copies—there were more than a hundred pages to go through. "It was next to the legend—handwritten." She turned another page. "Wait, here is the notation. It says in quotes Highland Project NP #367-44. Does that mean anything to you?"

McGaven thought a minute. "Sounds somewhat familiar and I'm not sure why." He sat down at his computer and typed in "Highland Project Sequoia County California." "Okay," he said. "It was the first area where the county and state government wanted to build a low-income housing development, but the community was outraged and didn't want it in their neighborhood. A crazed group of so-called concerned citizens against crime actually torched the place—several buildings were burned to the ground and two firefighters were seriously injured. It was an ugly situation."

Katie shook her head; she wasn't familiar with that project.

"Oh, wait. I keep forgetting. It was when you were in Afghanistan."

"What's the status now?"

"Everything has been locked up in multiple lawsuits and the places have been just sitting. What else is new?"

"How big is it?" she asked. "It must be a crime zone."

"Wait," he said and hit a few keys to bring up articles about the housing project. He scrolled through several and stopped on one in particular. "There are only five houses still standing and the others were burned. I'm not sure why those five stood through that. This area is next to a large agricultural property of more than two hundred acres—making it pretty isolated. They originally wanted to build a small community and a small shopping strip mall, but protesters were adamantly against housing near agriculture fields that use pesticides. Protection of children, food, and the overall community, and so on."

Katie skimmed the stories and said, "Looks like they called it the 'Humanity Project,' which was originally planned for one hundred units, or single-family dwellings, but had been downsized to less than fifty. And now only five houses remain after the fire? Wow, it's so isolated," she said, studying the map. "Seems strange to build that there."

"Maybe that's where the contaminated water found in Amanda's hair came from?"

She stood up and scrutinized her preliminary profile. "Definitely possible. What makes you think that a killer would only stay to one small area? He would spread out, but remain in his comfort zone. Not keep all his victims in one place. His distinct signature is to keep his victims in condemned, foreclosed, and abandoned houses. Simple, but brilliant."

McGaven followed what she was describing. "You think that he's using another area."

"But," she back-pedaled her theory, "there was nothing in Sykes's background that had anything to do with this project. This project wasn't Jamison's Magna Group. So we can't link Dr. Jamison. What, or who, is the connection? Someone would have to be connected to this other project. It looks like Simms Construction took over." Katie was frustrated. They were close—very close.

"Who do we have now?" McGaven pulled up the three suspects they were able to link from First Memorial Hospital and the Basin Woods Development. "Okay, some of my reports have finally come through from the last background checks."

"What do you have?" she asked.

"Looks like Sebastian Harding has been doing time for robbery for the last year and half."

Katie frowned. "He's out. Whose this other guy?"

"It's for Chris D. Randall. He lived at Basin Woods, but it's weird. There's a big chunk of his history that just ends—it's missing. Like off the grid."

That caught Katie's attention. "Usually when people have clean chunks of history, it means that they are using another name. Everyone leaves some type of footprint, debit cards, applications, employment…"

"That's why I'm looking for aliases, monikers, and other names used. I don't see anything, no ID or driver's license, but he did work as a maintenance trainee at the hospital under that name. It looks like he was also paid under that name."

Katie had an idea. "Cross-reference anyone at the hospital with the first or last name Chris or Randall. I know we're assuming that the killer is currently employed. He could have quit by now, but let's see if anything pops."

McGaven keyed up the spreadsheet of all current employees at the hospital and did a quick search using Chris or Randall. He waited until a few things came up. "Oh, it can't be…"

"What?" she asked.

"Let me double-check a few things." McGaven had a pained expression that Katie had never seen before.

Katie began to pace in the small office that now had blueprints scattered everywhere.

"Crap. I hate this database," he said.

McGaven typed quickly and was clearly troubled. He stopped and stared at the computer.

"What?" she asked and stared at the screen.

McGaven said slowly, "Chris D. Randall also known as Randall Christopher Drake."

"Who is that?" Katie looked confused.

"It's a nickname—of course. Randall is Randy the security guard at the hospital that I've spoken to several times." He stared at the database. "He's the guy that gave me the video of Amanda and Marco Ellis. I can't believe…" He was out of words as things began to tumble into place.

"Wait a minute. What's his connection to Basin Woods?"

"From what I can see, he lived there with his wife."

"Is he still married?"

"It says he's a widower."

"What happened to her?"

"It just says that Tara Drake died. And Maggie Drake is also deceased."

"Who's Maggie?"

"Their three-month-old baby."

"Well, wait," Katie said. "Are they connected to the Highland Project?"

"It says that he and his wife lived there too—their last listed residence."

"Drake is off work now. Have patrol go by his house to see if he's there.

He picked up the phone. "On it."

Katie waited while he made the call.

"They're going by his residence now."

Katie grabbed her coat. "Let's go check Basin Woods out now—if Tess Regan was taken by the killer, she could be at this location. It's familiar. It fuels his internal need to fulfill a fantasy. I know it's almost dark, but we can still do a reconnaissance. We'll update the sheriff when we get there. We cannot afford to wait if someone's life is hanging in the balance."

McGaven followed suit by grabbing his jacket.

"You know that gut thing I'm always talking about?" she said.

"Yeah."

"It's working on overtime now."

CHAPTER 61

McGaven didn't have to argue about wanting to drive this time; instead, Katie handed him the keys before he could ask.

Katie had retrieved Cisco from the police department kennel and he padded alongside the detectives as they got into the police vehicle and raced out of the sheriff's office parking lot heading east.

The setting sun was behind them reflecting a burning orange in the rearview mirror as they raced down the freeway. McGaven set an ambitious speed but kept safety as his priority, especially with the dog unrestrained in the back seat.

Cisco stood up and watched the road with the detectives—he sensed something important was up and obviously wanted to be a part of it.

"What are you thinking?" asked Katie holding to the handhold.

"About?"

"The location."

"One thing I've been learning during my short time as a detective is that you never know what you're going to find. Jump in feet first and let whatever happens shake out."

Katie leaned back against the headrest and smiled. "That's the truth," she said, remembering her last case and the odds that were stacked against her.

"Did you want to call the sheriff?"

"No, I want to wait for when, and if, we find anything." She took slow even breaths, hoping that McGaven didn't notice that she was beginning to feel strange—that familiar chill of anxiety crept into her spirit again. She relaxed as much as she could, hoping that it would merely wash over her and vanish like it had before when work had taken over.

They traveled for more than a half hour. Katie watched the outside scenery change from cityscapes to rural settings and then change back to smaller communities again. The landscape in the area was diverse and it was reasonable, if not commendable, that the county as well as the state wanted to improve impoverished and abandoned areas pumping new life into the city.

The view finally transformed into miles of agricultural land for crops, which made it seem like they hadn't seen another house in ages; she noticed less traffic too. The light was waning, affecting their ability to conduct a thorough search of the "Humanity Project" also known as Highland Project.

"Turn there," she instructed.

McGaven slowed the car and turned down a heavily graveled street, but it was instantly obvious that it was going into no-man's land. Even though they were within ten miles of the freeway, the neighboring two streets remained like a ghost town: overgrown, deserted, and ultimately forgotten.

The area had been originally fenced to keep people out, but it had been put up so long ago that it was lacking in areas. The main gate hung askew, broken and rusted, and was just wide enough for a car to barely pass through.

"What do you think?" she asked.

"I didn't expect it to be so…"

"Creepy."

"That's an understatement," he said.

Katie strained her neck, surveying the open land. It appeared to go on for miles. There were areas that crops were growing: mostly vegetables like broccoli, lettuce, and zucchini.

"It's so strange," she said, for lack of a better description. She felt a cold chill crawl up her spine and moved her shoulders quickly to try and shake it away.

McGaven studied the areas as well but remained quiet.

Cisco circled in the backseat and pawed back and forth from window to window. He kept his watch on the area looking for bad guys, but nothing moved except for pieces of garbage and dead brush blowing down the dirt street.

"Let's take a look," she said and focused on her iPad showing an overview of the area. "I think we should make a left and park."

McGaven maneuvered the car around a large fallen branch in the middle of the road. There were telephone lines down too, making it a tight squeeze driving underneath. He finally parked.

It surprised Katie that there were still so many trees in the area: they hadn't burned, fallen down or been removed.

"This is good," she said. "There's visibility for this block. And if anyone comes near, Cisco will alert us."

"He's not coming with us?"

"No. I don't know what kind of condition the houses are in and I don't want Cisco in the middle of something that might go sideways. Some are burned down completely and others most likely have significant damage. Officially, he's just a ride along."

McGaven gave her a concerned look.

"Don't worry; I've still got the remote if there's an emergency."

They exited the vehicle, leaving behind a very restless dog.

"Okay, how do you want to do this?" she asked.

Walking around the car to the trunk, McGaven popped the lock and flipped it up. "We're going in prepared." He divvied up flashlights making room with the crowbars, extra magazines, and made sure his service weapon was ready.

"Okay, Rambo," she said, trying to lighten the situation, but in reality, she wanted to calm herself down.

"I'll take that as a compliment. The easiest thing to do is I'll take one side of the street and you take the other. You know," he said, "they say this place is haunted. There have been many accounts of people seeing ghosts."

Katie rolled her eyes in disbelief. "People see what they want to see."

"Okay. But a couple of the deputies saw some weird stuff around here."

"Maybe they did," she said flippantly. The last thing she needed to hear about was some demonic spirit, most likely someone sneaking around trying to scare people.

McGaven smiled. "You never know what you're going to find."

Katie took an overall survey around the area.

"What do you think?" he said. "It's only two and half houses each."

Nodding in agreement, Katie said, "You're right. That's the best way to handle the searches. If we can't find anything here, then we'll reassess."

"Okay," he said and headed to the first house on his side of the street.

"Hey," Katie said. McGaven turned around. "Anything doesn't seem right, you wait for backup. Check in every ten minutes and keep your cell phone open to the walkie-talkie mode."

"Ten-four."

CHAPTER 62

Katie walked up to the first house along a broken walkway still with remnants of caution tape; the house had been at one time charming and inviting. The front door no longer existed and several large pieces of burned plywood were the only things covering the main opening and windows on each side.

She looked down the street and behind the house. There were remnants of the other burnt structures, leaving only the cement foundations.

Before entering the house, Katie used her flashlight to search the front and backyards to see if there had been any recent activity, but they were bare and there were charred impressions of walls and porches. The upper windows were broken out, most likely from juveniles partying and throwing rocks.

It struck Katie as odd that there weren't any signs of graffiti or areas that had empty liquor bottles. The area would be a prime place for teenagers or gang members to congregate, but it seemed to lack their typical signatures.

Walking back to the front door, she carefully tugged at one of the loose pieces of plywood on the right side of the door frame. The sound of the screech of the long nails pulling away sent an eerie echo traveling down the street. She wondered if McGaven had heard it, but she was sure he had his own obstacles. She glanced across the street and saw the quick streaks of light from McGaven's flashlight bounce around inside the house.

Katie directed her flashlight inside and peered through the illumination from one side to the other: A large living room and open kitchen with small dining area on one side to the stairs leading up to the next level.

She entered the house with her gun ready but not directed. Standing at the threshold gaining her bearings, she saw the carpet had been removed and the appliances smashed and scattered around the adjacent rooms. The interior had a stagnant moldy smell mixed with smoke, but nothing that would make her gag. She was surprised that smoke still permeated the interior.

First looking around the living room walls, she was alert to seeing anything that appeared as if it didn't belong or might indicate a false room. She swept the entire downstairs area before she ascended the staircase, which still had some remnants of well-worn carpet attached to each stair.

With every other stair creaking underneath her weight, Katie made her way to the second story. She stood still to listen. It was quiet except for some mild wind blowing through the upstairs broken windows.

Directing the flashing in a systematic grid pattern, along the floor, walls, and ceiling areas, Katie combed through the second floor with tenacity.

She quickly searched the bedrooms and bathroom, but nothing appeared unusual or out of place with the layout.

McGaven's voice came from her speaker phone, interrupting her search, "Find anything?"

Pulling her cell phone from her pocket, she replied, "Nothing—yet."

"Just about to clear the first house. Over and out."

Katie jogged down the staircase and exited the house.

One down…

CHAPTER 63

McGaven was just about to clear the first house on his side of the street when he heard a crash. At first it sounded like it came from outside, but when he listened again it seemed to come from underneath the kitchen.

He retraced his steps and couldn't find where the noise originated. Then it dawned on him, there was a basement.

Walking back into what was once the kitchen, McGaven directed the flashlight in every corner and into areas without appliances. There was a regular door that he had mistaken for a pantry, so he opened it and shone the light down. It was indeed a basement. Slowly descending, he took the rickety wooden stairs down, searching from corner to corner, but nothing looked sinister or out of place. Perhaps it was the vacant structures settling, or an animal.

His cell phone alerted him, "You okay?" said Katie.

"Super. Clear here as well."

"Copy. Over and out."

Two down…

CHAPTER 64

Katie managed to explore the next house, but unfortunately had the same result and it was severely damaged and didn't look safe. Nothing unusual. She couldn't find clues indicating someone had stayed inside or if there had been foul play. Not one thing.

Katie's mood suffered the more she searched. Her enthusiasm for finding more evidence or something that would lead to the killer was waning with each empty room.

She approached the last small house standing: a small one-story structure which had been painted white with a dark trim. Standing in the walkway, she studied the siding, windows, and the weed infestation along the flower beds on both sides of the front door.

The night was in full force, dark, foggy, and a heavy mist clung to everything around her including her hair and clothes. She became chilled as she stared at the small residence. Something about the cozy home made her think of the type of people who had lived there. Did Randy and his wife live here? What happened to Randy's wife and daughter?

As she stared down the dark street in both directions, it seemed as if the few remaining houses, mostly burned out shells, sat in the shadows, as if the entire neighborhood was not only neglected but erased from time.

She strained to listen for Cisco's bark, but the dog was quiet. There were no other people or animals wandering around the area, which kept them safe for now. The remaining neighborhood was flanked by endless agricultural land as far as the eye could see.

Katie heard a soft bang from behind her and saw McGaven's large frame exiting the house opposite. His flashlight swung from left to right. She watched him approach with a long purposeful stride. He hesitated a moment and then headed straight to her.

"Hey," he said. "What's wrong?"

"What do you mean?"

"Well, you're not kicking in walls or anything at the moment." He tried to keep the conversation light under the circumstances.

"Just trying to get a grasp of the area." She still stared at the small white house.

"What does your profile say about this place?"

"Good question," she said. Looking at McGaven standing in the darkness, she hadn't realized before how lucky she was to have been promoted to the cold-case unit and to have such a good friend and loyal partner working with her.

"Katie?"

Her thoughts turned back to the killer. His motivations. His fantasies.

"Katie, what do you want to do now?" he asked.

"I thought we would find something here. I was overcompensating and just basically hoping to find something here, but…"

"We have to keep looking," he interrupted.

"You're right—you're absolutely right. This place seems perfect for a killer to use as his own private prison for his victims, but he's clever and no doubt there are other places that would suit his needs. We have to keep searching. It might be just one house—somewhere. It could be some property that he inherited."

"I'm going to move the car closer and take a look around at the land and a few of the burnt-out sections," he said. "Meet you there."

"I'm checking this place too—no stone unturned," she said and smiled as she headed toward the house.

Her phone buzzed, there was an incoming text from her uncle which read:

Small electrical fire at abandoned house crime scene at Basin Woods Project—fire department en route. Much of the evidence will probably be destroyed.

Katie was disappointed. She answered:

Thanks for update. We are checking leads at the Humanity Project—update soon.

She heard a car engine roar to life and drive around to the other street. McGaven had moved the police car to a better area near the fields.

Katie put the phone back in her pocket and didn't expect to hear any more from her uncle. The thought of losing crucial evidence made her almost nauseous. Her phone buzzed again and she didn't want to read the text, knowing that her uncle was going to give her a lecture about how impetuous she was and she needed to be careful. She wasn't disobeying an order; she was just ignoring it for now.

Her phone chimed once again. This time she glanced at it to find it was Chad calling her. She ignored it, hoping he would understand.

Katie entered the last house; staying at the doorway, just as with the other houses, she swung her flashlight beam slowly in a one-hundred-eighty-degree sweep. The house was different in the layout and condition. She didn't detect smoke. There was a new rug placed over the yellowing linoleum in the kitchen along with a roll of paper towels and some used napkins. She didn't see any evidence of food or wrappers or containers lying around.

That wasn't what stopped Katie abruptly and made her draw her weapon.

Spray-painted along the upper living room wall was the single word: "TRUTH."

CHAPTER 65

After parking the car on the next street, McGaven felt drained and definitely in need of some rest—or at least a large cup of strong coffee before investigating the large wide-open field. Sitting in the front seat, he grabbed one of the water bottles he had packed in the car, twisted the cap off, and immediately downed half of it. The cool water helped to revive some of his waning energy and gave him a lift—but it still wasn't as satisfying as a double cappuccino.

Cisco put his nose up against the side of McGaven's face, sniffing and snorting, until the officer gave him some attention.

"Hey, buddy, you thirsty?"

He smiled as he poured some water into a leftover plastic cup. The dog happily lapped it up with half of the water dribbling out the sides of his mouth.

"Nice going, Cisco. I guess Katie hasn't taught you proper water etiquette." He laughed and scratched the dog behind the ears. "Sorry, I need to get back to work, buddy."

The black dog whined and paced back and forth in the back seat.

McGaven got out of the car and took a moment to stretch his back. He hadn't been to the gym for more than a week and could feel the tenseness in his lower back and hamstrings building.

He stood in the middle of the street, completely still, watching and listening. If he stood long enough, the dark shadows began to play tricks with his eyes. One could imagine a couple of bad guys hiding behind a tree, or a dinosaur monster ready to attack—especially if you stood and stared long enough.

A pair of yellow eyes appeared on what was left of a wooden fence; he pointed the flashlight directly at a startled yellow-striped feral cat, causing it to cower and then dart off the fence, disappearing into the darkness.

His flashlight flickered.

"Crap," he said, trying to shake it back to full charge. There were extra batteries and another flashlight in the car.

McGaven pulled his cell phone to call Katie just as it rang. He pressed the talk button, "McGaven."

The voice on the other end was familiar and said, "This is Chad. I just heard about the fire over on the south end of town. I tried Katie's cell but it went to voicemail."

"Katie's fine. We're at the Humanity Project checking some things out."

"Humanity Project? I heard that's a bad place," Chad said.

"Nothing to worry about. Katie will call you later," he said and hung up as he moved toward the other street. He cut through several yards to get to the white house where Katie had called from, and then he dropped his phone. He bent down to retrieve it, and that was when someone whacked him on the head, throwing him to the ground. Groggily, he tried to get up to face his attacker, but his vision slowly faded. The last thing he heard before giving in to the darkness was Cisco's barking.

CHAPTER 66

The word "TRUTH" mesmerized Katie and she found herself drawn to the wall—not able to take her eyes away from it. On the floor in front of the message were several spray paint cans lying on their sides. Holding her flashlight above her directed Glock, she closely examined the letters of the word. Wondering if there were visible fingerprints still on the spray cans, Katie leaned over to have a better look.

She touched the back of her left hand against the wall and found that the paint was dry, but that still didn't lessen the chilling image.

This pleasant small house was the home base for a killer, or at least it was somewhere he hung out. She pulled out her cell phone. "Where are you?" she said softly.

There was intermittent static.

Katie couldn't take her eyes away from the message on the wall. She noticed that the spray-painted "H" at the end of the word "TRUTH" swept up and around, crossing the "T." It was an interesting personal signature.

She knew that McGaven would join her in a couple of minutes, so she hurried to walk around the main floor examining everything she could until he arrived. She realized she was in the area where the killer might have spent time, devised his plans, and masterminded his fantasies. It was actually a perfect cover and an ideal place to hide in plain sight. Again, clever and devious, which matched her preliminary profile—along with organized.

As she walked from the kitchen area back to the living room, she searched for a false wall and noticed a smudged area with what looked like grease about halfway up around the corner section. It appeared to be recent. Moving closer, she ran her fingertips down the side and felt an indentation where her index and middle finger fit easily.

She heard a weird noise, almost a raspy groaning, that sounded more like a dying animal, which made her instantly direct her gun and use her flashlight to sweep the area. Nothing was in sight—she half expected to see a cat or possibly a raccoon in the corner. But she was still alone.

Dammit! Where are you, McGaven?

There it was again. The strained sound as if it bubbled up from the bowels of the earth—chilling and creepy at the same time.

Katie retraced her findings on the wall and placed her two fingers into the niche again—this time she pressed and slid, and then pushed harder until the corner flexed. She pushed the wall as hard as she could and it wouldn't move. Using several different techniques of pulling, pushing, and sliding, she managed to move the hidden door wide enough for her to peek behind it. It was a cleverly designed entrance that most people would never know was there unless they looked for it. She never would have thought to look for it if it wasn't for her visit to the special effects company and all their masterful makeup and animated techniques.

Nothing was as it seemed.

Her heart pounded as her breath became erratic in anticipation. She needed to wait for McGaven, but she had to get inside the secret room. She peered into the opening. To her horror, as the flashlight beam crossed the small-sized bedroom, she saw a woman's body on the bed. Unmoving.

Not waiting another minute, Katie frantically attacked the secret door until she opened it wide enough to squeeze through. Her head roared with the sounds of her own heavy breathing and muttered words of hope. Images spilled into her mind and blurred her vision. Her mind played tricks on her as the stakes of the investigation rose.

The little girl and her mother were preparing food. Their eyes looking straight at her—pleading with her to protect them.

The boom—the flash—in an instant—they were gone. I couldn't save them…

She rushed to the bed where a woman lay still with her hands secured to the headboard and her ankles to the bottom posts. The restraints had bloodied her wrists and ankles; they had raw gaping wounds. The room reeked of urine, making Katie gag. She pressed her finger against the woman's neck for several seconds. There was a faint pulse.

"C'mon, wake up," Katie urged.

She carefully began to peel away the horrible duct tape that took part of her skin and hair with it.

The woman moved, startling Katie. First her hands and then her legs twitched.

His blood had saturated the front of Katie's uniform, leaving behind dark red streaks infused with tiny pieces of other matter.

She wiped the side of her face with the back of her hand; it too was covered with blood… I couldn't save him… Jack was gone.

"Hey, it's okay," Katie said. "You're safe now. I'm getting help." She kept a watchful eye, making sure no one was going to creep up behind her.

The woman moved her cracked bleeding lips and tried to say something.

Katie leaned closer and strained to listen.

The woman whispered faintly, "I told the truth."

Chills raced through Katie's body from the top of her spine and down her legs. "It's okay. I'm going to untie you. Okay?" She couldn't tell if the victim was the missing woman Tess Regan or another victim—she was in rough physical and mental shape.

The woman made a strange guttural sound and she repeated over and over, "Please… please…"

Katie looked around the room and saw a discarded screwdriver and a pile of painter's tarps in the corner. Whatever the killer was deciding to do he wasn't going to leave her alive.

She pulled out her cell phone with a slight trembling hand and pressed the saved number that directed her to Dispatch. Her phone responded with three beeps.

"Shit, no reception."

Katie moved back through the opening into the living room where her cell phone gave the tone that she was back in range again.

"911—what's your emergency?"

"This is Detective Katie Scott with the Pine Valley Sheriff's Office, badge number—"

She didn't get to finish her sentence when someone slammed her hard and threw her to the ground. Her smashed phone catapulted across the room.

Lying face down with her cheek against the stinking carpet, Katie struggled to keep her eyes open. She saw a pair of shoes—they weren't typical everyday shoes but the work shoes that police officers wore with a steel toe. Her phone dropped in front of her face as the person above her stomped its remains into tiny shattered pieces.

The next moment, her attacker pulled her weapon from her holster and she knew at that instant they were going to shoot her and be done with it. To her surprise, as she fought to keep herself conscious, trying to widen her eyes, she saw the outline of the person empty her magazine and the bullets drop to the floor one by one—each garnering a reflection from the low light. No matter how hard she fought, she closed her eyes.

Afghanistan. Her team had been searching a building when it was hit with heavy artillery. She and Cisco had been momentarily knocked out, tucked in a small area where the roof hadn't collapsed on

*them. She lay still as she heard the enemy speaking in their language
nearby in a hurried manner—it was clear they were arguing.*

*Play dead, she thought. Not moving a muscle, she remained still
and hoped that Cisco wouldn't move as she gripped him against
her body. The men bickered barely a foot from her. Something
made them move on, leaving her for dead. It hadn't been her
time to go yet…*

"Well aren't you a smart detective," hissed a man's voice, pulling
her from her past nightmare and into the current one. His voice
was a cross between a whisper and a stressed shout. "Too clever for
your own good and look where you are now." He took her empty
service weapon and threw it through the window next to the door.
Glass shattered in the aftermath of the impact, sprinkling pieces
of shards around the living room.

Katie blinked hard, still only seeing the man's shoes pace back and
forth. She pried open her eyes wider to gain her bearings, straining
to see who had ambushed her. His voice wasn't familiar to her, but
he obviously knew who she was by his tone and attitude. She caught
a glimpse of him. The man standing over her held her life in his
hands. She tried as hard as she could to identify him, but he wasn't
anyone she had spoken to or interviewed. That much she knew.

Then she suddenly realized he must be the security guard
McGaven had talked to by the photograph from the DMV. He
was the one that had helpfully copied security footage for the
investigation. He had access to the chemicals found in evidence
and it would have been easy for him to follow Amanda and the
others. He had watched and waited for the right opportunity.

*Randall Drake was the killer. The man Amanda couldn't identify
from his whisper, but was terrified would come back and kill her.*

Katie would bet that Randy had a high-end late model vehicle
that had left an imprint on Amanda's back—most likely during a
struggle. But all that didn't matter right now.

She fought to move her arms but the weight of them kept her pinned down. Fleeting thoughts of McGaven crossed her mind. Why couldn't she hear Cisco barking?

Cisco...

Katie closed her eyes again and played dead as her body slowly recovered from the intense blow, shattering her nerves and muscles. Her hands and upper body began to come back to life and she knew that the longer she waited, the more strength she would regain.

"You've ruined everything," Randy ranted. "This wasn't part of the plan. I have to dispose of you, so that it won't find its way back to me." He began to breathe hard, his fevered breath causing him to pace faster. "There's only one thing I can do now." He slammed the front door and locked it with a key.

He walked up to Katie and kicked at her leg. "Sit up. I know you can hear me. I said sit up!" He continued to pace. "Answer me! Sit up!" He kicked her hard again; this time it made a direct hit to her side. She felt the extra force from the steel toe.

Katie let out a wail of pain and rolled onto her back. It felt like her side had torn wide open.

"See, I knew you were awake." He towered above her. "Detective Katie Scott. I didn't get the pleasure of meeting you—just your partner."

As he waved his arms, Katie noticed several tattoos and heavy burn scars on his upper forearms. He kept rubbing his hands together, obviously fighting his urges and keeping his impulses in check—for now.

"Well, Detective, don't you have anything to say?"

Katie was winded and the pain in her side kept pulsing with pain. "Did you kill... Amanda Payton?" she whispered.

Truth...

"What do you think, Detective?" He laughed.

"Did you kill her?"

"Uh-oh, the secret is out now."

"Why?" she asked, trying to keep him talking so that she could gain strength.

"Why? You mean you haven't dissected or profiled me yet? Ah, but you have some blanks to fill in... like... I hated my mother—she lied. I hated my aunt—she lied. And..." he leaned down, bending over, and stared at Katie face to face, "I hated my foster mom too. Why? She lied." He laughed as a few specks of spittle hit Katie in the face. "I guess I have mommy issues. What do you think, Detective?"

Truth...

Katie watched Randy. His hair was dark, crew-cut short, and parted strangely on the right side. His eyes were dull, but darted back and forth, seeing everything in the room. She remembered what McGaven had said.

"What's the matter, Detective? Can't talk? All choked up?"

"Who was she?" she whispered.

Truth...

"Who?"

"Tara," said Katie.

He stopped, looked down at her. "What did you say?"

"Did you kill Tara too?" Katie braced for the worst.

"Don't you ever speak of Tara. She was an angel. I would never... NEVER hurt her, ever. You understand me?" He took another swinging kick at her side.

Katie closed her eyes. The situation was overwhelming but she tried to gain her breath. She wondered where McGaven was—her thoughts jumped to the worst conclusion.

No.

"You couldn't save Tara," Katie pushed in a low tone.

"How many times do I have to tell you? They *lied* to me."

"Why?" Katie managed to say.

"Why, you ask. Oh, I bet you think I hate women, right? Well, that's not true. What I do hate is the LIES! Lies that come so easily to women! I've heard them my whole life—so now I just like to hear them confess." He made strange sniffing sounds followed by clearing his throat.

Katie began to put together the clues that they had lived in this housing. "Did she burn in the house?" she guessed.

"Why are you doing this? Why are you bringing up Tara?" he said in anguish. "Why...?" he whispered.

"Why didn't you save her?"

"They said... they said," he began to unravel. "They said they would be fine... they said..."

It suddenly hit Katie. "You couldn't save Tara or the baby."

There was a sudden stilted silence.

"No," he whispered. "The doctor said they would be okay. The nurse said they would be okay. The paramedic said they would be okay. BUT THEY WEREN'T OKAY!" He attacked Katie. "Everyone LIED to me!"

There was nothing that she could do but take the hit—and the ones that came after. The pain radiated through her body causing her to grit her teeth. She couldn't catch her breath. The familiar prickly feeling that usually led to a panic attack—or worse—began to crawl up her arms and legs.

But then he became winded and seemed to calm down.

"You're tougher than you look, Detective. Oh, but did I read that you were in the army? Makes sense. But I'm afraid that your career is coming to an end. I've never killed a veteran before. Sounds like fun."

Katie tensed and was ready for the next assault—assuming it was going to be a stomp kick to her throat or her head.

Instead, Randy let out an anguished yell. He stormed about the house talking to himself and fueling his anger.

Katie heard him walk toward the hidden room. He began to curse out the wounded semi-conscious woman on the bed.

"It's your fault!" he yelled. "Why did you have to be so special? That wasn't in the plans. I was just going to let you go… Well… maybe not!" he yelled, half laughing and half seething in anger.

Katie heard a loud bang and another one against the wall, like the entire house was going to tumble down on top of them as he beat the walls with his fists. Then all was quiet. There were strange splashing sounds and the smell of gasoline permeated the air, and she realized what he was doing. Dark memories gripped her once again.

Smoke filled her nose and clouded her vision. The smoke. The fire savagely consuming the bodies. Death was everywhere. Few were left alive—bleeding—missing limbs—pleading for help.

Her mind spun. There was nothing she could do… she couldn't save them… it was human life… they mattered… there was nothing she could do…

She could save the woman in the torture bedroom. She had to. With every ounce of strength garnered in her body, Katie rolled onto her side. Blood was seeping through her clothes. She moved her arm slowly, inching it towards the small remote hidden on her waist. If she could just press it, she knew that Cisco would do everything he could to find her. The remote had a range of about a quarter mile. She had no other choice but to deploy him—and hope for the best.

Find me, Cisco…

Most of her strength crept back and she sat up, still hearing the rampage in the hidden room. Desperately looking around for something to defend herself, she saw garbage, straws, a doorknob, and old tattered baseboards. She heard the distinct crackle of fire. It reeked of the accelerant. Smoke began to billow from the room through the small opening. She was terrified that he had doused the woman with the gasoline.

Katie pulled her legs underneath her and pushed herself up, dizzy at first, but she managed to stumble into the kitchen area, holding her side, searching for anything—a knife, a frying pan, anything to fight him. In the corner, leaning against the wall, was a three and half foot long metal bar with a hook on the end used to open high windows.

She grabbed the pole, gripping it tightly, making fixed fists around the metal; feeling her balance return to about ninety percent, she crept toward the opening of the room.

Katie dared to look inside, where she watched in horror: Randy was panting for breath, standing in the middle of the room watching two of the walls begin to burn. As sweat dripped from his face the flames crept higher.

Without hesitation, Katie ran full speed into the room and swung the metal pole aiming for his stomach. It struck Randy in the arm and knocked him down against another wall leaving a large dent behind where his head had struck.

Katie took a fighter's stance and swung again downward, hitting Randy in the shins.

He screamed in pain, huddling over his wounded legs.

Her adrenalin spiked and she wanted to beat him unconscious—a strike for every woman he made a victim. Her head pounded. As she regained her stance, she hesitated, and tried to strike him again. Her hesitation was all that he needed, he lunged at her, taking her down like a linebacker on the field. They struggled as the flames began to build momentum.

Truth...

CHAPTER 67

A searing headache permeated throughout McGaven's skull, causing him to puke several times. He moved his arms and legs until he could push himself up and into a standing position. A few seconds passed before he realized where he was and that Katie was all alone.

He cursed himself for allowing someone to sneak up on him.

As he took a step forward, he groped for his weapon which amazingly was still in its holster.

Cisco ran at him, barking nonstop and running circles around him, waiting for a command.

Smoke filled the air and he realized that there was a house on fire.

Katie…

"Find her!" McGaven yelled. "Find her!" he yelled again. He realized that Katie must've pressed the release button for the back door of the cruiser. She was in trouble.

The dog barked again, gave McGaven one last look, and took off at full pelt, leaping over several tall bushes and scaling a fence before running at full speed down the street and disappearing from view.

McGaven followed as fast as his legs would carry him, stumbling every couple of feet, his head still spinning—probably suffering from a minor concussion. He knew that Cisco would beat him to the house, but he ran as fast as he could to get to Katie.

CHAPTER 68

Randy swung at her with his fists, but she managed to stay clear from any direct hits. Ducking and diving to her left, she lunged forward and pushed her thumbs into his eyes. The shock made him stumble back, giving her an opportunity to run.

She took the chance, turned her back on him and ran into the kitchen where she remembered there was a folding chair leaning against the wall. Not missing a beat, she grabbed the chair and swung it at him, knocking him to the side. She swung again, missing him.

As she readied herself to pummel him with the flat part of the chair, he anticipated her action and pivoted himself, causing Katie to lose her balance. She fell toward the floor with the chair knocking the wind out of her.

He frantically crawled on his hands and knees and found the steel pole. He stood up and swung it, striking the floor just inches from Katie's head. He stood above her. Sweat dripped from his face. His arms shook with fierce anger—rage he felt from all he had lost—the broken shell of a man who had lost everything and needed someone to blame.

Katie knew she couldn't fight anymore; *she* was now the woman that she couldn't save.

The fire licked into the room, doubling in velocity as it headed towards them and all around them.

Just when she thought it was over, she heard a thunderous crash over the roar of the fire and a black blur catapulted through the window, landed, raced through the living room and leapt. Cisco had his jaws clamped to Randy's shoulder, taking him down, simultaneously dislodging the pole from his hand. Once he was on the floor, Cisco shook him hard as he tried to fight back—to no avail. Cisco, trained to hold his grip, reattached his teeth into more areas, deeper and stronger each time.

The smoke thickened.

Flames crackled and flickered long tentacles of heat.

Randy screamed in pain, in rage.

Katie began to cough as the smoke filled her lungs.

Three loud shots rang out, splintering the locks as the front door burst open. McGaven filled the doorway with his gun positioned and ready.

Smoke billowed out in large rivers of black.

McGaven clamped his left hand over his mouth and nose for a moment—trying to control his coughing. Then he gripped the gun with both hands.

Katie yelled a command to Cisco: "*Aus*! Here, Cisco!"

The dog immediately released Randy and ran over to Katie, standing guard over her, tail down, waiting for the next command. Katie grabbed his collar.

Randy tried to get up to finish what he had started.

"Stay down on the ground!" McGaven yelled.

Randy grabbed the pole once again.

Cisco barked nonstop.

Katie pushed the dog to her side the farthest away from everyone, readying herself for what was about to happen. She kept them both low to the ground and began to crawl as they had done in the heat of battle—on their bellies, using elbows and legs to push them along.

"Drop it! Don't do it, Randy!" McGaven yelled. "Don't do it! Don't make me do it!"

Randy stared back at McGaven; hesitating a moment as if he reflected their previous conversations, he slightly tilted his head—his eyes still crazed. Then he raised the pole toward Katie.

McGaven fired twice, dropping the security guard facedown next to Katie and Cisco. Blood spattered the wall beside them.

Katie and Cisco continued to crawl toward McGaven.

"Save her!" she yelled. "In there." She waved to the room. "Please save her." Katie saw that McGaven wanted to help her, but she could make it outside with Cisco's help. McGaven rushed into the bedroom—and disappeared in the smoke.

The fire was in full force—the heat unbearable.

Katie and Cisco made it to the doorway and she rolled outside on her back feeling the fresh air, the coolness of light rain on her face, and knew that she had faced her demons and won this time. She pushed herself up and continued to crawl away from the house.

The crackling flames continued to build with smoke expelling from every broken window and crack in the house. Was it too late?

Moments later, McGaven stumbled out the front door carrying the lifeless woman. Trying to control his coughing, he gently put her on the ground safely away from the house. She moved subtly and murmured incoherent words. He took off his jacket and covered her as she lay there.

"You okay?" he said to Katie, helping her to her feet.

She grimaced. "Yeah, we're okay. You cut it a little close," she said.

"I'll work on that next time."

The light from the fire lit up the entire street and cast an eerie red-orange glow around them.

As McGaven helped her up on her feet, she contorted from the pain, and he guided her out of harm's way.

Cisco stayed right next to Katie and wouldn't leave her side.

"Good boy, Cisco," McGaven said, quickly checking him over.

"I tried to call it in…" she said.

"Don't worry. I think I've dispatched every first responder—cops, ambulances, fire trucks, forensics. I think maybe the army too." He held tightly to Katie. "Don't move, okay? Let's take a look at your side. We need to make sure the bleeding has stopped."

"Just one question," she said.

"Damn, that's a nasty injury," he said, ripping part of his shirt to press against the wound. "You might have a broken rib or two."

"I have a question," she insisted. "Hey! One question."

"What's that?"

"Is every cold case going to be as tough as this one?"

McGaven held her tight. "God help us."

CHAPTER 69

A week and half later...

Katie stood eagerly at the outside entrance to the Silver Springs Hospital, holding a large bouquet of yellow roses. It still hurt to walk, but she was healing up nicely—as for her emotional wounds—it would take more time.

After a few minutes, she saw Madeline Thomas emerge with her sister holding her arm. She looked frail, but there was an expression of relief on her face. Just as she stepped into the light, she looked up and marveled at the sky and everything around her. Life again. A smile washed across her face: It was clear that she was joyful and thankful to be out of the hospital and to have survived her ordeal.

Madeline looked around and then she saw Katie standing there. She stopped for a moment and gently took her sister's hand away.

Katie walked up to her and said, "I'm so glad to see you, Madeline. It's nice to know your name. I wish you all the best."

"Thank you," she replied.

"These are for you—your favorite, right?" Katie said, giving them to her.

"Oh, thank you. Yes, they are." She smiled at Katie and said, "I knew you were going to catch him."

"I'm so glad you're safe." Katie hugged her. "You take care of yourself, okay?"

Madeline nodded.

Her sister spoke. "Thank you, Detective, for giving us our lovely Madeline back."

Katie nodded and turned, heading back to her car. She didn't let them see the tears in her eyes as she wiped them away.

CHAPTER 70

Katie sat on her couch finishing another novel—it was her third since she had been ordered to stay home to recover. She had many good days, and some bad ones where the memories of the fire at the Humanity Project and memories of the battlefield sometimes merged into one disturbing event. It was difficult to be her own company and not be busy with another cold case. In some ways it was good; she thought about many things: Chad, being a detective, what she wanted in life.

Cisco snugged closer to her, never allowing her to feel alone. She looked down at the black dog and smiled. He had been there through her toughest times and he was here now.

Katie put the book down, pulled her feet up on the couch, and drew a blanket over herself. It was another day that she was still here and she was thankful. As she closed her eyes, she willed only the good memories to fill her mind. Having dinner with Chad, spending time with her uncle, and laughing at McGaven's jokes, those were the cherished times that she needed to hold onto.

There was the sound of car doors slamming outside.

Cisco stood up on the couch and barked.

Katie got to her feet and went to the door. She saw several people coming up her driveway carrying bags, bowls, and casserole dishes.

She opened the door; Cisco ran out to greet everyone. "What's going on?" she asked, surprised by the group.

Chad was the first to enter, holding several grocery bags. "Look who I ran into at the store," he said with a smile on his face. He gave her a quick kiss on the cheek and headed to the kitchen. "It's amazing the people you can run into in this town."

Katie couldn't believe it. "I'm being ambushed."

McGaven, accompanied by Denise, greeted her. "You know me, I never turn down barbecues."

Katie was taken aback. "You two are together?" The two people at work who always had her back were dating. That made her happy.

McGaven grinned and entered the house.

Denise hugged Katie. "You doing okay? We miss you at work."

"I don't know what to say."

"About this?" Denise said, referring to the get-together. "Or about me and McGaven?" She smiled. "What can I say, we've been flirting for quite a while and then I decided to accept his first date offer."

"I'm happy for you," Katie said.

John from forensics greeted her next: "Lovely day for a barbecue."

"I thought you'd be working this weekend?"

"I'm on call. Point me to the grill." He smiled and then joined the others.

"Go on in," she said.

As happy as Katie was about her friends surprising her, she smiled even more when she saw Nick with his brother, James, and Nadine at his side. They looked happy.

Katie hugged Nick. "I'm so happy for you guys."

He kissed her on the cheek. "Things have a way of working out."

"I'm so glad that you're here. All of you. Please come in."

James said, "We haven't been formally introduced. I'm James, Jimmy to most, and this is Nadine."

"It's really nice to meet you both."

"Nice to meet you too," said Nadine.

Chad yelled from the kitchen, "Your grill still out back?" He opened the sliding door followed by Cisco.

"Yes," she said.

Katie was still stunned: She had thought that her only family was her aunt and uncle, when in fact, this was her family. She had a lump in her throat as she watched everyone talk and laugh as they readied the meat for the grill. Denise and Nadine unwrapped vegetables, salads, and pies.

"Alright, who's the grill master?" Chad announced.

Raising his hand, Nick responded, "That would be me."

"Who seconds that?" Chad said.

Several "Ayes," resonated in the crowd.

Katie watched McGaven and John heap ice in the sink and put bottles of beer, waters, and soda in.

McGaven walked up to Katie and handed her a beer. "Here you go, Detective."

"Thanks."

"You doing okay?" he asked.

Someone must've told a joke as loud laughter broke out in the kitchen.

"Yeah, I'm doing okay," she said.

"Well, c'mon," he said, making sure Katie followed him.

Katie and Chad stood in her kitchen watching out the back window as Nick and his brother Jimmy talked. They seemed to have much to talk about and old issues to straighten out. She wasn't sure what they were saying, but it was the first step to mending the past and to moving forward with their lives. There was no doubt in her mind that they needed each other.

Nadine sat at the picnic table and smiled every so often. She was now a part of the family and would be bringing another Haines into the family.

Katie watched as the brothers laughed at something that Nick had said. It was clear that the years apart were beginning to melt away. She hoped that it would only bring more happiness and a family closeness that they desperately needed and deserved.

McGaven, Denise, and John were eating dessert at the picnic table, McGaven taking a break from enjoying his dessert every now and again to throw a ball for Cisco.

"What do you think?" Chad asked.

"I think that it's going to take some time, but it's a solid beginning for the Haines. I'm happy for both of them. Actually, for all three of them, and a fourth one on the way." She continued to watch them converse.

"What about us?" Chad asked.

She turned to him and said, "I think it is a good beginning. Make that a great beginning."

He leaned in and kissed her. "I hope your next case isn't as crazy as this one was."

"I'm so glad that Tess Regan will recover," she said.

"Well, she's lucky you were there. Any longer, she would have been… well, let's just say, she's lucky."

"Lucky that McGaven was there."

"True. He's a good man."

"I still cannot believe that we almost missed the clues that led us to Randall Drake. It makes perfect sense now—he made the evidence point to Dr. Jamison and caused so much collateral damage. He could watch his victims from security cameras and blended in without anyone suspecting him. Bobby Sykes must have known what was going on and was really trying to help, somehow; he felt compelled. One thing bothered me," she said. "Amanda mentioned the smell of jasmine. When they searched his house, they found two dozen bottles of jasmine hand-washing soap."

"Wow."

"There's still some things that we don't know why—like why Amanda had such a rich, fancy dinner in her stomach, but that's just the way it is."

"Why do you think he did it?" he asked.

Katie still watched the brothers as she spoke. "He suffered such a tremendous trauma of losing his wife and three-month-old baby in a fire that he blamed anyone and everyone at the hospital who told people that their loved ones were going to be okay—when they weren't. We're still not entirely sure of the number of his victims—not much turned up at his house. This case is officially closed, but sadly, there will probably be other victims we don't find or ever know about."

"I don't know how you do it."

"Remember, I'm not alone in this."

"I know." He hugged her tighter.

She turned to Chad. "I need a favor," she said.

"Name it."

"Since I'm supposed to be taking it easy, can you drive me somewhere?" she said. "It's not far and it won't take long."

"Of course."

Katie gestured to everyone outside. "I think they'll be just fine for half an hour if we sneak out."

CHAPTER 71

Katie walked down the curvy walkway through a grassy area holding a single pink rose, cut from her garden. She searched several areas until she found what she was looking for. Taking a quiet moment, she hung her head forward in respect and said a short prayer.

Her attention was focused on a particular cemetery headstone:

Amanda Lynn Payton - Loving Daughter & Best Friend

Katie then knelt down and put the rose next to Amanda's grave.

"I'm so sorry that I couldn't protect you—but you helped others and brought a killer to justice. May you find everlasting peace," she said softly.

She stood up and slowly walked back, filing Amanda's death away in the heavy box of people she couldn't save, which she carried inside of her like a lead balloon.

Standing up at the top of the hill, she could see the outline of Chad and Cisco waiting for her with the sun beaming behind them. It was as if there was a new awakening for her—a chance for a new day—a new life.

Realizing that life really was truly not long enough, Katie vowed to never skip any moment to tell someone that she loved them, mend any feud or argument, and never take those she loved for granted. Life was too fragile to take any chances of not expressing those sentiments. Life was indeed too short.

A LETTER FROM JENNIFER

I want to say a huge thank you for choosing to read *Her Last Whisper*. If you did enjoy it, and want to keep up to date with all my latest releases, just sign up at the following link. Your email address will never be shared, and you can unsubscribe at any time.

www.bookouture.com/jennifer-chase

This is a special series for me, and I have enjoyed writing it. Forensics and criminal profiling have been something that I've studied considerably and to be able to incorporate aspects of them into a crime fiction novel has been a thrilling experience for me.

One of my favorite activities outside of writing has been various levels of dog training. I'm a dog lover—just in case you couldn't tell by reading this book. I've loved creating a supporting canine character for my police detective.

I hope you loved *Her Last Whisper* and if you did I would be very grateful if you could write a review. I'd love to hear what you think, and it makes such a difference helping new readers to discover one of my books for the first time.

I love hearing from my readers—you can get in touch on my Facebook page, through Twitter, Goodreads, or my website.

Thanks,
Jennifer Chase

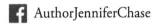 AuthorJenniferChase

 JChaseNovelist

 authorjenniferchase.com

ACKNOWLEDGMENTS

I want to thank my husband Mark for his steadfast support and for being my rock even when I had self-doubt. It's not always easy living with a writer.

A very special thank you goes out to my law enforcement, police K9, forensic, and first-responder friends—there's too many to list. Your friendships have meant the world to me. It has opened a whole new writing world and inspiration. I wouldn't be able to bring my crime fiction stories to life if it wasn't for all of you.

This continues to be a truly amazing writing experience. I would like to thank my publisher Bookouture and the fantastic staff for helping me to bring this book and the entire Detective Katie Scott series to life. A very special thank you to my editor Jessie Botterill—your unwavering support and amazing guidance has challenged me to become a better writer.

Made in the USA
Columbia, SC
29 November 2020